THE NEW GIRL

BOOKS BY RUTH HEALD

The Mother's Mistake

The Woman Upstairs

I Know Your Secret

The Wedding

27: *Six Friends, One Year*

THE NEW GIRL

RUTH HEALD

bookouture

Published by Bookouture in 2022

An imprint of Storyfire Ltd.
Carmelite House
50 Victoria Embankment
London EC4Y 0DZ

www.bookouture.com

ISBN: 978-1-80314-174-9
eBook ISBN: 978-1-80314-173-2

PROLOGUE

She looked out the window of the wooden hut into the misty darkness. He was gone now, but he might come back. Was she safer outside or inside? The photos of laughing children mocked her from the walls. There were reminders of other people's happy holidays everywhere: a jet-ski perched on a platform at the back, a lone frisbee on a shelf piled with snorkels, a shoe rack full of flip-flops and deck shoes.

Above her was a shelf of tools. Hammers. Screwdrivers. Duct tape. She steadied her breathing. She could use them to hurt him if she needed to.

She grabbed a screwdriver and gripped it tightly as she pushed open the door to the outside, her heart pounding. She stayed still for a moment, eyes darting left and right, holding the weapon out in front of her. She could only hear her own ragged breaths. There was no one else out there.

In front of her, she could make out the faint outline of the lake, the reason she'd come here; the promise of a ride on the boat. How easily she'd been charmed, led away from the others.

Behind her was the wood, stretching out for miles. There

was a path through, back to civilisation. She'd stumbled down it earlier, drunk and laughing, on an adventure.

She had to go back that way. She didn't have her phone anymore. At some point she'd lost it, or he'd taken it, she wasn't sure which. Instead, she had to guide herself by the moonlight. Mud seeped through her velvet shoes as she made her way into the dark wood. Her thin red dress that had seemed so appropriate for the celebration now felt like little more than a sliver of material.

A twig snapped under her foot, and her heart jumped. She was being too loud. If he was out here he would know exactly where she was. He would find her.

She wouldn't let that happen. She had to keep moving, no matter what. She had to get out of the woods. But she'd already become disorientated. She couldn't remember the way back. She knew that just a short distance away the party would still be going. She needed to get there, to ask for help.

She stumbled into a clearing, tripping over a tree root. She didn't remember this, didn't remember coming this way.

His voice echoed round the woodland and she froze. 'There you are.'

It was a moment before she saw him, standing tall and broad between the trees, his jeans and polo shirt spotless.

She started to run, but he grabbed her arm.

He looked down at her disgustedly. 'You're covered in mud.' She had hardly noticed it before, she'd been so focused on getting away, but now she could feel it sticking to her bare legs.

'I—' She was shaking with fear, desperate to get away from him. But she knew she was trapped.

'Never mind. We need to get you cleaned up and back to the party.' He grinned then, as if they were in on it together, as if everything that had happened in the hut was just a joke between them. She felt bile rising in her throat.

'If we go back now,' he said, 'then no one will even notice

we were gone.' He squeezed her arm just hard enough to hurt. Her heart raced as she flinched away from him. He smiled at her fear, amused, then pulled her closer, his stale breath on her face. 'Don't act so worried. We don't need to tell anyone.' His eyes were hard as he let go of her suddenly and she stumbled backwards. 'I know you wouldn't want to cause any upset. This can be our secret.'

ONE

Sophie heard Charlie's key in the door and shut her laptop, closing the job application she'd been working on for most of the day. She could hear tourists laughing and chatting outside the fish and chip shop below their flat, and she was grateful to have had the day off from serving hot drinks at the café on the seafront.

'Good day?' Charlie asked, and she felt the weight of his hand on her shoulder, smelled the oil and glue that he carried home from work beneath his fingers and in the fabric of his overalls.

'Yeah,' she said, as he leaned down to peck her on the cheek, his stubble grazing her skin. He started to strip off, whistling. She heard the whoosh of the water as he turned on the shower.

He was taking her out tonight, for their anniversary. Ten years since he'd kissed her, as they'd sat on a rock overlooking the sea as the sun went down, when she was fourteen. It had felt special, and she could remember the taste of the sea salt in the air and the stale smell of smoke embedded in his vintage leather jacket.

While he was in the shower she picked up her phone and

double-checked the Google alert she had for her name. It was a daily ritual, one she wished she could stop. The websites hounding her had disappeared years ago, but she felt a compulsion to check, just in case. She was afraid they'd come back, that the horrible things they wrote about her would be up there for all to see.

She held her breath as she flicked through the results. Today a Sophie Williams had appeared in court for dangerous driving. Another Sophie Williams had celebrated winning a local art competition. Nothing about her. She let herself breathe normally again. She was lucky that Sophie Williams was so common a name. It was unlikely that her friends and family had ever stumbled across the hateful websites in such a sea of information, and now so much time had passed that even those who had known what had happened to her would have forgotten. It was only her that was still caught up in the past, still checking.

Reassured that there was nothing new, she went to her wardrobe and pulled out the trusty dress she always wore for special occasions: her aunt's sixtieth birthday; drinks in town with the girls from the café; a rare treat of afternoon tea with her oldest friend, Keely. It was marine blue with a black floral pattern weaving across it, and it hid her stomach and her flabby arms.

Tonight she was going to tell Charlie that she was looking for jobs in London. She knew he wanted to stay put where they were in Dorset, in the place they grew up, but there weren't many advertising agencies in Dorset and she'd been rejected by all of them. If she wanted to get a foothold in the industry, she had to go to London. She hadn't wanted to go back there, not after what had happened to her at university, but now she'd set her fears aside, forcing herself to put her name forward. She knew that her online marketing degree wouldn't be looked on as highly as the degree at the University of South London she'd dropped out of, and she needed to maximise her chances. She put on her mother's necklace, carefully doing up the delicate clasp. Since her mother had died five years before, she always tried to wear something of hers on special occasions, a necklace or bracelet or ring. She liked to feel the silver against her skin, knowing that it had once touched her mother's skin in the same way. Standing in front of the mirror, the sun shining brightly into the bedroom, Sophie felt hopeful. She had a sense of purpose that she hadn't had in a long time.

'I can't believe it's been ten years since we got together,' Charlie said as they sat by the window in the restaurant, watching the sun go down over the sea. Behind them the door to the kitchen swung open and there was a burst of noise as harried waiters shouted back and forth to each other as they rushed to fulfil orders.

'Me neither,' Sophie said. Her life over the last ten years had been punctuated by bigger things: her mother's death, dropping out of university, her father's fall and injury. Charlie had always been there, by her side, and she'd been grateful. But she hadn't been counting off the years, and she'd been surprised when she realised they'd got to ten already.

He reached out and took her hand, the candle on the table in front of them flickering. It felt surreal, a romantic fairy tale. She felt strangely distant from him, as if she wasn't there at all, as if she was watching the scene in a movie rather than living it.

'I don't know why anyone ever bothers to holiday abroad when we have everything on our doorstep right here,' Charlie said, letting go of her hand and gesturing towards the view.

'It's beautiful,' Sophie agreed. 'But I'd like to travel, see the world.'

'We have the whole world right here.'

She squeezed her knife a bit tighter as it sliced through the fish. 'There's more, though, isn't there? Other cultures, other histories.'

'I suppose so.' He changed the subject, drawing a line under their differences. 'So what have you been up to today?'

She took a deep breath. 'I've been applying for jobs,' she said.

'That's good. You'll need something for the winter when there aren't any tourists.' The café she worked in closed for the winter season. The locals weren't interested in overpriced paninis and machine-made coffee, and the terrace that was so lovely in the summer took on a dystopian feel in the wind and rain. For the last few winters she'd picked up local marketing jobs, designing and delivering flyers for the local dry-cleaning business, developing branding for the ferry company and working on an advertising campaign for the tourist office. She'd set up her own website showcasing her freelance work, but it was still hard to get new projects.

'Now I've finally finished my degree I want to put it to good use,' she said.

'Great. I'm sure there are lots of jobs locally,' he said pointedly.

Sophie swallowed. 'No, there aren't. Believe me, I've looked. Most of the jobs I've been applying for are in London.'

Charlie raised his eyebrows. 'Really? Why? London is so dirty and polluted. And I thought you hated it there. That you didn't ever want to go back. Not after what happened. I can't protect you if you go back there.'

Sophie swallowed. She knew Charlie was right; she'd said she'd never go back. She'd come back to Dorset shaky and panicky, and she'd wanted Charlie by her side. His sheer physical presence had made her feel safer. She'd told him she'd been violently mugged by a stranger, that it had terrified her. She couldn't bear to tell him the truth.

It had always been convenient for Charlie that she hadn't

wanted to work in London. He'd never encouraged her to face her fears; he was more than happy for her to stay where she was, working in the café. She reached out and touched his hand. 'Look, it won't be that bad. We could live apart for a bit. Like we did when I was at university. We could see each other every weekend.' Sophie glanced out the window. The sun had set now and there was nothing out there but the flickering lights of the boats dotting the dark sea. 'I appreciate everything you've done for me, Charlie,' she added.

Charlie gripped her hand. 'Let's not ruin our evening by talking about this now.' He smiled at her. 'Besides, I've got a surprise for you. When you find out what it is I think you'll change your mind about London.'

On the bus back home, Sophie leaned her head against the window, woozy from the wine and overstuffed from the three-course meal. They bumped along the poorly surfaced road, winding round the coast.

'Ready for your surprise?' Charlie said suddenly, pulling her out of her thoughts.

'Oh, Charlie – you've done enough. The meal was perfect.' She'd offered to pay half but he'd refused to let her. She didn't want to feel any more indebted to him.

Charlie pushed the buzzer to stop the bus and hurried her towards the doors.

'Why are we getting off here?'

'You'll see.'

They were still a few miles from their flat. The cold night breeze blew Sophie's hair around her face and she shivered, pulling her shawl tighter around her. There was no one else about, only the sound of their breathing, their footsteps on the pavement and the gentle wind. She recognised the village; it was where Charlie's grandfather had lived until he died. They were near the secluded rocks where she and Charlie had had their first kiss.

They walked up a small hill, Sophie's high-heeled shoes rubbing against her ankles as she stumbled on the uneven paving. If she'd known they would be walking any distance she'd have brought her trainers.

'Is it far?'

'Just a little bit further.'

He led her down an unlit lane, winding upwards, and her eyes darted to the bushes on either side. She swallowed her fear as the blood rushed to her ears, and tapped her left wrist three times with her right hand. It was a ritual that calmed her when she was nervous. She reminded herself that her fear was completely irrational with Charlie by her side.

An old stone cottage was perched at the top of the hill, silhouetted against the night sky. Upstairs, the lights were flickering, like someone was home. It took a second for Sophie to recognise the house. Charlie's mother had inherited it in Charlie's grandfather's will. Charlie's grandfather had been born in the cottage into a family with six children, and then many years later, died there alone.

'Here we are,' Charlie said, smiling. His voice was muffled against the roar of the sea, which was just behind the cottage. He took out a key and opened the door, reaching in to turn on the light.

'Mum says we can live here,' he said, a huge grin on his face. Sophie thought of her job applications as she forced a smile.

'Wow,' she said.

In the hallway there was a haphazard mix of building materials and his grandfather's things; pots of paint balanced precariously on piles of yellowing books, a ladder leaning against the wall.

'I'm doing it up,' Charlie said proudly, 'but I haven't started on the downstairs yet.' He took her into the living room where flowered armchairs pointed towards patio doors with views down to the rocky shore. A walking stick leaned against an armchair, and Sophie felt a pang of grief for the man who had lived there. She thought of her own father, still unable to walk properly after his fall.

In the kitchen there was a rusty cooker, some of the knobs broken off, a huge sink and two overhead cupboards with the doors hanging off the hinges, revealing misty wine glasses and tins of baked beans and sweetcorn.

'We can get this all ripped out and done up as good as new,' Charlie said.

'Wow,' Sophie said again, but her stomach lurched. She could feel the walls starting to close in on her, London a distant dream. Instead, she'd be trapped in domesticity a few miles from where she grew up. This might be Charlie's dream, but it wasn't hers.

He grabbed her hand. 'Let me show you upstairs.' His palm was sweaty in hers as they climbed up the frayed green carpet. A cobweb brushed against her bare arm and she swept it aside.

'Remember, I was planning on finding a job in London,' she said softly. She felt sick as she said it, as if she should have given him a little more time before crushing his hopes. But she had to be honest.

He paused in his stride.

'Well, I guess you'll just have to withdraw your applications. We have everything we want now. We won't need to work ourselves to the bone to save for a house anymore. We have one right here.' She couldn't see the expression on his face, but she could hear his heavy breathing.

Charlie reached for her hand, pulling her towards the top of the stairs. 'Let's not discuss this now.' But Sophie could already feel the noose of the house, of Charlie's expectations, tightening around her neck.

. . .

Upstairs, she was assaulted by smells. New paint thinly disguised an underlying layer of damp. There was something else, too, the less abrasive scent of pine, as if Charlie had sprayed something around. He told her the bathroom needed doing up, and then took her into the back bedroom.

It was freshly painted yellow and there was a wonky border round the top, an odd mix of dinosaurs and unicorns.

'I decorated this for the kids,' he said. 'I thought we'd probably have two, so I made it unisex. They could share. We could get bunk beds when they're older.'

He never listened to her, always just assumed she wanted the same thing as him. She'd told him she wasn't sure if she wanted children, and she certainly didn't want them now. She had her whole life ahead of her.

'You know I'm not sure if I want children.'

'But you said that before Grandad died, before the inheritance, before this house. I thought it was just because we couldn't really afford them.'

'It's not that... I just want to live my life first. Before I settle down.'

'We have everything we'd ever need right here. The sun, the sea, our families, this house.'

But Sophie wanted to feel the buzz of the city, to be part of something bigger. She wanted to spontaneously go out to the cinema or a theatre, not plan a three-hour round trip to the nearest town. She wanted a completely different life.

He wrapped his arms around her. 'Is this about London? I don't think that's for you. You didn't feel safe there. And you did well at school and all that, but you dropped out of university. You're not really a career girl, are you?'

She winced, thinking of the online degree she'd worked so hard for. He didn't even seem to think that counted. 'You know I've always wanted to work in advertising.' Even as a child she'd been obsessed by ads; their bold colours, their promises of a better life. As a young teenager she and her mother would play a game when they watched the television, seeing who would be first to guess the product being advertised. Her mother always won.

'I thought you'd grown out of it,' he said. 'And I've done all this for you.' He indicated the room, and Sophie felt guilty for not being more grateful. Tears started to well up in her eyes and she felt an impulse to run out of the house, away from all this pressure to be someone else, to conform to the life Charlie wanted for them. But she stayed.

'And now,' Charlie said, as if the conversation they'd just had hadn't even happened, 'let me take you to the master bedroom.' He lifted her in his strong arms and carried her through the next doorway. Flickering battery-operated tea lights surrounded the bed, creating the illusion of candlelight. The room was newly painted a pale blue, reflecting the sky.

'I thought we could sleep here tonight.' He nodded to the metal-framed bed, covered with creased, white, freshly washed sheets. She wondered if the bed had been his grandfather's. 'The start of our new life,' he said.

She went to the window and opened it, listened to the sound of the sea just beyond the garden. The realisation hit her that she couldn't do this, couldn't be with Charlie. She didn't want to live in this house with him, to have kids with him. His hard work doing up the cottage only made her feel trapped.

She turned. 'Charlie,' she said, as gently as she could.

He was down on the floor. On one knee. She swallowed.

He opened the ring box and held it out towards her.

'Sophie – will you marry me?'

TWO

Sophie stared down at Charlie, his eyes eagerly awaiting her response. The ring sparkled. Outside the window the waves lapped across the rocks. It would have been the perfect proposal, but her chest was tightening and her pulse was racing. Her future flashed before her eyes: a marriage to Charlie, kids, living in this house, in this village so close to where she grew up, until the day she died. Living in his shadow, tiptoeing around his short temper.

She felt faint and woozy, the wine sloshing round her body, slowing her thoughts.

'Charlie—' she said, her voice soft. Her heart pounded in her chest. She couldn't say no, she couldn't do that to him, not after everything he had done for her. But she couldn't say yes either. This evening had clarified things for her. They wanted to live completely different lives.

'You're crying,' he said, standing up and wiping the tears from her eyes gently with his fingertips.

He grinned at her and she realised that he thought she was so overcome with emotion she couldn't speak.

She shook her head, trying to get the words out. 'Charlie—'

'Is that a yes, then?'

He took the ring out of the box and held it towards her hand, a cluster of diamonds set around a blue stone. It must have cost a fortune. She pulled her hand away.

She shook her head. 'I can't do this, Charlie. I'm so sorry.'

His smile collapsed in on itself and his eyes darkened. 'What do you mean?' He stepped towards her, clenching his hands together. She knew him well enough to recognise he was trying to control his fury.

She backed towards the window, the wind blowing through the gap at the top and lifting her hair.

'Look, I have to go. We'll talk tomorrow.'

'No, don't go, we can work this out.' He grabbed her arm, and she tried to pull away from him, but his fingers tightened on her skin.

'Charlie—'

'What's wrong with you? I've spent ages preparing the house for you.'

'I know. And I'm sorry.' She spoke quietly so as not to anger him further. 'Can you let go of me?'

He released his grip suddenly, flinging his arm out as he did so and catching her across the chest, knocking her to the ground. She got up slowly, anger building inside her. He'd made her decision easy, confirmed she was doing the right thing.

'I'm leaving,' she said firmly.

'Good riddance,' she heard him mutter, as he kicked the bed. But she was already halfway down the stairs, longing to get out of the stale cottage and to inhale the fresh sea air and her own freedom.

Sophie woke the next morning to the sound of seagulls. When she opened her eyes she saw the comfortingly familiar sight of her mother's photo on her bedside table and the overflowing wooden bookshelf. She was back in her childhood bedroom, not in the flat above the fish and chip shop she shared with Charlie. Outside her window, she could hear children shrieking as they fished for crabs in the rock pools.

She threw on her dressing gown, manoeuvred her way past her father's stairlift and went downstairs.

'Morning, Dad,' she said as she went into the kitchen.

'I heard you come in last night,' he said, putting down his paper. He looked at her with concern, waiting for an explanation.

'Sorry if I woke you.'

He shook his head. 'Don't worry. Is everything OK? Did something happen with Charlie?'

Sophie sighed. 'We've split up.'

Her father wrung his hands together. 'I'm sorry to hear that. Do you want a cup of tea?' he asked. It was the way he always dealt with stress. He thought a cup of tea could fix everything.

'Yes, please.' He got up slowly and limped over to the kettle. His leg had never recovered from his fall, but he was determined not to lose his independence and he pushed himself to do all the everyday things around the house. He never let her make her own cup of tea.

As they waited for the kettle to boil, her father put his hand on her shoulder. 'I wasn't expecting this,' he said. 'I've always liked Charlie.'

Sophie nodded. Charlie and her father had always got on well, and he'd even helped her father in his handyman business for a while, before he'd completed his apprenticeship as a plumber.

'I saw him earlier in the week, you know. He said he was doing his grandfather's house up for the pair of you. I thought it would make a lovely family home.'

'It will do, for someone. It's just not what I want.' She felt relieved to say it out loud, as if a weight had been lifted.

He nodded, and brought her her tea. 'What is it that you want?' he said, kindly.

She smiled at him. 'I want to go back to London, to find a job there.'

He nodded slowly, his face a mixture of pride and concern. 'You feel ready to return?' he said.

She nodded.

He squeezed her arm. 'I always knew you wanted something different. Your mother said you'd move out after university, that you wanted a career. But after she died and you left London... well, I wasn't sure if you wanted the same things anymore.'

Sophie smiled at him. 'I really want to see if I can build a career in advertising.'

'I'm sure you can, love,' he said, tears in his eyes. 'Your mother would be so proud.'

Sophie felt tears forming in her eyes, too, and she hesitated for a moment. Since her dad's fall, she'd worried about him. 'Will you be all right on your own?' she asked tentatively.

'Of course,' he said. 'I'll be fine. You go to London.'

She smiled at him through her tears. She was free of Charlie now, and she had her father's blessing to go. Now all she had to do was find a job.

After her shift at the café, Sophie met up with her oldest friend, Keely, on the seafront. They walked barefoot along the water's edge like they used to do when they were teenagers, when they'd always leave their houses to catch up, both worried about their parents overhearing their phone conversations. Keely's mouth fell open in shock as Sophie told her about Charlie's proposal.

'What did you say?' she asked, her eyes wide.

'I felt awful, but I had to say no.' Sophie felt guilty as she explained. Keely had been waiting for her own partner to propose for years.

'You did the best thing for you,' Keely said encouragingly. 'If it didn't feel right then it wasn't right.'

'Yeah,' Sophie said. 'I already feel more free.'

'How are the job applications going?' Keely asked.

'OK,' Sophie said. 'I've applied for a lot of advertising jobs in London. But I'm not getting interviews. I'm not sure if it's because I took so long getting my degree.'

'That's hardly your fault, Sophie. After what happened.'

Sophie sighed. Keely didn't know what had really happened either. Sophie hadn't been able to bring herself to tell her. Keely thought that Sophie had been mugged, and that it had pushed her over the edge when she was already fragile, still grieving for her mother.

'I know,' Sophie said. 'I think Charlie thinks I'm getting ahead of myself. That I think I'm better than I really am.'

'Don't pay any attention to him. He's just jealous.'

'Maybe he's right. I don't seem to be getting anywhere.'

'Are you looking through social media, or just sending your CV off and hoping?'

'I'm spending days filling in long application forms,' Sophie said. 'Honestly, you wouldn't believe the amount of stuff they ask for.'

'Hmm...' Keely said.

'What?' Sophie said.

'You know, you really have to be out there to get noticed. Network. Use social media.' Keely was on Instagram all the time, sharing photos of her three kids and running her tourist business, offering local tours of the most picture-perfect views. She made everything seem idyllic, from her own life to the town where they lived.

'I don't know.' Sophie hadn't been on any social media since university. She hadn't liked laying her life out like that for anyone to see. You never knew who was looking.

'You want to work in advertising, you've got to be able to sell yourself,' Keely said with a smile.

'You're right. It's just...'

'Just what?'

But Sophie couldn't explain that she was scared of being found, scared of the past catching up with her. 'I'll have a look into it,' she said.

Keely laughed. 'You'll look into it? You're not getting away with it that easily. I'll make you a profile tonight.'

After half an hour Keely had to get back to her kids. Sophie wandered home, feeling calmer. She unlocked the door of her father's house and shouted out to him. There was no reply. He must be out.

She went through to the kitchen.

'Hello, Sophie.' Charlie was sitting at her father's kitchen table, waiting for her, as he munched on a bacon sandwich.

'Why are you here?' she asked.

'You said we could talk today, but you weren't answering your calls. I was worried about you. Your dad was out, so I let myself in.'

'I'm sorry, Charlie,' Sophie said softly. 'We're over.'

He stood up. 'But I don't understand. I've done everything for you. The house. The ring. What more do you want?'

'We want different things. We've outgrown each other.'

'You've outgrown me, you mean. You think you're better than me, don't you?' He stood up, came closer to her.

'Look, Charlie. You'd better leave.'

He sneered at her. 'If we're breaking up, then I want the money you owe me back.'

Sophie felt sick. Charlie had cleared all of Sophie's credit card debt and paid for private physiotherapy for her father. She owed him a small fortune.

'You know I can't pay you now. I'll get it back to you as soon as I've found a job.'

He nodded and walked to the door. He took one last dismissive look at her. 'You need me a lot more than you think you do, Sophie,' he said, slamming the door behind him on his way out.

THREE

TWO WEEKS LATER

Sophie sat on the train to London, going over her notes for her interview. Keely had created a LinkedIn profile for her and put out a heartfelt post explaining how her mother's death and her father's accident had forced her to drop out of university and move back home, and how she was struggling to find a job, even though she'd recently completed her online degree. It wasn't quite true; the reasons she'd dropped out were different. Sophie would never have written the post herself, but it had worked. It had been shared hundreds of times and had attracted the attention of the people at One Pure Thought, a new advertising agency that had been set up the previous year by a trio of young entrepreneurs.

As Sophie stepped down from the train onto the platform, she got caught up in the stream of commuters, rushing by on either side of her, heads down, faces determined. Her body tensed as a tall blond man brushed by her, memories of her time at university flooding back. She'd lived on campus in south-west London, a short train ride from the city centre. She hadn't been back to London since university and she hadn't expected to feel like this, for the sights and sounds to remind her so much. After all, what had happened could have happened anywhere in the world. The city was blameless.

She paused on the concourse and pulled out her phone to check the directions. She was in plenty of time, so she walked out of the station into the grey cloudy day and found a small, cramped café.

She freshened up in the toilet, touching up her make-up and practising her smile in the mirror, wondering if the green shirt she'd bought specially was too bright. Finding a stool by the window, she hung her bag on the table hook, took out her phone and went over what she knew about the company. It had been set up by a Max Laithwaite (recently featured in a national newspaper's article, 'Thirty Under-Thirties to Watch Out For'), alongside his sister Cassie, the Client Relationship Director, and James, the Creative Director. There was a photo of the three of them on the website, sitting in distressed red leather armchairs. Max was the only one smiling. James was staring thoughtfully, his serious eyes slightly obscured by his crop of dark hair, while Cassie was looking determinedly at the camera, meeting the eyes of her viewer straight on. Sophie reread their vision statement and biographies and looked at their client list, which included many of the major food and drink brands, alongside some up-and-coming start-ups. She couldn't quite imagine herself working with brands of that calibre, shaping how they were presented to the world.

She stared out at the London pigeons fighting over scraps of bread in the street and wondered if she was brave enough to do this, to start a new life in London. She'd have to find a room in a shared house, and the thought of living with strangers terrified her. They could be anyone. When she'd lived with her father and then with Charlie, she'd known who was in the house each night. There were never any surprises. But in a house share anyone could bring anyone back. She wouldn't be able to lock strangers out. They'd be inside with her. She swallowed her fear. She had to face it, to live normally. She couldn't let everything that had happened in her past hold her back from a brighter future.

When she got to Soho, she passed the entrance to the office several times before she noticed the small door with the name One Pure Thought on a tiny plaque above the intercom. Sophie had been expecting a modern building, all glass and chrome, but this door seemed to lead to the area above a pub. She took a deep breath and pressed the buzzer. Nothing. Around her, people walked by, and she felt oddly conspicuous in the dark doorway. She thought she felt eyes on her and looked up to see a small security camera.

She pressed the buzzer again. This time she heard the static sound which told her it had been answered and then the click of the door being unlocked.

'Hello?' she said. But the other person said nothing and she heard the click of the door locking.

She sighed and pressed the buzzer again. Perhaps they weren't expecting her, or thought she was a delivery person. She pushed her hair back from her face, peered up into the security camera and forced a smile.

Again, she heard static and the door unlock. This time she pushed it open and climbed the staircase.

At the top there was a woman a few years older than her, dressed in boot-cut jeans and shiny silver heels with a neatly ironed shirt. Cassie. She looked better turned out in the flesh, all neat lines and sharp colours.

'You must be Sophie,' she said with a warm smile. 'I'm so pleased to meet you. Come through and sit down. I must introduce you to James.'

'Thanks so much for offering me the interview,' Sophie said, blushing.

'Oh, no problem at all. Your friend's post really resonated with me. And we're looking for a variety of people with different life experiences for our roles. We tend to attract the same type of people, all from the same universities. It makes us quite linear in our thinking. We want someone different, to challenge that.'

'That's brilliant,' Sophie said. 'And the company sounds like such an exciting place to work.'

'We like to think so,' a voice with a slight lilt came from behind them, and Sophie turned.

'James,' the man said, holding out his hand. 'Nice to meet you.' He smiled under his long lashes and Sophie felt a jolt of electricity rush through her as his hand gripped hers in a firm handshake. His eyes were a penetrating blue and they held hers until their hands separated, and his smile turned into a grin. 'Firm handshake,' he remarked. 'You can always judge someone by their handshake. At least, that's what some of our clients would say.'

'And did mine meet the standard?' Sophie asked, already feeling relaxed in his company.

'Oh, it far exceeded the standard,' he joked. 'Top marks for the handshake. Now you only have to pass the interview and the tests.'

Cassie's eyes narrowed slightly and she punched him playfully on the arm. 'Stop messing about. Let's go to the meeting room.'

She led them through an open-plan office, the modern desks and office chairs a contrast to the old brick building. Everywhere she looked there were huge advertising posters covering the walls, with the brands she would find in her dad's kitchen and on supermarket shelves around the world.

'Do you work with all these clients?' Sophie asked, in awe.

'Some of them,' Cassie said with a smile. 'We're targeting

the others. We'll work with them one day, I'm sure. At least if I have anything to do with it.'

There were a few people scattered around, bodies bent over desks, computers lit up with logos and photos. But mostly the office was empty, a desert of vacant space. 'A lot of the team are with clients today,' Cassie explained, as she pushed open a door in the corner to a huge room. Light beamed through vast arched windows. Sophie could see the pub sign outside the window blowing back and forth in the wind, creaking. The room didn't have a table or office chairs like she'd expected. Instead, there were the three comfy leather chairs that had featured in the photo on the website, alongside low-slung gamer chairs. When she looked at the leather chairs more closely she could see the rips in the arms of the fabric, smell their slightly stale odour.

'These chairs are from the pub originally,' Cassie said. 'Max didn't want them to go to the tip.'

Sophie nodded. Cassie sat in one of the gamer chairs, exposing the red soles of her Louboutin shoes. Sophie sat in the seat opposite her, trying to keep her back ramrod straight, while James took the armchair next to Cassie.

'So,' James said, 'what brings you here? To One Pure Thought? And what interests you about the brand strategist role?'

Sophie soon began to relax as they interviewed her. They ran through the questions on branding and advertising quickly and then focused on getting to know her. Their main goal was to employ someone who was a good fit for the team.

'Honestly,' Cassie said with a smile. 'We've had such bad luck lately, employing graduates. I really wanted to find someone with a bit more life experience this time. So can I hear about that? Your friend's post said you'd been looking after your father for the last few years.'

James's eyes softened in sympathy as she spoke about her parents, her mother's death and her father's accident. Cassie tilted her head as she listened intently.

'It's OK,' Cassie said gently, as tears formed in Sophie's eyes. 'We understand. I lost my stepmother when I was young. It was after my parents had had a difficult divorce, which made it worse. Max and I still use our mother's maiden name even now. And James... well, James is the kind of guy who understands. He's always been there for me.' Sophie saw a flicker of a look between them. A knowing, affectionate glance. Was there some kind of romantic relationship between them?

'I'm sorry I got emotional,' Sophie said, wiping away her tears with the back of her hand, irritated with herself. She'd always been so in control, kept her emotions in check. But here, in front of James and Cassie, she was falling apart.

Cassie passed her a tissue. 'Don't worry. We appreciate your honesty... it's rare. And you've been through so much. It's completely understandable for you to be upset.'

James was staring at the floor. 'It's OK,' he said. 'The thing is, we get so many young graduates here... and we feel that although they may understand the principles of marketing, they lack something fundamental. They don't understand people, they don't have empathy. And in a creative agency like ours, that's what we need. We need to understand our clients, and we need to understand their customers. Not just the data and the stats – we need to understand them at a human level. Your personal story... it's distressing, but at the same time it's given you a maturity, a wisdom and an empathy. And those are qualities we're looking for now.'

Sophie half smiled, shocked. She hadn't blown it. 'It's great to be talking to a company that has values,' she said.

Cassie smiled at her. 'We pride ourselves on ours.'

They stood up and Sophie followed their lead. 'Have you had a lot of applicants?'

'We didn't advertise the job this time, but we always have a few speculative applications, and we've sifted through those. We're being very selective in who we invite for interview. We wouldn't want to waste our time.'

'So, Sophie,' James said, as they walked down the corridor. 'Do you have any questions?'

She nodded. 'Can you tell me what the role involves?'

'Well, we really want someone who can be flexible and contribute to all aspects of the business, not just the brand strategy, but also competitor research, pulling together campaigns and creating copy. We're a small agency, so we need someone who can chip in. We'll also want to put you in front of clients and get you involved in selling new projects to keep our business ticking over.'

Sophie felt a rush of excitement, her heart beating faster. Everything about the company seemed perfect. She could imagine herself working with James and Cassie, getting involved in everything the agency did, learning all the time and developing new skills. She wanted the job so badly.

'Any other questions?'

Sophie asked about the most challenging parts of the job and the company's growth ambitions. After James had finished answering, he turned to her and grinned. 'Aren't you curious about pay at all? Or perks?'

'The pay isn't really what's motivating me,' Sophie replied. 'I just want to come to London, use my degree and do interesting work with people I like.' She worried she was coming across as desperate, but she really wanted the job, and she hadn't been offered any other interviews.

'I see,' James said.

'I'd just need enough to afford to live in London.'

James smiled at her. 'You won't have to worry about finding a place in London. The company owns a few flats here, very close to the office. They're for our employees. You can live there.'

'Who would I be sharing with?'

James looked amused. 'No one, you'd get a flat to yourself.'

Sophie thought of the money she owed Charlie. She'd been planning to live in a cheap house share so she could save the money to pay him back. There was no way she could afford to live by herself in central London.

'How much is it?' she asked tentatively. Perhaps it was subsidised.

James raised his eyebrows, as if surprised by her question. 'It's an employee perk, so rent-free. So perhaps you'll consider it.'

Sophie's mind was spinning. Rent-free? And he was asking her to consider it, which meant...

'Have I got the job?' she asked, her voice an embarrassing squeak.

James laughed. 'Of course you have. Congratulations. You can start next week.'

FOUR

ONE WEEK LATER

Sophie got into the taxi gratefully, sinking into the back seat. She'd been surprised to see the driver with a sign with her name on it when she'd got off the train, tired from dragging two heavy suitcases up and over the stairs and then across the concourse.

In the comfort of his black cab, it felt like she was a world apart from the London she'd lived in as a student. She could see how everything connected and fitted together, unlike being underground in the cramped darkness of the Tube. They drove over Westminster Bridge, the river sparkling beneath them. Her driver pointed out the London Eye, as it retreated into the distance, and then they drove past the Houses of Parliament on the other side of the river.

The streets were filled with life; in every direction there was movement and sound. Cyclists weaved in and out of the traffic and a bus trundled by. Suited workers walked down the streets stuffing sandwiches into their mouths in their hurry to get back to the office.

Sophie felt more relaxed. She'd been nervous this past week, wondering if she was making a mistake coming back. But she needed to take the next step in her life and start her career.

She thought of the flat she'd live in. She supposed most flats were in high-rise blocks in London, towering into the sky. Would she feel safe there? She'd live on her own, be able to lock the door, which was surely better than a house share. But how would she sleep if she was completely alone? She was so easily frightened by noises in the night and she worried about intruders. Before now Charlie had always been by her side; she knew he could fight them off. But in a big block there'd always be noises, the sounds of other people walking by.

When they got to Soho the taxi made its way along the backstreets, past the empty theatres and bars doing lunchtime trade to workers sitting at the outside tables. They turned right into a street of Victorian town houses, standing tall against the sky. They were whitewashed and beautiful, window boxes with flowers on each one.

'Here we are,' the taxi driver said.

The house looked like all the others in the street: four storeys tall, built for accommodating a well-off family and their servants. Sophie could see a figure at the window, which moved away as the taxi pulled up. As the driver got her bags out of the boot, James opened the front door and propped it open with a wedge.

'Hello, Sophie.'

'James – I didn't expect to see you here. I thought you'd be at the office.' It was the middle of the working day.

'One of my most important jobs is welcoming new staff,' he said with a smile. 'Let me take your bags for you.' He lifted the suitcases easily and carried them up the stone steps to the house.

Inside, the hallway was wide with high ceilings and a black and white mosaic tiled floor. The light fitting looked expensive, chandelier-style, with glass crystals hanging down, sparkling. But the light itself seemed dim, barely casting a shadow in the long windowless hallway.

James led her up the wide carpeted stairs. The house was eerily silent. There must be six or seven flats in the building, but she couldn't hear any other signs of life. Everyone else must be at work.

He opened the door to a flat on the third floor, and a huge living room greeted her. Light shone through the big sash windows. Sophie and her suitcases seemed small inside it. She didn't have enough stuff for this place. It was so different to the cramped flat above the fish and chip shop she'd shared with Charlie, and the cluttered house by the sea that he had been doing up for them. This flat was sparse, recently decorated, a blank canvas ready for her to make her own mark on it.

The walls were painted white and the high ceilings dwarfed the four pieces of furniture: a two-seater sofa, a coffee table, a sideboard and a small bookcase with nothing on it. She'd have to fill it up. When she got the chance she'd go round the charity shops, look for books and ornaments to make herself at home.

'Do you like it?' James asked, smiling.

'It's huge,' she replied. 'I love it.'

He pushed his dark wavy hair back from his eyes. 'Phew,' he said. 'I'm glad.'

He led her onto the balcony through the narrow door, and for a second she brushed against him and electricity rushed through her. She looked up at him, into his penetrating eyes. It felt strangely intimate to be in the flat with him, almost as if they were a couple moving into their first home together.

'There's a great view from the balcony,' he said. 'Although watch the railing. It's a bit low.'

Sophie looked over at the houses opposite. Outside one of them, a person stood leaning against a green electricity box, in a royal-blue rain jacket. They seemed to be looking up at her, but they quickly turned their face away when she looked back. They must have heard the balcony door opening and been curious. Perhaps they were a neighbour.

'If you turn that way, you can see the park,' James said. 'And over the top of those buildings, there's the Shard.'

'Wow,' she said. There were two chairs and a small table on the balcony. Bright flowers were in the window box. The soil was wet from where they'd been freshly watered.

'These are beautiful,' she said. 'Who planted them?'

James blushed. 'Oh, I did. I wanted to brighten the place up a bit. It's quite stark here. And I needed a break from the relentlessness of the office. It was good to come here and do something with my hands, feel the earth beneath my fingers, you know? After staring at a screen all day.'

'I can understand that. So how come the company owns this flat?'

'We own the whole house, actually. Our investor has a lot of money. And so when we set up the company, he bought this converted building, too, so we could house our employees.'

It reminded Sophie of the way companies in the early twentieth century used to build housing for their employees. Like the Cadbury family, or the railway houses.

'What made them do that?'

'Well, they know that the cost of living in London is expensive. And Cassie and I want people from all backgrounds to be able to work here. Cassie thought if we took away the problem of rent, that would really help us attract the best people. And the owner is a shrewd businessman. He knew buying flats in London was a good investment anyway, as they were likely to go up in value. So he could kill two birds with one stone. House the employees and make some money.'

'Makes sense,' Sophie said, although she couldn't ever imagine having that much money.

James touched her arm. 'I know it can all seem a bit intimidating. Max has so much money he doesn't know what to do with it. But not all of us are like that. I'm not from the same background.'

'Really?'

'Nope. My parents were teachers.'

'My mother was a teacher. She taught English at my secondary school. I hated being in the same school as her.'

'Yeah, that can be a pain. Luckily I went to a school miles away from home, so it wasn't a problem for me.'

They came back into the flat. James opened up his shoulder bag and pulled out a MacBook and a box containing the latest iPhone.

'I set these up for you this morning,' he said, placing them down on the coffee table. I've put a Post-it with your username and password for the Mac on the keyboard. You should be good to go as soon as you get to the office.'

'Wow, thanks,' Sophie said, staring at the iPhone and thinking of the old phone she'd kept for the last four years.

'Do you want a drink?' James asked. 'Tea or coffee? I put some milk in the fridge, but nothing else, I'm afraid. You'll need to pop to the supermarket.'

'I'm OK for now. I'd like to see the rest of the flat.'

'The bedroom and bathroom are through here,' James said, leading her into a spacious bedroom with a king-size bed in the centre, a large wardrobe and chest of drawers next to the wall and a desk in the corner.

There were no sheets on the bed. James saw her looking.

'I thought you'd want to choose your own bed sheets and curtains and the like. Hang up your pictures. Make the flat your own.'

'Sure,' Sophie said. She felt overwhelmed. Cassie was expecting her at a meeting this afternoon. She wouldn't have much time.

'Oxford Street's not far. I can come with you if you like.'

Sophie looked at her watch. 'I need to get to the office. I have an introductory meeting with Cassie.'

'Oh, she'll understand. Don't worry. I'll drop her a line

now.' James typed quickly into his phone. A few seconds after he'd sent the message, it beeped.

'All fine with Cass,' he said. 'She says you can have your meeting tomorrow. Now let's go shopping.'

'Don't you need to get back to work?' Sophie asked.

James's eyes twinkled. 'This is my work,' he said, with a cheeky smile. 'Helping new employees settle in.' She felt his arm brush against hers and she was suddenly aware of the scent of his aftershave. 'Unless you don't want me to come with you?'

She shook her head. 'I'd love it if you accompanied me.'

He grinned and took her arm. 'Let's go then.'

James locked up the flat and handed Sophie the key. When they got down the stairs and made their way out into the autumn sunshine, Sophie felt happy. She shielded her eyes from the low-lying sun as she went out of the building, a sudden movement across the street attracting her attention.

It was the person in the blue jacket she'd seen from the balcony. Once again, they had been looking at her house. She'd assumed they were a neighbour, and she expected them to come and introduce themselves or go back inside. She gave a small wave. But instead of responding they turned and walked briskly away, breaking into a run as they got to the end of the street.

FIVE

Sophie chatted to James as they walked towards the Tube station. He was giving her the lowdown on everything there was to do nearby; the theatres, bars and clubs. As they neared the station entrance, they were interrupted by his phone.

'Excuse me,' he said, holding his finger up to say he'd only be a minute while he answered it.

Sophie flicked through the news on her phone while she waited.

'That was Cassie,' James said, when he'd hung up. 'She said she wanted to be the one to go shopping with you. I should get back to the office.'

'OK,' Sophie said. She thought of Cassie's Louboutins and hoped she could afford the shopping trip with her.

'Cassie can never resist the urge to shop,' James said with a smile. 'I'll see you later.'

'Thanks so much for showing me round the flat.'

'No problem. You'll be at the drinks this evening, won't you? They're in your honour. To welcome you to the company.'

'Of course,' Sophie said, but she felt a shiver of anxiety. She didn't like going home on her own when she'd been drinking. She hadn't done that since she'd been at university.

'Bye, then,' James said, and there was an awkward moment when they didn't know how to say goodbye. They were work colleagues, and yet it didn't feel like it. After the hour in her new flat, she felt like she already knew him. And they hadn't even been in the office yet.

He hesitated for a moment, searching her eyes, and then settled for giving her arm a small squeeze. She felt a strange combination of relief and disappointment. As he'd leaned towards her, a small part of her had wondered if he might kiss her.

'See you later, Sophie,' he said.

She met Cassie in John Lewis on Oxford Street. After struggling through the throngs of people, listening to the mix of languages they spoke as they strolled down the street with their heavy shopping bags, she was pleased to see a familiar face waiting for her near the make-up counter.

'Welcome,' Cassie said, wrapping her arms around her. Sophie was surprised by her embrace, but she returned it, and Cassie air-kissed her, once on each cheek.

'Thank you,' Sophie said. 'I'm sorry about our meeting. I would have come, but James said it was easy to rearrange.'

'No problem. Look, we can talk as we shop. I want to tell you all about the company, our goals and ambitions. And I want to talk to you about your role. I have high hopes for you. We need more strong female leaders at the agency.'

Sophie felt a flush of pride and excitement. Cassie had already picked her out as someone who had leadership potential. She had a plan for her. 'I'd love to talk more about my role,' she said.

'We can sort out the things you need for the flat at the same time.'

'It's a beautiful flat. I feel so lucky to have it.'

'I'm so glad you like it. I chose it myself.'

'You did?'

'Well, the building. The company wanted to invest in property and I went off on a search. There are six flats for employees. We've given you the nicest one. The others aren't taken yet.'

Sophie thought how quiet the house had seemed. She'd assumed it was because everyone else was at work.

'Are you going to offer them to new employees?'

'Yeah, that's the idea. But no one else has taken us up on it yet.'

Sophie frowned. Who would turn down a rent-free flat in the centre of London? Unless she'd got the wrong idea. Was she expected to pay for it? She dreaded to think how much that would cost. Her whole salary probably.

'How come they weren't interested?'

'They already have their own places. Family-owned, usually. You might notice we employ a type. Men who went to private school mainly. I'm trying to increase our diversity, but it's an uphill battle.'

'Right.' Sophie wondered if she would fit in.

'So,' Cassie said gleefully. 'Let's get shopping. What do you need?'

'Not too much,' Sophie said. 'Just sheets and curtains. And some pictures and decorations – something to brighten the place up.' She thought of the flat's white walls, how much of a blank canvas it was.

'I can help with that,' Cassie said. 'I love everything about design, including interior design. I'm a creative person. I studied graphics at university.'

'Did you?'

'Yeah. That's why I got involved in founding an ad agency. I always loved the immediacy of ads, how they communicate so much with a single image.'

'Me too,' Sophie said enthusiastically. 'I love branding because of the psychology behind it, how a good campaign can address consumers' needs and satisfy their aspirations. I can't wait to work on my own campaigns.'

'Between us we'll be a great team,' Cassie said. 'Shall we look at the sheets then?'

Sophie coughed. 'I'm not sure I want to buy bed sheets in John Lewis. They're much cheaper in Primark.' She blushed, thinking of Cassie's expensive shoes.

Cassie's face fell. 'Oh, Sophie, I'm sorry. We'll pay for the sheets.'

'You really don't have to.'

'Oh, don't worry. It's not my money. It's on the company credit card. Whatever you need for your flat, you can put on it.'

'It's fine,' Sophie said. 'I don't want to have debts.' She thought again about the money she owed Charlie.

'You wouldn't have to pay it back. Just consider it another perk, along with the flat.'

It was 6 p.m. by the time they'd finished shopping, and they were both laden down with bags. Cassie had talked non-stop the whole time, explaining the company's strategy and their plans to grow the business. Sophie had felt like she should have been taking notes. She wasn't sure if she'd remember everything.

Cassie hailed a taxi and they took the bags back to Sophie's flat before heading to the pub below the office for Sophie's welcome drinks. Everything was on her doorstep, her flat only a couple of streets from work.

As Cassie walked in, she waved to the woman behind the bar who raised the glass she was cleaning.

'Max knows the landlord well,' Cassie said. 'We come in here a lot. Have you met Max yet? I suppose you haven't had time.' She smiled. 'I'll make sure I introduce you.'

'Your usual?' the barmaid called over to Cassie.

'Do you prefer white or red?' Cassie asked, turning to Sophie.

'White,' Sophie said automatically, remembering too late that she'd planned to stick to soft drinks, at least at the beginning of the evening.

Cassie ordered a bottle of white and took it over to the table. 'Here's Max,' she said, introducing a boyish-looking man, blond, with piercing green eyes, who was sitting next to James at the table.

'Max,' said James, 'is the guy you need to impress.' Sophie felt a fluttering of nerves in her stomach and swallowed. She thought of the photo of Max on the website, reminding herself he was only a few years older than her.

'This is Sophie,' Cassie said. 'She just started today.'

'Great,' Max said, without much enthusiasm, his accent a private school drawl. He studied Sophie's face, then looked her up and down, reaching out his hand to shake hers.

'Why didn't we meet at your interview?' Max asked, and Sophie felt a shiver of alarm. Didn't he like her?

Cassie smiled. 'I thought you trusted me on staffing, Max. I promise she won't be like the last one.'

Max glanced at James. 'If you say so.'

He turned to Sophie. 'So which university did you go to?'

Sophie swallowed. 'I did an online degree, actually. In marketing.' There was no need to mention her abandoned course.

'Online?' Max raised his eyebrows, and looked over at Cassie. 'Well, let's see how you get on here.'

'Sophie impressed us in the interview,' Cassie said quickly, before Sophie had the chance to defend herself.

Max was looking over her shoulder, his mind elsewhere. 'Look, Mercedes is at the bar. Excuse me a minute.'

James put his hand on Sophie's arm. 'Don't worry about him. He can be a bit prickly at times.'

'He lacks social skills,' Cassie said.

'It's OK,' Sophie said. 'He seemed distracted.'

'I'm afraid it takes a certain skill set to work with my brother,' Cassie said with a wry smile.

Sophie nodded.

'You'll need to be able to deal with his mood swings. But I'm sure you can cope with that.'

'Of course,' Sophie said, thinking of the difficult customers she'd dealt with at the café. 'Honestly, I can deal with anyone.'

They had nearly finished the bottle of wine when Max wandered back over with a woman in an expensive suit.

'That's Mercedes,' Cassie whispered. 'She started six months ago.'

Mercedes smiled at Sophie as she approached the table. 'You must be the new girl.'

'Yep, I am.' Sophie stood up and stuck out her hand. 'Sophie.'

'Mercedes.' Mercedes gave her hand the briefest shake and then looked Sophie up and down the way Max had. Sophie folded her arms across her chest, suddenly aware of her H&M shirt and her Next skirt. Mercedes managed a half-smile, as if she had decided already that Sophie wasn't worthy of her time and attention.

'More drinks?' Max asked the table, and Sophie saw him lower his hand to rest it on the back of Mercedes' skirt. She didn't move away. Sophie took a big gulp of her wine. So that's how it was.

'More wine,' Cassie said, waving the empty bottle at him.

'Sure,' Max said.

And with that, he and Mercedes returned to the bar.

'They're dating,' Cassie said, when they were out of earshot.

'Right.'

Some others from the office arrived, and everyone shifted up so they could sit at the end of the table. James budged up closer to Sophie, their legs touching. 'Max has always been a bit of a ladies' man. Irresistible to some, I suppose.'

'Really?' Sophie asked, and Cassie laughed heartily.

'Don't let him hear you say that. You'll damage his ego.'

'It's a combination of his money and his persistence,' James says. 'After a while it's hard to say no.'

Sophie nodded.

'He's worked his way through a lot of the female staff,' Cassie said.

'Right.' Sophie glanced at James beside her, who smiled ruefully. He was far more attractive than Max.

They quietened down as Max came back to the table with Mercedes.

'So how are you settling in?' Max asked. 'James said you've moved into one of our flats.'

'Fine, thanks,' Sophie said. 'The flat's lovely. And so close to the office.'

'That will be useful when work gets busy. As it will do. We have a work hard, play hard culture.'

'I'm more than willing to work hard.'

'People say that...' Max said. 'But they don't all mean it.'

Cassie looked at him. 'Believe me, she means it. Just trust her.'

'I'll always be in the office until the work's done.' Sophie intended to excel at this job. She'd been given the opportunity and she wasn't going to waste it.

He smiled. 'The work's never done.'

. . .

Sophie left the pub with the others, her mind slightly fuzzy from drink. Max had his arm round Mercedes and they kissed on the pavement outside. Sophie hesitated for a moment, wondering if she should wait to say goodbye to him or slip away.

Then Max pulled away from Mercedes. 'Do you want me to walk you home?' he asked Sophie, seeing her standing there.

'No. It's only round the corner. I just wanted to say goodbye. And thanks for organising the drinks. I'll see you tomorrow.'

'No worries. See you tomorrow. Good luck on your first day.' He said it seriously, as if he thought she would find it difficult.

Cassie and James said goodbye, and Sophie set off back to the flat. Although it was only a couple of streets away, the noise of people leaving the pubs faded quickly as the streets became more residential. Sophie felt her body tense as she realised how deserted the street of huge, terraced houses was. She stuck to the route under the street lights, clutching her keys between her fingers. Despite the alcohol coursing through her veins, she was alert, her eyes darting around the shadowy corners as if someone might jump out.

As she got to her road, she was sure she felt someone watching her. She had a heightened awareness of a small movement in her peripheral vision, but when she turned round, all she saw was a homeless man across the street, bedding down for the night in the porch of a house.

She kept walking, relieved to climb the steps to her building, but feeling very conspicuous as she stood at the top. As she fumbled with her key in the stiff lock, she realised she hadn't opened the door herself before. James and Cassie had always done it for her.

She fiddled with it for a moment, unable to turn the key, a rising sense of panic engulfing her. She didn't know anyone in London except the people she was working with. If she couldn't get in she'd have to call James or Cassie. She pulled out her phone, trying to shield it from view. She didn't want to be a target for muggers. People got mugged in London all the time. You had to be more careful here.

She found Cassie's number, but then hesitated. She couldn't phone her saying she was locked out the night before she started the job.

She reached up and tried the key one more time. It must have been a slightly different angle, because suddenly the lock gave and the key twisted and she was inside. The hallway stretched out before her and she could see the dark shadows of the stairs. She waved her hands around expecting a sensor to flick the lights on. Nothing.

Glancing at her phone she saw it was nearly out of battery. The torch wouldn't run with low battery, and besides, she needed to conserve it until she got to her flat. She wasn't safe yet. What if the key didn't turn for her own door either?

Using the dim light from the phone screen to guide her, she ran her hand along the wall. Eventually she felt a light switch, sticky and tacky with something unknown. She pressed it hopefully and a dim bulb came on in the centre of the chandelier above her, casting a tiny circle of light around it. She started to make her way up the stairs. She could just about make out a bare bulb hanging from the landing above that led to two flats. It felt odd to be in such a big building without the noise from other occupants. No talking. No television. Only the sound of her own footsteps.

When she got to the landing she reached for the switch for the next light and quickly flicked it on, the light chasing away the shadows as she climbed the steps to her doorway. Looking from left to right, she placed the key in the lock and was grateful when it turned. Inside the flat everything was as she'd left it, and she felt relieved as she turned on the final set of lights. Her shopping bags from her trip with Cassie were still by the sofa and her suitcases were in the living room.

She felt a slight breeze on her face and turned to see that the balcony door was wide open. It creaked as it moved back and forth. Sophie froze, staring at it. Had someone been in her flat, or had she just not shut it properly?

She tried to be rational. The only things in the flat of any value were her shopping and her suitcases and both were still there. No one had broken in. She'd just left the door open. But still she went round the flat checking every room, inside every cupboard, even under the bed. There was no one hiding here. She was alone.

She needed to get to sleep before her first day at work tomorrow. Wearily she took the bed sheets out of the shopping bags and made the bed. She couldn't be bothered to find her nightclothes, so she stripped off and crawled under the sheets.

It was only when she was about to drop off that she noticed the amber glow from outside and realised that she hadn't bought any curtains. From the bed, she peered out into the street. But there were no lights on in the houses opposite. No reason to think anyone was looking in.

SIX

Sophie felt the warm glare of bright sunlight on her eyelids and rolled away from it. She wasn't ready to wake up. But even facing the other way, the room was still far too bright. She opened her eyes slowly and remembered she was in the new flat. The huge bedroom windows that she had so admired yesterday were letting in the October sunshine.

Her stomach rumbled. Last night she'd managed to knock back three glasses of wine without eating anything, and now she was ravenous. She picked up her phone from the floor by her bed where she'd put it on to charge and looked at the time. Her alarm was due to go off in a few minutes. She needed to get up and get ready for her first day in the office.

As she eased herself out of bed, her head throbbed. She wasn't used to drinking alcohol anymore. She hardly drank anything at home in Dorset. In the kitchen, she opened each cupboard in turn, hoping some food had appeared there overnight. But no. She hadn't even remembered to buy cereal yesterday.

Sighing, she went to the bathroom and turned on the shower. Stripping off, she stared at her face in the huge backlit mirror that lined the wall. There were dark circles under her green eyes and her blonde hair was all over the place. She'd need to be on her A-game today, but she felt exhausted.

She went over the night before, running through what she'd said to everyone. The whole office's first impression of her would have been formed at the pub. She'd let her guard down, but she didn't think she'd said anything stupid. It had been quite a different introduction to the formal one she'd imagined.

She showered and dressed quickly. At the local coffee shop she had a Danish pastry and a hot chocolate, loading up on sugar and carbs to take the edge off her hangover. Stopping in Tesco, she added paracetamol to her gurgling stomach with a swig of water.

When Sophie got to the office just before 8.30 a.m., it was already busy with people at their desks, the clacking of keyboards and the quiet rumble of music through headphones.

James looked up from his desk as she approached.

'You're here early,' she said, with a smile.

He laughed. 'Not really. I've been here since six. I like to get here early and work on my graphics when it's quiet. Later in the day there are a lot of interruptions and lots of meetings. Every morning I see the sunrise through the huge glass windows. There's something uplifting about starting the day that way.'

Sophie nodded.

'Don't worry,' he said, seeing her expression. 'We don't expect everyone to get in at six. Like I said, I like it because it's quiet. A lot of the others are night owls and prefer to work late. I do that, too, of course,' he said ruefully.

'It sounds like everyone works hard,' Sophie said.

'Yeah, I suppose we do. But it doesn't feel like work, you know. I love it here.'

Sophie felt a buzz of excitement. She couldn't wait to get started.

'Is Cassie around?'

'She won't be in until a bit later. She's with a client. Why don't I give you a tour?'

'Great. If you have time, that is.'

'Of course.' He rose from his desk and Sophie got a waft of his aftershave. He seemed fresh after last night, no signs of a hangover.

'Do you want a coffee?' he asked. 'Cassie bought a Nespresso machine.'

'Yes, please.'

'Come this way,' he said, as he walked her over to the kitchen.

They made their coffees and then he took her round the office. 'I think you met most people last night,' James said, smiling. 'But I'll just take you round so you can see where everyone sits and introduce you formally. This is Peter, Damian, Daniel, Luke.' The men looked up and nodded at her. Although James had said the others liked to work late rather than get in early, most of the desks were already occupied. And they were all men. Sophie frowned, remembering something Cassie had said about their problems with retaining women, how they needed more female leaders. She was going to need to keep Cassie on her side.

'Right, you sit down and settle in. I'm going to email you over a few files on a new campaign for energy drinks that your predecessor was working on. And you can see what you think.'

Max appeared then, bustling in with Mercedes. Mercedes went to sit at her desk, while Max came over to say hello.

'Are you getting her up to speed, James?'

'Yep. Just passing over Lydia's campaign planning.'

Max sighed. 'I'm not sure that will be much help.'

Sophie wondered why, but the expression on Max's face stopped her from asking.

James shrugged. 'I might as well share it. Maybe Sophie can make sense of her ideas, work out what to do.'

'I'll take a look,' Sophie said, hoping she wasn't out of her depth. If the woman before had struggled with them, then she might too. Suddenly she felt nauseous, as if she was a fraud, about to be found out.

As she waited for James's email to come through with Lydia's files, Sophie quickly checked her emails on her phone. There was a new one to the business account she'd set up when she'd been doing freelance marketing work. She thought she'd told all her clients that she'd no longer be available, but perhaps this was a new enquiry.

She opened the email, and put her hand to her face in shock.

From: user198274928@gmail.com

To: sophie@sophiedoesmarketingandgraphics.com

The police want to talk to you again. You know what will happen if you speak to them. Don't make the same mistake again. Watch your back.

SEVEN

Sophie stared at the message, her breath caught in her throat. How had they found that email account? How could they have possibly known it was her? She didn't give her surname on her website, and all her clients were locals down in Dorset. And yet somehow they had tracked her down.

What did the police want from her now? The last time she had spoken to them had been when she was still at university. Everything that happened was so long ago. It had taken her years to recover from it. But she'd thought she had finally escaped.

'Sophie?' James appeared over her shoulder and she quickly locked her phone and put it down on the desk. 'Did you get the files I just sent you? I can talk you through them now.'

Sophie forced a smile as James pulled up a chair beside her and she opened her emails on her laptop. 'Here they are,' she said.

After James had left, she tried to get on with her work, but she couldn't stop thinking about the email about the police.

Whoever had sent it had managed to find her business in Dorset. And yet, she reassured herself, they wouldn't know she was in London, wouldn't have any idea that she'd moved for a job. Sophie just needed to focus on her work, make a good impression and move on with her life. She tried to forget the email as she looked through Lydia's campaign ideas.

Cassie breezed into the office mid-afternoon.

'Sophie,' she said, placing her hand on Sophie's shoulder and pushing her sunglasses onto the top of her head. 'How are you getting on?'

'OK,' Sophie said. 'How was the client meeting?'

Cassie grinned, excitement radiating from her. 'Good, actually. I just pitched a huge campaign for a start-up upmarket gin brand. And they want to work with us... In fact, they want us to start right away.'

'Wow,' Sophie said. 'Congratulations!'

'How's the work going that James gave you? Do you think you'll be able to help me with the new campaign as well?'

'Yes – that would be brilliant,' Sophie said, thrilled. The new campaign would help her really make her mark. 'I'm still getting my head round the energy drinks campaign that Lydia was working on, but I'm sure I'll be able to work on both.' At first Lydia's ideas had seemed off the wall, but the more she looked at them, the more they made sense. They were daring and original. Sophie liked them, but obviously the company hadn't. Max had said as much. Sophie would have to come up with something different.

'Excellent,' Cassie said. 'Well, as it's your first day, why don't we meet and discuss the various things you're going to be working on, and where you see your career going.'

'Sure,' Sophie said, glad for a break from her desk and excited about the work for the gin company. She grabbed a notebook and pen and stood up.

'You'll need your coat, too,' Cassie said. 'We're going out.'

. . .

Cassie hailed a black cab as they left the building and they weaved through the London streets until they got to Mayfair. They got out of the cab and Cassie shoved a couple of notes into the taxi driver's palm before walking across the pavement, to a suited porter standing outside a discreet black door. She showed some ID, explained that Sophie was her guest and he waved them in. Once they were inside Sophie assumed they were in an expensive hotel. There was a wide staircase, pictures of distinguished men lining the walls. They took a small, rickety lift to the sixth floor and Cassie led her to a small bar, overlooking Green Park.

'Wow, what a view,' Sophie said, walking up to the window and staring out over the expanse of grass. 'You wouldn't know you were in central London.'

'That's why members' clubs like this cost so much,' Cassie said, as she lowered herself carefully into an armchair, keeping her back perfectly straight.

'Ah – it's a members' club?' Sophie was vaguely aware of the concept but wasn't sure what one was, or why anyone would join.

'Yes, my husband and I are members. There's a waiting list as long as your arm. His parents put him on it as soon as he turned eighteen, and luckily we got in, eventually. All the best-connected people in London come here. Even Max hasn't managed to become a member yet.' She smiled smugly. 'It's the one thing my father is proud of me for. Belonging here.'

'It's lovely,' said Sophie, fully aware she'd never be able to afford to be a member of a place like this.

Cassie called the barman over and ordered coffees for both of them. 'Unless you want something stronger?' she said to Sophie, just before he left.

'No thanks,' Sophie said. 'I'm still recovering from last night.'

'Don't worry, you'll get used to the pace. Everyone works hard and drinks even harder at One Pure Thought.' She laughed. 'That's what comes from working in an office full of men. I'm glad to have some female company for once.'

Sophie smiled.

'So tell me,' Cassie said. 'How are you settling in?'

'I've only been working half a day,' Sophie said with a smile, 'but everyone has been very kind to me, helping me out. And I'm really looking forward to getting stuck into the work.'

'Not homesick then?'

'Not really.' Sophie thought of her father and felt a flicker of worry, imagining him on his own in his house. 'I'm going to miss my father.'

'How is your father? You mentioned in your interview that he had poor health.'

'Yeah, he's not very mobile. He's had problems walking ever since he had a fall.'

'That's so sad,' Cassie said, placing her warm hand on Sophie's arm. 'You know, my stepmother had a similar accident. Fell down the stairs, never the same again.'

'I'm so sorry to hear that.'

'It's OK to miss home, you know.'

Sophie thought of her home life, how much she'd needed a change. 'Other than worrying about my dad, I'm just glad to be here. There's not much I'll miss.'

'No boyfriend then?'

Sophie shook her head. 'There was someone, but we split up before I got the job. We wanted different things. He wanted to get married and I didn't.'

'Ah. That sounds difficult. But there are loads of eligible men in London. James is single, you know.' She gave Sophie a knowing look and Sophie flushed. Was it so obvious that she found James attractive?

Her thoughts were interrupted by her phone. She recognised the ring tone as her personal phone. She would always carry it with her because her father had told her he didn't want to call her on her work mobile. He was old-fashioned about keeping work life and personal life separate. She looked at the screen.

Charlie.

Why was he calling her? Her first instinct was not to answer, but then she remembered telling him to watch out for her father, to call her if anything happened to him. She stared at the phone, hesitating.

'Take that if you need to,' Cassie said.

'I'll be quick,' Sophie said. She was probably overreacting, but she just needed to check that her dad hadn't fallen again.

'Of course, go ahead.' Cassie pulled her iPhone out and read her messages.

'Charlie – is everything all right?' Sophie's voice came out in a rush.

'Hi, Sophie.'

'I'm in a work meeting. Is Dad all right?'

'He's fine.'

'Oh good.' Sophie felt her shoulders loosen. 'I can't speak right now.'

Cassie looked up from her phone and smiled, waving her hand to let Sophie know she could continue with the call.

'Don't worry. I'm in London. I came up to talk to you – I can meet you later.'

Sophie swallowed. She didn't want to see him. 'I'm busy later.'

His voice hardened, taking on a familiar edge that made her body tense. 'Sophie, you owe me a lot of money. I'm only asking to meet you. You owe me that much.'

EIGHT

Sophie felt sick as Charlie reminded her about the debt. She needed to get him off the phone. She didn't want Cassie to hear this.

'Look, I'll see you, but not today, it's my first day at work. How about we meet on Saturday?'

'Where will I stay until then?'

'What do you mean?'

'I came all the way to London to see you. I don't have anywhere to stay.'

'I didn't ask you to come.'

'I could stay with you.'

Sophie thought of her new flat, her fresh start. She didn't want him there, creeping back into her life. Cassie was looking up from her phone now, her eyes full of questions. Sophie needed to end the call.

'No, you can't. I'll sort out the money. Don't worry about that. Just go home.' She hung up the phone and smiled at Cassie.

'Everything OK?' she asked.

'Yeah, it's fine. I'm so sorry for the interruption. I wouldn't normally take personal calls – I just thought it might be about my father. With his health, I always worry that something might have happened to him.'

'Of course. I understand. If you ever need any help with anything, just let us know.'

'Sure,' Sophie said. Although she didn't think Cassie really meant it, it was nice of her to say it.

'We consider our employees like family. We look out for each other.'

Sophie smiled. 'I've really appreciated you and James helping me settle in.'

'No problem at all. How's the new flat?'

'It's great,' Sophie said. 'I just need to get some curtains sorted.'

'Curtains?' Cassie raised her eyebrows. 'I thought it already had some. They must have been taken down when the last woman moved out, so it could be cleaned.'

'Oh,' Sophie said. She hadn't realised someone had lived there before her. Hadn't Cassie said she was the first employee to accept a flat?

'I think the curtains must be in one of the storage cupboards in the building. We can go over straight after this and I'll see if I can find them for you.'

Sophie smiled. 'That would be amazing, thanks.'

'No problem. You need curtains. You never know who might be trying to look in. Especially in London. Lots of strange people about.'

Sophie nodded.

'Hey, don't look so worried,' Cassie said, reaching out and touching her arm. 'No reason why anyone would target you.'

When they got to the converted townhouse an hour later, Cassie opened the front door and led Sophie up the stairs, to a cupboard on a middle landing.

'Ah, here they are,' she said, pulling out dark red material from the bottom. The curtains were thick and lined. 'The last tenant left the place in a bit of a state, so we gave it a thorough clean. Someone must have forgotten to put the curtains back up.'

She pulled the huge bundle out of the cupboard, and Sophie held out her arms and felt the weight of the heavy material.

'Great, I think that's all of them,' Cassie said, with a smile. 'You can sleep easy tonight.'

She paused for a moment, peering into the cupboard. 'What's that down there?' She pointed, but Sophie couldn't work out what she was meant to be looking at.

'Oh God,' Cassie said. 'Not again. Those are rat droppings. I thought we'd got rid of the rats, but these old houses – they're built for them. They live in the walls, under the floors.'

Sophie shivered. 'Do they?'

'They say you're never more than six feet from a rat in London. Which is fine if they're outside and you never see them. But you don't want them in the house.'

Sophie hated the thought of rats scurrying around at night. 'Do you think they're in my flat too?'

'I don't know. I suppose they might be. Your flat's the only one occupied, so they might be after the food there.' Cassie put a comforting hand on her arm. 'But don't worry. I have a pest controller on speed dial. I'll sort it out.'

By the time Sophie got back to the office with Cassie, it was early evening, and Sophie knew she had a late night ahead of her if she was going to get her head around Lydia's campaign for the energy drinks and start looking at the material Cassie had sent her about the new gin company. Most of the others were still at work, and she could see Max through the glass panels of his office, typing furiously. She went back to her desk and immersed herself in the documents on her laptop. After a while, her vision started to blur, as she read the same lines over and over.

She tried not to think about Charlie, the money she owed him. She wouldn't be paid for another three weeks, and even then she'd only be able to pay back a small part of her debt. She thought of her father's physiotherapy. There was another bill due soon. He was making so much progress, but she wouldn't have been able to pay for it without Charlie.

She was going to have to talk to Charlie, make an effort to be nice to him.

'How are you getting on?' James said, making her jump.

'OK,' Sophie said, looking back at the computer screen at Lydia's work. 'I think I've got the gist of what we need to do about the energy drinks campaign. Lydia's files have really helped.'

'Have they?' James raised his eyebrows.

'What do you mean?'

'Lydia really struggled with that campaign, and her work wasn't of a particularly high standard. She just wasn't very focused, particularly at the end of her time here. And she offended one of our major clients. Max had to work hard to make sure they didn't leave the agency.'

Sophie frowned. She hadn't seen anything wrong with Lydia's work.

He smiled. 'Don't worry, you're completely different to Lydia.'

'What happened to her?'

'Well, we were going to let her go. It just wasn't working.

But then she left of her own accord. That made things a lot easier.'

Sophie nodded. She didn't want to disappoint them all, for the same thing to happen to her.

'Are you hungry?' James asked, interrupting her thoughts. 'Do you want to go and grab some dinner? There's a great café round the corner.'

Sophie was tempted. She longed for some fresh air and to have a break. But she needed to crack on, to work out how to avoid letting them down the way that Lydia had.

'I'm OK, thanks,' she said. 'I want to focus on this.'

When Sophie eventually packed up her laptop and dragged herself out of the office, she was exhausted. the walk home refreshed her and she intended to make one final adjustment to Lydia's recommendations when she got in. But instead, in the privacy of her flat, she found herself rereading the threatening email, telling her not to go to the police. Why had they sent it now, after all these years?

She didn't want to talk to the police, didn't want to bring back the past. But something must have happened for them to be emailing her. Maybe there was new evidence, although who knew what it could be? She shivered. She needed to know what was going on.

She opened Google on her laptop and typed his name into the search bar. Will Baron-Taylor. It was something she hadn't let herself do for the last five years. At first, she'd googled him all the time and had become a voyeur on his life, feeling a burst of anger every time she saw a photo of him having fun at a party or laughing with his mates. She didn't understand how his life was continuing as normal, while she was the one who'd had to leave university.

But the NHS therapist she finally saw helped her to stop

her obsessive behaviour. The six sessions were enough for her to realise that keeping up to date with Will's life was doing her no good at all. She'd drawn a line under it, not wanting to know where he was or what he was doing, whether he was successful or whether his past had caught up with him. She needed to focus on her own life.

But now things had changed. She needed to know why the police might contact her. She needed to find out what had happened to him.

He was an investment banker now, high up in some complicated department of an international bank. In his spare time he liked squash and golf; and the first thing that came up when she googled him was a sponsored run, for the survivors of domestic abuse. She felt sick with the irony.

He'd followed the path laid out for him. He'd been the kind of boy who was built for success. He'd had everything stacked in his favour; privately educated, confident and sporty. She sighed. What he'd done to her hadn't stopped him – it hadn't even slowed him down.

She looked at the next link and saw that he was running for political office. He wanted to be an MP and had started his campaign. There wasn't much information in the profile, just a couple of paragraphs where he talked about his political views and policy proposals. He pitched himself as a family man, concerned about working families. He didn't have kids, but was 'devoted' to his wife. Sophie knew he wouldn't want anything coming out about the past.

His constituency was in north London, far away from the centre. And the investment bank was in Canary Wharf. She thought of all the times she'd seen tall, blond men on the Tube and how they'd made her jump. None of them had been him. He was far away from her. He couldn't hurt her; he didn't even know she was in London.

Sophie stared at the computer screen. She needed to stop

getting distracted and get on with her work. She had a new life now, the foundations of a career. Cassie and James had taken a chance on her. She had to show them she was worth it. No one else was likely to offer her a job as good as this one. She needed to focus; she couldn't throw everything she'd worked so hard for away. She couldn't be dragged back into the past.

NINE

By the time Friday came round, Sophie was exhausted. It was early evening, and everyone was still in the office, staring at their computer screens. Sophie had sent her ideas on the energy drinks campaign to James, and some analysis on the gin company's customers to Cassie. She'd also been doing some work for Max on company performance. The budgeting problem that he'd set her had seemed like a test, as if he'd wanted to catch her out, but she'd worked out a solution easily. The other part of the task was to write a presentation on the company's growth, which she would tackle next week.

'All right?' James said, coming up and standing behind her.

'I'm fine.'

'How did you get on with those numbers Max sent?'

'I've finished them.'

He smiled. 'I thought you'd find it easy. I've got some real work for you now. Do you want to get started?'

'Sure,' she said, ignoring how tired she was.

'Don't worry, you don't need to do it over the weekend. I'll just explain it to you now and you can get on with it next week.'

He pulled up a blue swivel chair beside her desk and rested

his muscled arm on the table. And then he set about explaining the brand ideas he'd come up with for the energy drinks company. His eyes sparkled as he gesticulated, taking her through the key concepts. Sophie could see how passionate he was about his job. He'd managed to create slogans that completely captured the brand's essence, and he wanted her to develop the ideas further. She was buzzing at the thought of getting started.

Two hours later, Sophie was bleary-eyed as she focused on the computer screen, immersed in images, looking for just the right one to exemplify James's branding idea.

James came up behind her and put his hand on her shoulder. 'Time to go,' he said.

'There's just one more thing I want to do. I'm nearly there.'

'Sometimes a break is best. Ideas come when you least expect them.'

She looked up and saw the others in the office were starting to put their coats on.

'We're going to the pub,' Pete said.

'Celebrating?' she asked, watching a group of them file out, chatting.

'Nothing special. Just nearly the end of the week. Are you coming?'

She hesitated.

'Come on,' James said softly. 'Don't keep working. Let's drink to celebrate the end of your first week. You look like you need a glass of wine.'

She smiled. 'I think I do.'

The rain took Sophie by surprise. Her desk was in the corner of the office away from the window and she'd hardly left it all day. She'd had no idea of the weather outside. James held his umbrella over her as she shivered and tried to avoid the puddles in her open-toed shoes.

It was only a few steps to the pub and they rushed into the warm building in a flurry of umbrellas and damp coats. Cassie went straight over to reserve their usual spot by the fireplace, and Max got the first round in. There were only twelve of them there, but he brought back four bottles of wine and a bottle of vodka with a tray of shot glasses. They started with shots, and Sophie pitched hers back reluctantly as Cassie raised a toast to the day.

Cassie was the only other woman there. Mercedes had left the office earlier for a client meeting and Harriet, the admin assistant, had gone at five to collect her children from their after-school club.

The wine was all going down rather too easily. Sophie felt relaxed and happy in the whir of conversation and friendly voices. Soon Cassie was making her excuses and leaving herself.

'Date night with the husband,' she explained. Sophie realised that Cassie couldn't see much of her husband with the hours she worked. Somehow, she couldn't imagine Cassie in a partnership with another person. She was such an individual, so strong-willed.

The rest of them chatted until closing time. Sophie was surprised they were all still there. No one had made excuses to get home to girlfriends or partners, or said they were tired. It was good; she supposed that they all got on so well. The evening had been full of laughter. It felt like she'd known them for years.

'Time to leave,' James said gently, encouraging them all out the door.

As they exited the pub onto the street, the rain had got heavier, battering the wet pavement. Sophie hunched in on herself, pulling her coat above her head, knowing she was going to get drenched. James tapped her on the shoulder. 'You can take my umbrella,' he said. 'I don't want you to get wet.'

'There's no need. It's not a long walk.'

'You'll be soaked through. Take it.' He pointed at the bright sign of the Underground station about twenty-five metres away. 'I'm only going over there, to the Tube. I can make a run for it and I'll hardly be wet at all.'

'OK, then,' she said, the rain already lashing her feet through her ill-advised open-toed shoes. 'Thank you.'

Her fingers touched his as she took the umbrella from him, and she held it over him for a moment. They had to stand close together for it to cover both of them, and he was taller than her, so she had to hold it slightly above her head. His chest was almost brushing against her.

She glanced at the others. They were all heading off in the other direction, waving their goodbyes.

He looked down at her, and she gazed into his blue eyes. For a moment they paused, their eyes locking. He leaned down towards her and she tilted her neck upwards. She blinked, anticipating his lips on hers.

But then he pulled away and smiled sheepishly. 'See you on Monday, Sophie,' he said. And with that, he ducked out from under the umbrella and made a run for it, dashing towards the station.

She was soaked to the skin when she got home from the pub, despite James's umbrella. The rain had been horizontal, dragged this way and that by the wind. As she'd neared her house she'd seen a discarded, broken umbrella, its metal guts facing skyward, defeated by the elements. Useless.

She climbed the stone stairs then shook out her umbrella in the porch before she opened the door, wondering if she could leave it in the hallway. She knew there was no one else in the house, but somehow it felt like only her flat was her domain, as if the hallway belonged to someone else.

Relieved to be inside, she climbed up to the third floor, feeling the wine starting to sink in, slowing her footsteps. She'd enjoyed the day. She'd loved immersing herself in the brief for the gin company, and the camaraderie of the office and the pub.

As she climbed the stairs, there was no noise except for the creaking pipes, no light creeping out from under the doors of the other flats. She opened the door to her flat with relief, and immediately went from room to room switching on all the lights. She thought of her father and his insistence that you only needed to light the room you were in, and felt a pang of longing. She missed him; that feeling of having someone who loved her living nearby. In the two weeks she'd stayed with him after she'd split up with Charlie, she'd enjoyed sharing breakfast with him each morning. But most of all, she missed his conversation and his sage views on life. She'd ring him tomorrow, check how he was. Tonight she needed to put the curtains up before she went to bed. She had meant to do it the day Cassie had retrieved them from the cupboard, but she hadn't been able to find curtain hooks, and she'd had to rush out in a lunch break to buy some.

She pulled a stool from the kitchen and wobbled on it as she hung the curtains in the bedroom. She felt conspicuous standing on the stool, and she thought of what Cassie had said about anyone being able to see in. Across the road she could see the homeless man in the doorway, sheltering from the downpour. He wasn't looking at her, but if he looked up he'd be able to see straight in. She stumbled for a moment on the stool and reached out to the window to get her balance. The glass shook beneath her weight and she quickly pulled away, almost falling. When she glanced back to the street, the man's face was turned towards her, his eyes meeting hers. She managed a half-smile, then continued to hang the curtains.

The flat was completely silent. She thought of the other flats in the house, cavernous and empty. In a way, she had even less to fear, being on her own in the building. There was no risk that someone else would leave the front door to the house open, like they might have done in a house share. She was in control.

She went to the living room to hang the remaining curtains. As she finished attaching the heavy material to the final hook, the sound of a car horn outside made her jump. The street was usually so quiet. When she looked outside, there was no traffic. The horn must have been from another street, the noise travelling through the cold night air.

She saw the shadow of a man or woman at the end of the road, head bowed. Just standing there, looking at something on their phone. Waiting for someone in the middle of the night, in the pouring rain. Sophie shivered, and quickly drew the curtains. She was so isolated here, alone in the centre of the city.

In the bedroom, she stripped off her clothes, cleaned her teeth and climbed into bed. She opened a book but couldn't concentrate on the words. Then she heard something. A gentle plod-plod. She was sure it was footsteps coming up the stairs.

Sophie froze.

The footsteps stopped.

Should she do something? Check out who it was? Perhaps one of the flats was occupied now, but James hadn't let her know. Or hadn't known himself. Cassie could have put someone in there. Or Max. Or perhaps it wasn't footsteps at all, just her overactive imagination.

She slid out of bed and crept into the living room towards her front door, double-checking it was locked. Silently she reached for the chain and pulled it across. It made an almost imperceptible scraping sound.

Sophie held her breath. She was sure she could hear breathing on the other side of the door. She stood staring at it, convinced it might burst open at any second. She told herself that it wouldn't, that there was no one there. It was just her mind playing tricks.

She backed slowly away from the door, into the living room, looking round at the furniture for something heavy. There was a small bookcase in the corner that she hadn't yet had the chance to fill up. She dragged it across the room awkwardly. It made a horrible scraping sound against the wooden floor. If there was anyone outside, she knew they would hear her, know what she was doing.

But there wasn't anyone outside, she reminded herself. She was only moving her bookcase in front of the door for her own peace of mind. Knowing it was there meant she'd be able to sleep. Towards the end of her time at university, she'd done the same thing every night, putting her bedside light on the floor and moving her bedside table so that it blocked the door.

Once the bookcase was blocking the entrance she felt better, and she crept back to bed. It was only when she was under the covers with the light turned off that she heard footsteps move away from her front door and make their way downstairs. They left the house and let the front door shut with a bang

TEN

An insistent buzzing woke Sophie, and it took her a moment to realise it was the entryphone for her flat. She rolled over and ignored it. It had taken her ages to get to sleep last night and she wasn't expecting anyone.

It rang again and she reluctantly dragged herself out of bed and across her living room to answer it.

'Hello?'

'I'm here about the rats.'

'Oh, right.' It was the pest controller Cassie had mentioned.

She clicked the buzzer to let him in, then ran back to her bedroom, threw on some clothes and ran a brush through her hair. By the time he knocked on the door, she looked more presentable.

She pulled the bookcase away from the door and opened it, forcing a smile.

'Hi,' he said. 'I'm Ben.' His broad body filled her doorway, and his handshake nearly crushed her fingers.

'Sophie,' she said. 'I'll take you down and you can see where we found the droppings.'

She showed him the cupboard on the landing and then left

him to it. When he came back twenty minutes later, she was eating her breakfast.

'I've put some bait and traps down in the cupboard,' he said. 'Couldn't see any signs of them elsewhere.'

'Oh, that's good.'

'Seen anything concerning in your flat?' he asked.

Sophie shook her head. 'No.'

'Right, that's good.' He peered curiously at the bookcase that was still in the middle of the floor. 'Best to keep the place clean and tidy, so they have nowhere to hide.'

She shivered. 'Will do,' she said.

'Old houses like this... rats can be everywhere. They live in the chimney stacks, in the walls. Sometimes you can hear them running up and down at night.'

Sophie thought back to the night before, the person in the house. The nights on her own terrified her. 'I haven't heard any rats,' she said.

'Well, good. And don't worry if you smell anything bad over the next few days or weeks. Rats tend to go back to their nests to die. Usually out of sight in the walls, or below the floorboards. So you won't have to see them. But you will smell them. Nothing I can do about that, I'm afraid,' he said cheerfully. 'But I do like to warn people.'

After Ben had gone, Sophie got out the Hoover. She was determined that the rats would have nowhere to hide in her flat. On the surface, her home seemed clean, but behind the sideboard there was a thick layer of dust. It was the same in the bedroom, and she attacked the area behind the wardrobe with the Hoover attachment, feeling strangely satisfied as she watched the thick dust disappear. Suddenly, she heard a sucking sound. Looking down, she saw a silky piece of burgundy material caught in the

Hoover. She turned it off to let the suction release, then carefully pulled the item out.

It was a dress, silky with lace at the neckline, covered in a thick layer of dust. She brushed it down. It was beautiful, well cut and a size twelve. Her size. She looked at the label and saw a brand name she didn't recognise. Googling it on her phone she saw it was a high-end independent fashion brand, based in Kensington.

She took off her jeans and shirt and slipped it over her head. It fitted her well, but was perhaps a little tight. She swirled round in it in front of the mirror, wondering who had owned the dress. Someone who'd lived in the flat before her. The dress was so dusty, it must have been there a long time. Clearly whoever had owned it had forgotten about it. If she got it dry cleaned, it would be as good as new.

After she'd finished vacuuming, Sophie ran herself a bath and then lay there, letting the stresses and strains of the week wash away. Her weekend stretched out emptily before her. She hadn't made any new friends in London except for the people she'd met at the office. Perhaps she'd walk over to Leicester Square later, go to the half-price theatre booth and buy herself a ticket for the evening. She thought about going down to the river and wandering along the South Bank, but the weather was drizzly and raining.

Her phone rang, but she ignored it, letting her head sink under the bathwater. It was probably Charlie. He'd been calling her all the time. At first, she'd picked up, worried something had happened to her dad. But now she let it ring. She needed to figure out how to pay back the money she owed him, so she could cut ties with him.

When she got out of the bath, she rang her father to check how he was. He seemed cheerful.

'So how was your first week at work?' he asked.

'It's been brilliant. They're letting me work with some of their big clients already. How have you been?'

'Getting by well enough. Charlie says he'll look out for me, so you don't need to worry,' he said. 'Always been a kind boy, that one.'

She grimaced. 'Great,' she said, her voice clipped. 'But you don't need him, do you? You can manage on your own?' She didn't want him becoming dependent on Charlie. He could still turn to Sophie if he needed help.

'I can manage. I just like his company. But of course he's down in London this week.'

'Is he?' She'd thought he might have gone back home.

'Haven't you seen him? I thought he was there to meet you. Still pining after you.'

As soon as she finished the call with her father, Charlie rang. Again.

'Hi,' she said wearily as she picked up.

'Hi, Sophie. You said we could talk today. I'm in London. How about we meet on the South Bank?'

'Look, Charlie, I'm not sure we have much to say to each other. I've promised I'll pay you the money back as soon as I can. Now I'm earning it will be easier. As soon as I get my first pay packet, I'll give you as much as I can.'

'So what are you up to today?' he asked.

Sophie sighed. 'I don't know.'

'It seems silly for me to have come all the way to London and us not to meet up.'

She stared around her empty flat. She didn't have any plans and she craved company. And he'd travelled all that way. She would see him. It would give her a chance to draw a line under their relationship, make sure they remained on good terms. 'I need to get some food in first,' she said.

'How about this afternoon?'

'OK, then. But Charlie—'

'Yes?'

'It's not a date.'

'I know that. I just want to talk to you.'

Sophie was surprised to find she was enjoying herself as she went round Tate Britain with Charlie. He had always made her laugh and she felt relaxed in his company, talking and joking like they used to. She told him about the job and how hard they all worked. Being with Charlie was like slipping on an old coat, comfortable but something she knew she couldn't keep on forever. She'd forgotten how easy it was to be with him when he was in a good mood.

After they left the gallery, they crossed the river and wandered along the South Bank together, past the London Eye and the street performers. Sophie had to stand close to Charlie to be under his umbrella. It was the second time a man had held an umbrella over her in the last couple of days, but this felt far less comfortable than it had with James. When she saw a little kiosk selling them, she went in and bought her own. All they had were Union Jack ones, and she held it over herself like a tourist.

After a while Charlie started to reminisce about the past, the pubs and the beaches of their childhood in Dorset.

'I loved growing up there,' Sophie said. 'Life was so simple. I do miss it sometimes.'

'Do you think you'll come back one day?' he asked.

'I hope so. I'll want to be close to Dad.'

'I'll take care of him while you're not there,' Charlie said. 'I love the guy. He's like family.'

Sophie grimaced. She had always loved how Charlie and her father got on so well, but now his close relationship with her father felt like an imposition. He was telling her he'd always be a part of her life, a part of her family.

'I'm not sure I'll be living down south forever, though,' he continued.

'Oh – why?' Sophie asked, wondering if he'd met someone new.

'I've been thinking,' he said. 'About London. About you.'

Sophie sighed. They'd been having such a nice afternoon.

'Maybe I got ahead of myself a bit before,' Charlie continued, 'saying I wouldn't move to London. I just thought with inheriting my grandad's place... well, it all seemed so perfect, like destiny. But we don't need to rush things. We could live in London together, at least for a few years.'

Sophie's eyes widened in surprise. 'You want to move to London? But what about your business? What about your life?' She thought of how he'd proposed, how important it was to him to live near where he was brought up. Was he really willing to sacrifice living in the place he loved for her?

'I can leave the business for now. I'm sure I'll find work here. I love you, Soph. We've always had such a good time together,' Charlie said. 'I thought we were made for each other.'

'I thought so too, Charlie,' she said softly. 'At the time.'

They stopped by the Millennium Bridge, looking over the river towards St Paul's Cathedral, Charlie holding his umbrella above hers so he could stand closer to her.

'Do you remember when we came up to London together for the day?'

'Yeah,' she said, staring out over the murky river. She hadn't thought about that trip for ages, but now it came back to her. They'd only been sixteen, and they'd just wandered the streets and had lunch in McDonald's. But it had been fun. It had been that day that she'd set her heart on going to London to university.

'I think we stood in this exact spot.'

She felt him move closer, and turned her head to look at him.

Before she knew it, he was coming in for a kiss, his mouth moving towards hers.

She pushed him away just as his lips touched hers.

'No, Charlie,' she said.

'I'm sorry,' he said quickly.

She sighed. 'This won't work. I only want to be friends. And if you can't handle that, then perhaps it's best we don't meet up.'

She turned and walked away, striding across the Millennium Bridge on her own, blinking back tears.

She decided to walk home, going down Fleet Street and then wandering through Covent Garden. She passed crowds of drinkers standing outside pubs and weaved her way through the hordes of tourists, stepping into the road to pass them. Then she turned into her road a few streets away. She could still hear the faint sounds of life from Soho, but the street itself was quiet.

She looked over to the doorway where she'd seen the homeless man the other night, but there was no one there, and no belongings, not even the remains of his cardboard box. She supposed he must have been moved on. The residents must have complained.

She pulled out her keys from her bag as she approached her doorway. As she got there, a man stepped out in front of her. She jumped back.

'Charlie?'

'Hi, Sophie.'

'What are you doing here?'

'We still need to talk.'

'What about?' Sophie said, irritated. 'I thought I made myself clear.'

'I can be friends, if that's what you want.'

'Charlie, did you follow me home?' As she said it, she realised he couldn't have. He'd been waiting for her.

'You weren't answering your phone.'

'Charlie—'

'I don't know how we'll manage to be friends if you don't answer your phone.' His face was petulant. 'And we haven't sorted out the money.'

'I'll pay you back as soon as I can.'

'Can I come in? Can we talk?'

She touched his shoulder gently. 'Not now. I'm tired. I'll ring you tomorrow, OK?'

'OK,' he said, reluctantly. 'Let's speak tomorrow.'

'Great,' she said, managing a forced smile. 'Speak to you then.'

She turned and let herself into the building, opening the door just a fraction and slipping inside so he couldn't follow her. She stood behind the closed door for a moment, waiting until she saw his shadow retreating through the glass pane. It was only then, as he walked away, that she realised she'd never given him her address.

ELEVEN

When Sophie arrived at the office on Monday morning, it was a hive of activity. She said good morning to Harriet at the desk beside her, and as she put her bag under her own desk, Max strode across the office towards them.

'Harriet!' he said loudly, startling both Sophie and Harriet, who had just taken the first sip of her cup of coffee. 'The kitchen – it needs clearing and cleaning.'

Sophie's mouth dropped open in astonishment. Harriet worked in admin, she wasn't a cleaner. And besides, the kitchen was always messy. It had never bothered Max before. If you went to the kitchen any time after 10 a.m. it was impossible to find a clean mug. Instead, there would be loads of dirty cups piled up in the sink and on every available surface. Breakfast bowls, too, spilled milk and leftover cereal. Sophie could guarantee that the microwave would be sticky with spillages from someone's overheated porridge.

Harriet looked up in surprise at Max, standing imposingly over her desk.

'Can you tidy it up, please,' he repeated.

'Sure,' Harriet said, frowning. 'After I've finished going through these files.'

'No, not after you've finished going through these files. Now.' Max's voice was firm.

Sophie raised her eyebrows at Harriet in solidarity. Why should she be the one to clear up after them? Surely everyone could put in a bit of effort. After all, everyone had contributed to the mess. But Harriet was getting up resignedly and going over to the kitchen.

'I can help,' Sophie said quickly.

Max turned to her. 'No. How's that presentation I asked you to work on coming along?'

'The one you mentioned to me on Friday?'

'Yes, that's right. About company performance. Is it ready?'

'No, not yet.' She hadn't prioritised it over work for their clients. When Max had given her the task he'd made it sound unimportant, like something she should be doing if she had a spare moment.

'Well, I'll need it in an hour.' He looked round the office. 'Everyone,' he said loudly. He banged on the table and those who hadn't been watching the drama unfolding looked up. 'Right, we need to make this office look good. No mess on the desks. Everything neat and tidy, no slouching. We have an important visitor coming.'

Sophie looked down at her desk. There was nothing on it. She should clearly get on with the presentation. She put her headphones in to block out the sound of the others and got to work.

For the next half hour, she saw Max pacing up and down out of the corner of her eye. She'd never seen him this nervous.

And then finally he left. Five minutes later he was back with a suited man with grey hair, standing rod-straight. They disappeared into his office together with Cassie and James. Max shouted a coffee order to Harriet as they went through the door, throwing his wallet at her and telling her to go to the posh coffee shop up the road.

Harriet missed the catch and scrambled around under the desk to get the wallet. Then she grabbed her coat and hurried out to get the coffees.

When the door of the meeting room swung open an hour later, Max was red and flustered, and the man looked calm and collected.

'Right, so are you going to introduce me to your staff?' he said.

'Sure.' Max put his hands to his mouth in an exaggerated gesture and shouted at everyone to gather round. No one moved at first, and James repeated his request. 'Come here, guys. Come and meet Mr Price.'

They got up from their desks slowly and headed over.

'Mr Price is the investor in One Pure Thought,' James began. 'And he wanted to see all you people who put in the hard work and dedication that keeps this company on its toes and ahead of the competitors.'

'Hello,' Mr Price said, looking at them each in turn. His eyes rested on Sophie, running up and down her body. She shrank under his gaze, folding her body in on itself.

'This is Sophie,' Max said, jumping over to where she was standing. He placed his hand on her waist and pushed her forward a bit. For a moment, she was so surprised by the gesture, she didn't say anything.

'Nice to meet you,' she said finally, holding out her hand to Mr Price. He shook it, his own hand clammy.

'Sophie is our newest brand strategist. She's been working on a presentation showing just how much we've grown over the last six months, how we're going to secure you a high return on the investment you put into the company.'

'I don't need a presentation to tell me that,' Mr Price said, sharply. 'I can use my own judgement.' He grinned at Sophie, then smirked at Max. 'Although I do admire your taste in employees. You always could pick them.'

Sophie reddened and looked across at James. Mr Price had already moved on, following Max for a short tour of the office.

Sophie turned to James. 'So he's the investor?'

'Afraid so.'

He looked familiar, as if Sophie had met him before. She was sure she knew him from somewhere. 'I thought I recognised him.'

'You might have done,' James whispered, glancing across to Max and Mr Price at the other side of the office. 'His face was all over the papers a few years ago.'

'Oh,' Sophie said. 'Why? Who is he?'

'He's Philip Price.' The name rang bells but Sophie couldn't think why. And then it clicked. The politician. He'd been caught in some kind of sex scandal and had to leave office.

'Ahh...' she said.

James smiled. 'You remember now? The press weren't kind to him. But without him we wouldn't have a company. He's our only investor, so we have to keep him onside.'

'Max seemed so nervous around him.'

'He is,' James said. 'That's because he's Max and Cassie's father.'

TWELVE

Sophie left the office at around 7.30 p.m., leaving most of the others still at their desks, bathed in the light from their computer monitors. She'd been working on Lydia's campaigns and she still couldn't find much she wanted to change about her work. She must be missing something.

She grabbed her laptop, put it in her handbag and went down the stairs and out of the office. The street outside was lively, the pub full of people spilling out and drinking on the pavements. Next to it, shops and coffee shops had left their lights on, displaying their wares. She hurried home, turning into her quiet, empty street.

'Hello?' A voice came out of the shadows, making her jump.

The woman was blocking the entrance to her house. 'Hello?' Sophie said uncertainly, her heart thumping.

'I'm sorry. I didn't mean to startle you. Are you Sophie Williams?' She held out her hand. 'I'm DCI Jameson. I want to talk to you about Will Baron-Taylor.'

Sophie swallowed her nausea. The email had been right. The police did want to speak to her. So much so that they'd found her in London. She felt a rush of heat wash over her as she thought of Will.

'Do you have ID?' she asked curtly, delaying the inevitable.

The police officer got out her badge and Sophie studied it intently. She had no choice but to take her up to the flat. They walked up the stairs and Sophie unlocked the door in silence.

The police officer perched on the edge of Sophie's grey sofa, and Sophie wished she was anywhere but there. She'd left all of this behind her. It had taken a Herculean effort, but she'd managed to accept what had happened to her and move on with her life, focus on her future.

'Do you want a drink?' Sophie asked.

'No, thank you.'

Sophie paced the room, her heart pounding.

'You can sit down,' DCI Jameson said, and Sophie perched awkwardly on the other end of the sofa.

'I want to talk to you about what happened when you were at university. Your allegation against Will.'

'Sure,' Sophie said, trying to control her shaking hands. It was the last thing she wanted to talk about. She didn't even want to think about it. 'Although I told the police everything at the time.'

Suddenly, the new life she'd worked so hard for seemed to be built on sand. At just the mention of Will's name she felt like she was coming apart at the seams. After all the effort to rebuild herself, to build her resilience, it was unravelling so easily.

'Would you mind taking me through it all again?'

Sophie felt a rising panic and bit the inside of her cheek hard, trying to control her mounting stress levels. It didn't help. She got up and walked over to the window, opened the double doors onto the balcony to get some air in. She looked at the bright flowers, heard the voices of strangers chatting in the street. Life went on. Her life went on. Will was in the past.

She could feel herself shaking and she took deep breaths, trying to calm down.

'Sophie, are you all right?'

She didn't answer. Couldn't answer.

'Why don't you come and sit down?'

She did so obediently, sat back on the sofa, her face hot, her head pounding. She couldn't do this. She thought of the balcony outside, the drop. She needed to get out.

'Breathe,' the police officer said. 'It's OK. Do you want me to get you a glass of water?' She stood up without waiting for Sophie's answer and opened the cupboards until she found a glass and then ran the tap.

'Here you go.'

'Thank you.'

'Sophie,' DCI Jameson said softly, 'I need to understand exactly what happened back then. With Will.'

Sophie shook, tears forming in her eyes. 'I – I haven't thought about this for a long time.' But that was a lie: she had thought about it every day, checking her Google alerts for her own name to see if Will and his friends had set up any more websites about her, warning the world that she was a liar. What she meant was that she hadn't had to confront it head-on like this, that someone else hadn't forced it on her.

'OK then, well, I've got the notes from your previous interviews. I just want to go over a few of the details with you.'

Sophie thought of the email she'd received, telling her not to speak to the police. What was she going to do now? Tell them the truth? It hadn't got her anywhere before.

'I really don't know how I can help you,' she said. 'I don't have anything new to say.'

The police officer reached out and touched her arm. 'It's OK,' she said. 'We don't have to do this now. I can come back another day.'

'Why?' Sophie asked. 'Why do you want me to go back over

it now? It didn't help at the time.' She could hear the note of accusation in her own voice, the anger. Had the police let her down, or had she let herself down? She was the one who had withdrawn the allegation.

DCI Jameson looked at her. 'I'm here because there's been another report against Will.'

'What do you mean?' Sophie said. 'Who reported him?'

'I'm afraid I can't tell you any details. But what I can tell you is that there are multiple similarities between your allegations against Will and the current one.'

He'd done it again. But of course he had. She hadn't met him before that night, but she'd learned a lot about him afterwards. How he had a reputation. How she wasn't the first person to hang around with him and wake up with no memory of the night before. She hadn't even been the first person to report him to the university or the police. She'd just been the first person who had got near the courts. But she had dropped her case.

She felt filled with regret. If she'd proceeded, would he have been locked up, stopped from doing it again? But she knew he wouldn't have been. The police had been clear she didn't have a strong enough case, and there was little chance of a conviction. Her palms started to sweat as she thought back. What could she have done but get on with her life? She just hadn't realised how withdrawing from the case would look. Suddenly it had been her on trial, not him.

Sophie took a deep breath. 'What do you want me to tell you about?'

THIRTEEN

The next day at work Sophie was still thinking about her conversation with DCI Jameson. The detective inspector had wanted her to go through everything that had happened with Will again, and Sophie had gone over every last detail. She thought of the email warning her not to speak to the police and her stomach churned. Will and his friends thought they could bully her into not telling the truth, withdrawing her statement like she'd done before. But that wasn't going to happen. Not this time.

She thought of Philip Price. When she'd researched him, she'd seen that he'd slept with a string of his younger employees, promising them promotions that never materialised. Sophie remembered him looking her up and down and shivered. She thought of Max dating Mercedes, a much more junior member of staff. Like father, like son. Philip's affairs had come out when someone had leaked the story to the papers, with photos of each of the girls with Philip. It had seemed like before then none of the girls had known about the others.

She brought his name up on Google, looked at the string of companies he owned. He'd made his money from the business he'd set up when he was in his teens, selling used parts that he rescued from cars that were being scrapped. He'd expanded rapidly until he'd started investing in property all over London, which was the foundation of his current wealth.

'All OK?' Cassie said, coming over to her desk.

'Yeah,' Sophie said with a smile.

'I see you're looking up my father.'

Sophie blushed. 'I just wanted to understand his background.'

'Of course, that makes sense. He's an entrepreneur. Always had good business sense. Anyway, how do you feel about going to your first client meeting?'

'Really?'

'Yeah, it's just an initial introduction. Big energy company looking at the branding of their sustainable energy business. They want it to look younger and more innovative.' She grinned. 'I thought we'd make a good team.'

'Sure,' Sophie said, smiling. 'I'd love to come.'

Cassie looked at her. 'Brilliant. You'll need to get changed, of course. Pop back to the flat and then come back here as quick as you can. I can brief you in the taxi over.'

Sophie was back in the office half an hour later. She'd changed out of her jeans and into a skirt and blouse, hastily applying make-up. She looked OK, and she hoped she'd meet Cassie's standards. Cassie always looked perfectly put together, with everything colour-coordinated. She always seemed sophisticated and assured, and walked with an unusual confidence.

Cassie smiled at Sophie when she came through. 'Great,' she said. 'Let's go.'

In the taxi, Cassie briefed Sophie on the client. Philip had provided them with the introduction. He played golf with one of the senior directors.

'How involved is Philip in One Pure Thought?' Sophie asked. She hadn't liked what she'd read about him, or the way he'd looked at her.

'Not so much,' Cassie said. 'He just set the company up as a vehicle for Max, really. Max didn't know what he wanted to do with his life, and mentioned creative media in passing, and voila, he had a company,' Cassie said bitterly.

'What about you?' Sophie asked. 'What did you want to do?'

'That's the irony. I'm actually interested in this area. But he made Max the CEO, not me.'

'That must have been frustrating.'

Cassie shook her head, brushing Sophie off. 'It doesn't matter, not in the long term. I'm going to prove myself, get my own investment.'

'Break away from Philip?'

Cassie frowned. 'Not necessarily. My father... well, he inspires me. I want to be at least as successful as him. I want to learn from him and then surpass him.'

'Right,' Sophie said uncertainly, thinking of what she'd found out about Philip.

Cassie sighed and stared out the window. 'There's a lot of rubbish written about him online. About those girls. None of it is true. They were just after his money.'

Sophie didn't know what to say.

'Honestly, Sophie, the lies are so upsetting. They completely ruined his career. I'm so glad he's managed to bounce back. It was all so unfair.'

When the meeting finished, Sophie shook hands with the clients, looking them confidently in the eye. As she picked up her papers, she felt on air. The atmosphere in the room had been electric, as she and Cassie had bounced ideas off the clients.

'You were very impressive,' Cassie said, once they were outside and the clients were out of earshot. 'Congratulations.'

'Thanks.' Sophie blushed.

'We make a great team. Soon we'll be selling more than Max and James put together.' Cassie wound the window down in the taxi, letting the noise of London in, her hair fanning out in the breeze. She turned to look at Sophie. 'We're a small company, a family company. And it really feels like you fit right in. You're lucky, you know, joining at this time. If you like, I could mentor you, show you the ropes. I really think you have a lot of potential.'

'That would be brilliant, thanks.' Sophie grinned.

'But there's one thing, Sophie.'

'What's that?'

'We need to get you some new clothes. You know what they say: dress like the job you want.' She glanced at Sophie's pencil skirt. 'Listen, I'll take you shopping, sort out your wardrobe, so you'll soon be wowing all the clients.'

Sophie shifted uncomfortably in her seat. She couldn't help thinking that Cassie didn't just want to fix her clothes – she wanted to build Sophie in her own image.

FOURTEEN

James put a capsule in the coffee machine as Sophie reached into the cupboard above him and took the last mug from right at the back. There was no space to put it down amid the litter of dirty mugs balanced precariously on top of each other on the work surface, so she held it in her hand as she waited for James to finish with the machine.

'Harriet wasn't in yesterday afternoon,' James said apologetically. 'No one put the dishwasher on.' He opened it up and shoved a tablet in from the cupboard above, then switched it on.

Sophie bit her tongue at the idea that the office dishwasher was Harriet's responsibility. At least James was putting it on now, which was more than the others had done.

'Cassie told me your meeting with the energy company went really well yesterday. She thought you gave a great performance.'

Sophie glowed with pride. 'Thanks. She's offered to be my mentor.'

'That's brilliant. She never usually shows much of an interest in the junior staff. You can really learn a lot from her. She's a shrewd businesswoman.'

'I can tell.'

'What did you think of Philip?' James said with a smile.

Sophie blushed. 'I didn't know what to think... He's... a character.'

'Yeah, he is. Sometimes he's a bit much. But he does own the company.'

'What's he like to work for?'

'I don't have much to do with him, really. Max runs the business day-to-day. Philip just pops in occasionally. But he is in charge overall. His money started the company. Plus he owns the flat you're living in, of course.'

Sophie shifted uncomfortably as she remembered the footsteps she'd heard at night. 'Does he have a key?' she asked.

'I'm sure he has one to the house, yeah. But I wouldn't have thought he would use it. He owns dozens of properties all over London. He probably doesn't even know where they all are.'

'I heard someone in the house the other night. I thought I was on my own. It... it scared me a bit.'

James smiled. 'That will just be Max. He often used to take girls back to the empty flats there. It's close to the office and convenient.' James looked thoughtful. 'I wonder who it is this time? I wouldn't have thought it's Mercedes. They usually go back to her place.'

'You mean he's cheating on her?'

'I wouldn't say that. I think she knew the score when she started dating Max. She knew about the fling with Lydia before her.'

'Lydia?'

'Yeah, she lived in your flat before you. He used to go over to see her after work.'

Sophie imagined Lydia, living in the flat where she lived now. She wondered why Cassie hadn't told her that she was the previous tenant.

She thought of Max. Had his fling with Lydia happened

because of the convenience of her living nearby? Did Max put the women from the office in the flat for that reason? She shook the thoughts out of her head. She was being ridiculous.

Just then her phone started ringing, its cheery ringtone echoing round the office. She looked at the screen and saw it was only Charlie. She swiped to dismiss the call. 'Sorry about that,' she said.

'Is everything all right?' James asked. 'You've seemed stressed lately.'

'It's just my ex – Charlie. He rings all the time.'

'And you don't want to speak to him?'

'Not really.' She'd spoken to him after their trip to Tate Britain, but it was like speaking to a brick wall. He refused to accept they were over.

'I can beat him up if you like,' James joked.

Sophie shook her head. 'He's a good guy underneath it all. Without him... well, my father wouldn't have had the physio he needed. Charlie lent me the money for it.'

'I see. And now you feel you owe him.'

'I literally owe him.' She didn't mention he'd also paid off her credit cards. She'd got into debt when she'd had to fund a lawyer to counter Will's private prosecution against her, claiming she'd lied to the police and damaged his reputation. In the end his case had been dropped, but by then she'd spent thousands of pounds on legal advice.

'That sounds tough. Let me speak to Max. Maybe we could arrange an advance on your salary. We'd lend you the money now and you could pay it back out of your salary each month over the next year. Then you could pay Charlie back straight away.'

Sophie's heart leaped. That would solve so many problems. 'Do you think that would really be possible?'

'Let me speak to him. I'm sure I can persuade him.'

Sophie hesitated. 'It's a lot of money.'

James frowned. 'Is it? How much?'

She sighed, reluctant to admit how much it was. She looked at her feet as she said it. 'Ten thousand pounds.'

But James laughed. 'Oh, that's not a lot to Max. It should be fine to lend you it. Besides, it's for a good cause. And I know you're going to be one of our best employees.'

'I haven't even been here two weeks,' Sophie protested.

'I know talent when I see it, Sophie.' He squeezed her arm.

Later, when the darkness had descended over the London rooftops, Sophie was still in the office. Her computer screen glared brightly. If she could just crack the key aspiration behind the sustainable energy brand, then she'd go home and rest.

She felt a hand on her shoulder, saw a shadow above her. She jumped.

She looked up. It was only James. She let out a sigh of relief.

'You're here late,' he said gently.

'Yeah, I'm just working on the sustainable energy branding. Trying to come up with a real connection to its customers.'

He pulled up a seat beside her and leaned over the piles of brochures on her desk that she'd picked up from the company. Then, he reached for a pen and circled a picture of a happy-looking couple clasping hands. 'Focus on them,' he said. 'What is it they want from life? Who do they aspire to *be*? And how can sustainable energy help them achieve it?'

'You're good at this,' she said, grinning.

'Years of practice,' he said with a smile that lit up his whole face. She couldn't help noticing his perfectly straight teeth, and the smell of his aftershave. She breathed it in.

'You smell good,' she said before she could stop herself.

He smiled. 'So do you.'

'I haven't even got any perfume on.' *Or make-up*, she thought. In fact, she probably looked awful. She'd been working so hard she'd hardly seen any sunlight in the last week.

'I like your natural smell,' he said, and somehow it seemed so shockingly personal that Sophie laughed.

'What's so funny?' he said, swiping her lightly across the shoulder. The physical contact made her tingle.

'Nothing,' she said.

But then he started laughing too, and they were both in fits of giggles, without really being sure what they were laughing at.

'You know, it's quarter to eleven,' he said when they'd finally stopped. 'You'd really better get home.'

She nodded. 'Sure.'

'I'll walk you, if you like.' She hesitated for a moment, unsure what he meant. Usually she'd turn down anyone who offered, not wanting to get into any awkward situations. But today she craved his company for just a little bit longer.

'OK, then,' she said.

She closed her documents and shut down her computer, while he went to the other side of the office.

He flicked the lights off and for a second she felt a shiver of fear and excitement. As if he might come up behind her and put his arms around her. She tried to stop the thoughts, but there was no denying that James was attractive.

'Are you ready?' he called out from across the office. He was disappointingly far away, by the door to the stairs.

She grabbed her phone and her bag and made her way over to him, carefully navigating around the desks in the dark.

Her leg knocked into the corner of a desk. 'Ouch,' she said.

'Are you OK?'

'Yeah, just bumped my leg.'

'Want me to have a look?' He was definitely flirting with her now, and a part of her wanted to lift her skirt and show him where she'd bumped her leg, to see what would happen next. Would he touch her? Lean in to kiss her? More?

She shook the thoughts out of her head. 'I'm fine.'

'Do you like it here?' James asked as they stood by the lift.

'I do. I'm really enjoying the work.'

'And the company of the other employees?' he asked, his eyes twinkling.

'Yes, that too.'

The lift beeped and they stepped in together. He brushed against her as they went through the narrow doors and she felt a shiver run up her spine.

She glanced up at him, saw his strong profile, but he was looking away.

She wanted to kiss him, but she knew it was a bad idea. She shouldn't get involved with anyone in the office. Especially not one of the bosses. But then she was single. And she didn't think he was seeing anyone either. Surely there would be no harm.

When they got outside the building, there was a gentle drizzle. She had the umbrella she'd bought the other day in her handbag, but she let James hold his over her, and snuggled up close to him to avoid the drips. She could feel his arm against hers, the warmth coming off his body.

They chatted easily all the way back to her flat. She was disappointed when she got there. It signalled the end of the evening.

He looked down at her from beneath the umbrella.

'I suppose I'd better go.' There was a question in his eyes, or perhaps she was imagining it. Did he want to come up? No, it was just her reading too much into his expression.

'Yes,' she said. 'I'll see you tomorrow, at the office.'

His eyes searched hers and then he leaned forward towards her. She took a small step closer to him. Her mind was telling her she shouldn't kiss him, but now the moment was here, and she couldn't pull away.

She shut her eyes. But instead of feeling his mouth on hers, she felt his lips on her cheek.

She opened her eyes again, and blushed.

'Night night, Sophie,' he said with a smile.

FIFTEEN

Sophie sat on her balcony with her laptop, the sun streaming down. The week had rushed by and she had so much work left to do over the weekend. The company philosophy involved being always on, always available to clients. There was no request too small. Sophie loved throwing herself into her work, loved the thrill of getting it right and satisfying the clients, and the idea of the generous bonuses she'd been promised for performing well.

Sophie had spent the whole of Saturday morning hunched over her desk in her bedroom, working on the gin company's branding. She'd wanted to come out to the balcony to get some air, thinking she could work outside. But now all she could see on her computer screen was her own reflection. She tried to move position so the laptop was in shade, but the sun was still too bright. She couldn't read the document on the screen.

She shut her laptop and tilted her head back to catch the sun. Sipping her orange juice, she told herself she deserved a short break. She could go back inside and return to her work after she'd spent ten minutes enjoying the sunshine. Across the street a woman walked by with a pram, looking up at the houses as if in awe. She glanced up at Sophie, as if she'd felt her watching her, and then hurried on. Sophie remembered the feeling of being watched the other day, the sounds of someone walking around outside the flat. She wondered if that would ever stop, the feeling of being constantly alert. She'd hoped it might change when she moved to London, started a new chapter in her life. But now she had spoken to the police she was even more worried. What if Will's friends somehow found out she had gone against their wishes? What if they tried to punish her?

Sophie sighed and went back inside. Whenever she let her thoughts wander they always went to the same place. Will. For years she had put him to the back of her mind, but now he was here again, front and centre.

She decided to take a proper break and pop to the shop down the road for milk. She needed to buy candles, too, something to make the flat smell a bit nicer. Since Cassie had hired the pest control man to put poison down, she'd been acutely aware of the sounds and smells in the flat, convinced she could hear rats scuttling through the walls at night. They would be dead soon, the pest controller had told her matter-of-factly. But they would rot wherever they died, in the brickwork or under the floorboards. They didn't bother to look for the corpses; they were too difficult to find. Since he'd said that, Sophie had been aware of every bad smell, sure that in the corridors she could catch the whiff of something stale and rotten, the tangy smell of flesh.

She walked out of the flat and down to the corner shop and picked up some milk. They didn't have candles, but she found some plug-in air fresheners gathering dust at the back. She bought all three of them and then went back home.

As she walked up the stone steps, a voice called out from across the street.

'Hello? Sophie?'

'Hi.' Sophie looked at the girl who had appeared from the side of the building. She was in her mid-twenties, wearing a long black winter coat, her face worn and tired. Her hair had been scraped back into a messy ponytail and loose strands were coming out. 'Are you OK?' Sophie asked her.

The girl's eyes darted from side to side. 'I need to speak to you.'

'What is it?' Sophie asked.

'It's best for us to speak away from the house,' she said quickly, glancing up at the building. 'There are cameras there.'

'Cameras?' Sophie frowned. The house didn't even have a video entryphone.

'Look, I need to talk to you. About the company. I don't know how you're finding it, but it's not good for you, it's toxic... they take over your life. I can explain when we talk.' The girl pulled a folded piece of paper out of her coat pocket and pushed it into Sophie's hand.

'Who are you?' Sophie asked.

'My name's Felicity. I used to work at One Pure Thought. I used to live here. In your flat. Look – I can't explain here. They're watching. Please call me, OK?'

Sophie stared at her, but she had already turned and scurried off down the road, head down.

SIXTEEN

When Sophie got inside the building she felt shaken, and she stood for a moment, leaning against the closed front door, gathering her thoughts. How long had Felicity been watching the flat, waiting to talk to her? Sophie was hardly ever in, either working late or at the pub. She thought of all the times she'd felt watched, from the very first day she arrived. Had that been Felicity? Her stomach knotted. She didn't like the fact that she'd been found so easily. Although Felicity had lived in her flat before her, of course she'd know where to find her.

In the back of her mind Sophie was always worried that Will or his mates would track her down. It was irrational, but she couldn't shake her fear. Especially not now, with the police asking questions. She was back in London, and although it was a huge city, a part of her felt like she was in his territory.

Sophie looked down at the small white plastic bag she was carrying and remembered the air fresheners. She could only see one socket in the hallway, so she plugged one in there and then went upstairs.

As she unlocked the door of her flat, she realised she was still clutching the piece of paper Felicity had given her. She put it down on the kitchen counter and turned the kettle on. What did Felicity want to speak to her about? She'd seemed so agitated.

Perhaps James would know. He must know her if she used to work for the company. It was strange that no one had ever mentioned her before. Perhaps she was one of the women they'd employed before Sophie, one of the 'mistakes' they said they'd made in their recruitment. She could speak to James at work, find out what he knew. Felicity had said the company was toxic. Sophie thought of Philip and his scandal, Max making his way through the women in the office. Maybe that was what she meant. It couldn't do any harm to find out.

Sophie took her phone out and crafted a text message to Felicity. She tried to make it as neutral as possible.

Hi, it's Sophie. I'm happy to meet you to talk on Tuesday. There's a coffee shop up the road – Element Café. I can meet in the morning before work. 7.30 a.m.?

It was the only time Sophie was available. She wondered if Felicity would want to meet her so early.

But the reply came back immediately.

What about this evening? In half an hour?

Sophie's curiosity was piqued, but she wanted to speak to James first, check what she was getting into.

Tuesday's the earliest I can do.

OK. Tuesday then. Element Coffee. 7.30 a.m.

Sure.

On Monday morning Sophie found James when she got into the office.

'Morning,' he said. 'How are you?'

'Yeah, I'm good. How long have you been in the office?'

He shrugged. 'Since six. You know me.'

'Ready for a coffee break then?' She smiled at him, and thought how easy he was to talk to. He was one of the most senior members of the team, and yet he was always friendly to everyone. She thought of how Max had spoken to Harriet the other day, when Philip had come into the office. James and Max were so different to each other.

'Sure,' he said.

Sophie put her laptop down on the desk beside him and turned it on, then they wandered over to the kitchen together.

'How was your weekend?' James asked.

'I had a visitor,' she said.

'Not a rat?' he said, eyebrows raised. She'd told him how she thought she heard scratching in the walls at night.

'No. A woman came round. I think you must know her. Felicity?'

A shadow crossed James's face. 'Felicity? She used to work here.'

'She turned up on my doorstep. She wanted to talk to me. She was saying all sorts of things. About how the company was toxic. That there were cameras in the flats.'

James sighed visibly, his shoulders slumping. 'I can't believe she's still doing this.'

'She's done this before?'

'Yeah.' James pulled the coffee out of the machine and handed it to Sophie, then put another pod in the machine. 'With Lydia.'

'Lydia? She lived in my flat before me, didn't she? Felicity said she had lived there too.'

'Yeah, they both lived there. After Felicity left she came back to talk to Lydia, tried to persuade her to leave too. I sometimes wondered if that was why Lydia eventually left. Of course, we were glad anyway. Lydia wasn't right for the company.' Sophie frowned. She still hadn't worked out why everyone seemed to think so little of Lydia.

'Why did Felicity want Lydia to leave?'

'Felicity's bad news, Sophie. She wants to sue the company, but she doesn't have enough grounds. She tries to get other people onside. She's tried it with all our employees. Including Lydia. And now you.'

'I see,' Sophie said.

James's eyes narrowed.

'Let me guess. She wants to meet you. Explain her crazy theories about the company?'

'Yeah,' Sophie said, thinking of the coffee she'd suggested.

He leaned forward, looked deep into her eyes. 'Look, you can't talk to her. I don't want her to get it into her head that you might support her case against the company.'

Sophie thought about how agitated Felicity had seemed. She clearly had some kind of problem. 'OK,' she said. 'I understand. Although I did feel a bit sorry for her. She seemed... very anxious.'

James sighed. 'I know what you mean. She just seemed to go completely off the rails after she left. Became obsessed with the company, obsessed with bringing us down. I don't think she's well. She believes all sorts of odd things, believes we dismissed her unfairly. It's a mess, really.' He put his hand on Sophie's shoulder. 'For your own good, don't get involved with her.'

SEVENTEEN

Sophie and James went back to their desks and slid into their chairs next to each other. Sophie was going to cancel her coffee with Felicity. She felt sorry for her, but it was clear that if she spoke to her, it would be damaging for Sophie and her career.

James turned to her. 'I'm sorry you had to deal with her turning up like that,' he said. 'Just let me know if she comes to see you again. We need to keep an eye on what she's doing.'

Sophie nodded. 'Of course.' But she was distracted by her phone. There was a new Google alert for her name. A website she hadn't seen before. She swallowed, praying it was about another Sophie Williams, winning a drama competition or being interviewed in a local paper.

She clicked on the link. It wasn't someone else. It was her. On the homepage of the website there was a huge picture of her smiling face. A photo of her on the beach in Dorset, squinting into the sunlight. They must have taken it from Keely's Instagram page. It was one of the only photos of Sophie on social media.

She scrolled down to see the rest of the page and her heart sank.

Whore. Bitch. Liar.

The words were like knives through her, reopening old scars. All the old accusations were there. Somehow Will and his friends must know she'd been to the police.

Sophie tried to calm her breathing. She shouldn't have spoken to the police. Not when she knew what Will's friends were like, how they'd made her life hell for so many years. Not when she'd worked so hard to escape them.

She remembered Keely taking the photo of her on the beach and posting it on Instagram just before she'd moved to London. She would normally have told her not to, but she'd let it go. She was tired of hiding. She'd even thought at the time that maybe she could risk getting social media accounts again, sharing photos, sharing her life.

But Will's friends had found the photo, put it up on the website. She went back to Keely's Instagram account, looked at the picture there. Underneath it Keely had written 'My beautiful friend Sophie. I'll miss her when she's in London'. They knew from Keely's comment that Sophie was in London. Sophie slowed her breathing as she thought about how huge London was. There was no way they'd be able to find her in it; in a city of millions of people she could be anywhere. She was more anonymous than she'd been before in her village, where she was always worried they could easily find her, any time they wanted to. She thought of the email they'd sent to her freelance email account. They had found her in Dorset. But they wouldn't find her in London. Would they?

Sophie read the whole website through again. There was nothing new on there. Only the claims and accusations they'd made before. That she was a girl who cried rape, who wrecked men's lives.

She took a deep breath. She could handle it. She'd endured

it for years, website after website about her put up and taken down. All the rumours about her. She'd dealt with it when she was nineteen and she could deal with it now. But still tears pricked the backs of her eyes as it all came flooding back. She used to be so scared that they'd come for her. Will had taken out a private prosecution against her, wanted to see her tried for lying to the police. She'd got into so much debt consulting lawyers, just so she'd be able to defend herself.

She wasn't that person anymore, running scared. She'd rebuilt her life. She was strong, and she could deal with this. Everything was going to be OK. But she needed to tell Keely to take the photo of her off her social media. They'd have access to anything Keely shared about her.

Sophie got up from her desk and went out of the office. She took the lift down and stood outside in the alleyway, with the smokers. She was about to take out her phone and ring Keely, ask her to delete anything to do with Sophie on her social media, when she felt a sudden surge of anger. She thought of the other woman who'd accused Will, how she'd have to go through everything Sophie had.

Instead of phoning Keely, she rang DCI Jameson and told her everything. She told her about the latest website. She told her how she'd withdrawn her accusation against Will because his friends had set up websites accusing her of lying, how they'd threatened to share naked photos of her. She told her how she'd been afraid for years that they would track her down and hurt her.

After she'd hung up the phone, she burst into tears. She knew there might be repercussions. But if the worst thing they could do was share naked photos of her, then she would cope. She had her new life now. And she was tired of running. Tired of hiding.

EIGHTEEN

Outside the pub, there were already crowds of pavement drinkers, revelling in the unusual autumn sunshine. The rain of the previous weeks had been momentarily forgotten as office workers sipped pints of beer and glasses of wine, the heat of the sun warming their faces.

Sophie squeezed past the drinkers in the bar area, her eyes taking a moment to adjust to the dark. The queue at the bar was at least three deep and just one barmaid was pulling a pint, while avoiding eye contact with the sea of people leaning over the bar. Sophie went straight to what she thought of as 'their' table, at the back. She wasn't sure if the barmaid reserved it for them each night, but someone from the office was always there. It felt as if it was their own private space, an extension of Max's domain.

Sophie needed a drink tonight, an escape from everything that was going on. At first, after her conversation with DCI Jameson, she'd felt on a high. Free. The detective inspector had said that the law had changed since Sophie was at university. If Will's friends sent out photos it would count as distributing sexual images without consent. They could be charged.

But the initial elation of telling the police was wearing off and she was starting to worry. She knew she might be called to the court to give evidence later, that her own rape might even go to trial now that there was a new accusation, but for now she just wanted to forget all about it, get on with her life, have a drink and relax.

A lot of her colleagues were already at the pub, and Sophie squeezed in next to James while he reached for the wine and poured some into an empty glass. He handed it to her and she sipped it gratefully. She was drinking more and more since she started at the office. She rarely had a day off. And she never had just one glass of wine either; she always had three or four. Although she never really knew exactly how many because she was always being topped up. It didn't matter, she supposed. She was often tipsy, but rarely drunk. And without fail, she was always at work at 8 a.m. the next day, no matter how dire she felt. She'd learned that that was what was important to Max and James. As long as you put in the hours and got your work done, the rest didn't matter so much. In fact, they probably preferred it if you put in the hours down the pub too. James and Cassie in particular were always talking about the importance of team cohesion and getting to know everyone.

Now they were chatting about their favourite films and Sophie relaxed into the conversation. It felt easy after a long day.

'I'll go and get some more wine,' James said. Sophie needed to move to let him out.

'I'll get it,' she said, as she stood up from the wooden bench.

'No, no, no. The bosses have to pay. Those are the rules.'

'I want to.'

'You're not paying.'

'I'll come with you then.'

Max was already at the bar paying for a few pints of beer.

'So,' James said to Sophie. 'How are you getting on?'

He had a twinkle in his eye and she remembered the other night when she thought he was going to kiss her. She blushed. She didn't want to make that mistake again.

But he was standing unnecessarily close to her, his leg touching hers. He rested his arm on the bar beside hers, their shoulders touching.

'Same wine again?' he asked, leaning towards her. She could almost feel the bristles of his stubble on her face. 'Or would something more expensive be more suitable?' His lips were so close to hers, she could feel his breath when he spoke.

His eyes met hers once more. She was sure it was about to happen this time. Their eyes were locked on each other and he tilted his head.

And then she felt hands on her waist, moving her to the side. She jumped and turned.

'Max!'

'Hello, you two. Thought I'd stop you before you ordered more wine. You can put it on my tab.'

James leaned back, away from her, the moment lost. 'Thanks, Max,' he said quietly.

Sophie frowned at Max as he picked up the pints he'd ordered from the bar and went past them towards their table at the back. She hated people unexpectedly touching her.

'Are you all right?' James said, noticing her expression.

'Yeah, fine. Max just... grabbed my waist.'

'Huh?'

'Not like that... just to move me out of the way. It made me feel a bit uncomfortable.'

'Oh, I'm sorry...' James paused, searching for the right words.

Sophie shook her head. 'It was nothing. I'm probably overreacting.' Sophie found it difficult to judge what was acceptable these days. Max was probably just a tactile person.

'If his behaviour ever bothers you I can always speak to him about it on your behalf. Just let me know.'

'I will do,' Sophie said firmly. 'Of course.' She thought of Felicity, who had said the company was toxic, and Lydia, who'd left under a cloud after a relationship with Max. Sophie needed to keep in with Max. The job was everything to her.

James put his hand on Sophie's arm. 'Max is a good guy. He's just lacks... tact sometimes. He doesn't always understand social norms. It's his upbringing. He's used to having everything his way. But I have some good news for you.' James paused and smiled. 'I spoke to him about giving you an advance on your salary.'

Sophie looked up, thinking of her debt to Charlie, how smothering it was to have him still in her life. 'And?' she asked hopefully.

'He's open to the idea, if you need it. I explained about your father, about the money Charlie lent you for his treatment. He was sympathetic. He understands about wanting to get an ex out of your life.' James smiled. 'So, if you just confirm how much it is you need, I'm sure we can sort it out.'

NINETEEN

Sophie studied herself in the mirror. The company was chasing a new client, a start-up TV streaming service, and she'd been slaving over the presentation for the last week. It was as good as she could make it, but now she had to make sure she looked the part too. The green striped designer dress she'd bought with Cassie on Bond Street the week before was perfect for the meeting. It somehow accentuated her figure without exposing it, and the colour complemented her blonde highlights. She had the perfect big, beaded necklace to go with it and a matching green handbag which doubled up as a laptop bag. She applied her make-up carefully and straightened her hair, then went to the balcony to check the temperature. There was a bitter wind, so she paired the dress with a black biker jacket and knee-length black boots from the high street.

She smiled at herself in the mirror, pleased with her efforts. She was determined to impress at the meeting. It was her chance to show Max just how good her work was, make sure he didn't regret offering her an advance on her salary. She dropped a slice of bread in the toaster to eat on her way to the office. As soon as it was out she buttered it while it was still hot. But when she picked it up, it slipped through her fingers, brushing over her dress, covering it in long greasy smears. She rubbed at it with a paper towel but it was useless.

She didn't have anything else to wear. Cassie hadn't thought much of the pencil skirt she had worn to the last meeting. Sophie looked in her cupboard at the long line of jeans and semi-formal shirts. They wouldn't do. Her favourite dress was in the wash, and besides, it was too casual. Then she saw the burgundy dress that she'd found down the back of the cupboard. She'd had it dry cleaned and it looked brand new. It was her only other dress, her only option.

She slipped it over her head. It was a bit tight, but otherwise fine. She took one last look in the mirror then left the house for work.

She felt nervous going through the doors of the office, self-conscious in her outfit, which seemed tighter now she was walking. The back of the dress kept riding up and she had to keep pulling it down. She told herself it would be fine once she was sitting in the meeting.

It was 8.30 a.m. and the meeting wasn't until 9 a.m., so she had half an hour to prepare. She read through the presentation at her desk, drawing out the key points she wanted to make. Out of the corner of her eye she saw the clients arriving, dressed in jeans and polo shirts. They must be young tech entrepreneurs. She regretted her choice of clothes immediately, but there wasn't time to change. James took them through the office, asking Harriet to get them some coffee. They were a bit early, but James had explained that he and Max would have a chat to them in the office first, and warm them up, and then Sophie would come in with her presentation.

'You're going to ace it,' he'd told her yesterday. 'I know you will. They'll be blown away.'

It was five to nine now and the men had been talking in the office for fifteen minutes. She could see them through the glass panels, smiling and laughing. They seemed relaxed. She went to the ladies' to check her make-up in the mirror, to make sure she hadn't smudged her mascara by mistake. She looked overdressed. She took off the necklace and shoved it in her bag, and wiped off some of her lipstick.

She walked back into the office, grabbed her papers from her desk and strode as confidently as she could towards the meeting room.

She knocked lightly, then let herself in.

There was a silence while Max and James just stared. She felt a flush rise to her face.

'Is that my coffee?' said the client.

James came to his senses quickly. He stood up and smiled. 'This is Sophie. Our newest and brightest recruit.'

Max was still staring at Sophie, his eyes on her breasts. She swallowed, suddenly aware that the dress was perhaps a bit tight, that she was a woman coming into a room full of men.

'Do you want to explain the pitch, Sophie?' James said when she'd sat down.

'Yes, of course,' she said quickly, flicking through her papers to find the right place. Max still hadn't taken his eyes off her, and she felt the hairs on her arms rising as she started to speak.

When they left the room, Sophie breathed a sigh of relief. The presentation had gone well, the clients had seemed to like it and were interested in working with One Pure Thought to develop the brand. Max said nothing to her as they left the room, but James congratulated her.

'Where did you get that dress?' he whispered as they returned to their desks.

'In the flat. It was behind the wardrobe... must have been there ages.'

'Oh... I thought it looked familiar, no wonder Max was freaked out. I think it was Lydia's. She must have left it behind.'

'Do you think Max would have recognised it?' She remembered how he'd stared at her. She'd thought he was being rude, but maybe it was just the dress. Perhaps he'd known it was Lydia's.

'Probably.' James laughed. 'It would have given him quite a shock seeing you in it. Like he'd seen a ghost.'

She wondered why Lydia's dress had made Max so anxious. 'Did Lydia and Max have a bad break-up? Did she leave the company because of him?'

'No, it wasn't that at all. This wasn't the right place for her. Her work really wasn't up to scratch.'

Sophie thought about how impressive Lydia's campaign ideas had been. How had they not realised she was good at the job? There was something no one was telling her, something more to why Lydia had left.

Max came over to her desk later that afternoon. He seemed to have recovered, returned to his usual self.

'Well done on the presentation,' he said. 'It seems like you're our star employee.' She should have been happy, but his tone was slightly sneering.

'Thank you,' she said.

'I'm really pleased with how your employment is going,' he said, running his fingers over her desk, a bit too close to her.

'What do you mean?'

He smiled at her, looked her directly in the eye. 'I'm sure you'll pass probation.'

Sophie swallowed. 'I didn't realise there was a probationary period.'

'There isn't,' James interjected with a frown. 'Not really.'

'It's more of a thing in our heads,' Max said. 'We observe our employees over the first three months, and if they aren't up to scratch then we get rid of them.'

'We ask them to leave nicely,' James corrected. 'It's not really about them so much, as the fit with the company. Some people... well, they don't fit... and it's clear they will never be happy here. We nudge those people towards the door.'

'You'll be different, won't you, Sophie?' Max said. 'You won't let us down.'

Sophie walked home that evening thinking of Lydia and Felicity. Had the company really treated them badly, or was there more to it? She considered messaging Felicity, to see if she could shed any light on what had happened with Lydia. But then she thought of what James had said about Felicity trying to sue the company and decided that she wouldn't get the real story out of her anyway.

As Sophie unlocked the door of the house, she was greeted by the sharp smell of the air freshener. Beneath it she thought she could smell a rotten scent, but it was so faint she couldn't be sure. She climbed the stairs to her flat. It seemed like the smell was getting stronger, but it was probably because she was moving away from the air freshener on the ground floor.

The light was dim outside her flat and she was just peering into her handbag to get her key out when she caught sight of a brown shadow on her doormat. She looked up from her bag and focused on the object, saw the long winding tail, the dark beady eye. A rat. She jumped away from it, but it was soon clear it wasn't moving. It was dead, lying against her door as if it had been propped up there, its tail curled round behind it. It wouldn't have died in that position on its own. Someone had moved it there. Someone had put it there to scare her.

TWENTY

Sophie stared at the dead rat in horror. She didn't know what to do. She didn't want to move it herself, and she didn't have the pest controller's number.

She reached forward to open the door of her flat and managed to unlock it with her arms outstretched. As the door opened the rat's body slid down into the entrance, blocking the door so she couldn't shut it. Swallowing the bile rising in her throat, she stepped over it into her flat, then propped the door open so the door didn't close on the body.

Unable to take her eyes off the furry brown rodent, she paced up and down her flat. She couldn't leave the door open all night; she needed to figure out a way to move the body as soon as possible. Picking up her phone, she rang James and asked him if he had the number of the pest controller. He told her he'd get it from Cassie and ring him himself. Sophie was relieved when her buzzer sounded half an hour later.

It was James.

'I'm sorry,' he said with a smile as he greeted her at her door. 'You'll have to make do with me. I couldn't get hold of the rat man.'

'You didn't need to come all this way,' she said. She remembered he lived the other side of London, in Battersea.

'It's no problem.' He stared down at the rat. 'There's a shovel in the outside cupboard, I think. Do you have a bin bag?'

Fifteen minutes later, James had carried the rat down to the outside bin and returned to the flat. 'All done,' he said, rubbing his hands briskly together, as Sophie scrubbed the doorstep with disinfectant. 'Such an odd place to choose to die, but at least it's gone.'

'I know. The pest control man said they usually choose dark, quiet places to die. Do you – do you think someone put it there?'

James looked thrown. 'Why would anyone do that?'

'I don't know.' Maybe she was being paranoid, imagining things. But then she had been sure she'd been imagining someone watching her before Felicity turned up. It was hard to know what was real and what was her imagination. But the rat had been there. That wasn't in her head.

James squeezed her shoulder. 'Hang in there. I can see why you would think that, but I'm sure it just died there on its own. After all, if you were out, the house would have been dark and empty. It would have seemed as good a place as any.'

Sophie nodded. 'I owe you one. Do you want a drink?'

'No, no. I need to be off. Early start tomorrow. I'm at a client's all day.'

'Ah, OK then.'

'I'll see you at Max's party, though, on Saturday?'

'Yeah, probably.' Sophie wasn't sure she felt up for a party. She was exhausted from her long hours at the office.

'Oh, come on. Everyone from work's going.'

She smiled. Even if she just went for a couple of hours, it would be nice to see James. 'OK, I'll see you there,' she said.

. . .

Saturday arrived, and Sophie was putting on her make-up in front of the mirror, getting ready for the party. She grinned at her reflection. It would be nice to see James and Cassie outside of the office and get to know them better. She turned back and forth in front of the mirror, checking her outfit from all angles. She was wearing a dark red skirt she'd bought with Cassie and a sparkly top that she'd had for years and often brought out for parties. She was just about to head out the door when her phone started to ring. Charlie.

She didn't want to talk to him. Not until the advance came through on her salary from Max and James. Then she could pay him back and be rid of him.

She cancelled the call, grabbed her bag, locked the flat and went down the stairs.

When she opened the door to the flats, Charlie was outside waiting for her.

'Hi,' he said. 'I've been trying to get hold of you.'

'I'm sorry, I've been busy. What are you doing in London?'

'I just wanted to talk to you. I feel... like you're just not interested in speaking to me anymore.'

She sighed. That was true. She just wanted him to leave her alone. 'We've split up, Charlie.'

'But you said we could be friends. And I'm in London again this weekend, crashing with a friend.'

She raised an eyebrow, wondering why he was in London so frequently these days.

He continued. 'I thought we could still do things together. Go to museums, tourist attractions, the theatre. Explore a new city together. But as friends. Just because you don't want the romantic part of the relationship doesn't mean we can't have the other bit, does it?'

Sophie put her hands to her temples. 'No, but—'

'I've got tickets to the theatre tonight. To *The Mousetrap*. I know you've always wanted to see it.'

'I do, yeah, but – I can't tonight. I'm busy.'

'Oh,' he said. 'With what?'

'I'm going to a party, with some of the people from work.'

'Aren't you bored of them, after spending all week with them?'

'No. Look, Charlie. I want to see them, OK?' She was going to have to explain to him again that she didn't want to be friends. But she didn't have time now. And she wanted to pay him back first.

'Maybe we can catch up later then?' he said.

'Maybe.'

'What time will you be back?'

'Around nine. I'm only planning to stay for a few hours. But listen, I don't think we should talk then, I'll be tired. We can talk another day.'

He nodded.

She walked down the stairs past him. When she glanced back behind her, he was watching her intently, a small frown on his face.

When Sophie knocked on the door of Max's Chelsea home she could already hear the bass pumping. She took a deep breath, feeling slightly intimidated. She felt confident in the office now, but it was different entering Max's house; it felt like a step into the unknown.

At first no one came to the door, and Sophie was just about to ring the bell when two people stumbled out, clutching each other, vapes in their hands. The girl, clad all in black, slipped slightly on the steps and Sophie reached out her hand to steady her. The girl turned her head, but her eyes were vacant as she stared through Sophie.

Sophie swallowed and hesitated for a moment. A taxi pulled up behind her and a blonde woman got out unsteadily and climbed the steps to the house. The front door was ajar now and Sophie pushed it open, and the woman slipped in behind her. 'I'm looking for Cassie,' the woman said to Sophie, slurring her words, her eyes unfocused. 'Have you seen her?'

'I only just got here,' Sophie said, and the woman stumbled past her, disappearing into the living room. Inside the house there were people everywhere, lounging on the sofas and leaning against the walls, chatting, drinking and dancing. Sophie stepped through the rooms unacknowledged, and wondered if coming here was a mistake.

In the living room, two girls sat on the sofa snorting lines of coke off the glass table. Bodies were crowded in groups, drinks in hands. The room smelled like a mixture of sweat, the sweet, fruity scent of vapes and stale alcohol.

Sophie felt a slap on her back and turned. 'Sophie!' Max smiled at her, his grin lopsided, his eyes unfocused. 'Sophie, Sophie, Sophie. I'm so glad you made it.'

'Thanks,' she said.

'Let me get you a drink from the kitchen.' She followed him through, nodding to the people in the corridor as she did so. She hadn't seen anyone from the office yet, and she didn't know anyone here.

Max kept stopping to talk to people and only occasionally remembered to introduce her. The crowd seemed to be mainly his friends from school, a collection of investment bankers, lawyers and entrepreneurs like him. Out of the corner of her eye, Sophie could see that the woman from earlier had found Cassie. Cassie had her hand on her shoulder, guiding her back towards the door.

In the kitchen Max made Sophie a cocktail and she took it gratefully. 'Have you seen James?' she asked.

'James? He's here somewhere.' He made a show of looking round the room. 'But why do you want to find him? My company not good enough for you?' He laughed, but there was something in his eyes that made her think he was serious.

'It's not that,' she said. 'It's just I said I'd see him here.'

'He's always popular with the ladies, James,' Max said. 'Never known what to make of it myself.'

It was typical of Max to think that he should be the centre of attention, not James.

'He's a nice guy, that's why,' Sophie said. 'He's been really kind to me in the office.' She wondered if now was a good time to ask Max when the advance on her salary would come through, but she decided it wasn't. It was best to speak to James.

'Piling on the charm, is he?' Max slurred, getting a bit too close to her. 'Well, make sure you don't fall for it.'

Sophie frowned at him, irritated.

'But seriously,' he said. 'You're a nice kid. You'd be better off with someone else.'

Sophie winced at the word 'kid'. She was only a couple of years younger than him. Luckily, Cassie came in then, and swept her away to meet people. 'Come and join us,' she said. 'All our better halves are on Jenny's fiancé's stag do, so it's the perfect chance for us girls to let our hair down.' She introduced her to a gang of women who'd gone to her school. 'This is Sophie,' she drawled. 'Our top new brand strategist.'

'Oh, brilliant,' they said, their eyes glazing over. The conversation went back to what their husbands and boyfriends might be getting up to on the stag do, and then moved on to girls they'd known at school, what had happened to them, where they were now. Sophie nodded and smiled politely, feeling awkward at the edge of the circle.

'Sophie – another drink?' Cassie asked, when she saw she'd finished her cocktail.

'I'm not sure.' She didn't want to drink too much, like she always did when she was nervous. It had been her weakness at university. Now she was older, she recognised the signs, but she still found it hard to say no.

'I'll get you a drink,' James said, appearing beside her. 'White wine?'

Her stomach clenched with relief at seeing him. 'Thanks,' she said. 'Could I have some water, too?'

'Of course.'

She hardly said anything while she waited for him to return.

'Shall we go and sit down?' he asked as he handed her her wine. He'd forgotten the water. He indicated a sofa a kissing couple had recently vacated, disappearing upstairs.

She sank into the sofa. She was aware that her sparkly black top and red skirt just weren't right for the party. The others had long talon-like nails, hair that had been styled by a hairdresser and designer dresses. She felt provincial here, like someone's younger sister, or the nerdy friend that had been invited as a favour. She didn't fit in.

James followed her gaze. 'Cassie can be a bit much when she's with her school friends.' They watched her back arch as she laughed uproariously at something one of them had said. 'She's different to them, though. She's shockingly, painfully smart. She could run rings around them if she wanted to. But she doesn't. I think it's because she thinks they might come in useful to her one day. She likes to network, keep all her options open.'

Sophie nodded. She needed to learn to network, but at the moment she felt too awkward and out of place.

'That's why she's such a good salesperson. I think Max gets a bit jealous sometimes. He's never been that good. But of course, because he's the man, his father made him CEO, and Cassie Client Relationship Director.'

'That must have frustrated her.'

'It did. But I'm sure she's got a plan. She could outwit both of them.'

Sophie laughed. 'I'm sure she could.'

James sipped his beer, and Sophie turned to look at him. From what Max had said earlier, she'd thought James was interested in her, but now he seemed more interested in Cassie.

'She's certainly impressive,' Sophie said.

'She's like a chameleon. She can be anyone you want in order to sell something.'

Sophie thought of when she'd first met her, and how well they'd got on ever since. Had that just been Cassie charming her? She and Max must have had a strange upbringing with Philip. Maybe it had hardened them both.

'I guess a lot of men go for that.'

'Yeah, they do. But I prefer less complicated people. Less fake nails, less fake tan, less fake person.'

Sophie's heart leaped, suddenly aware of how their legs were touching on the sofa. Did he mean her?

'Should we get a photo of the two of us?'

'Really? Why?' She looked at him questioningly.

'I don't know. I just thought it would be nice. We might want to remember this moment. Later on.' She thought he might kiss her then, but instead he stood up quickly, and collared a man ambling by with a beer.

'Rick – could you take a photo of the two of us?' He handed him his phone.

'Sure.'

Sophie tried to straighten up on the sofa, aware the angle wasn't at all flattering with Rick taking the photo from so far above. She felt James put his arm around her and she leaned in to his warm body.

'There you go,' Rick said, handing back the phone. 'I've taken a few.'

'Thanks,' James said, showing Sophie the pictures. James was grinning at the camera happily, and Rick had captured a strange expression in Sophie's eyes. She was looking at James adoringly, with a kind of drunken longing. She flushed, embarrassed.

'Those are *not* good photos.'

'I don't know, I kind of like them. We almost look like a couple.'

She looked at him, her eyes searching his, but he pulled away. 'Another drink?' he asked.

TWENTY-ONE

They sat on the sofa most of the evening, just the two of them, Sophie and James, only getting up to go to the kitchen and get more drinks, although James got up a lot more often than her.

Her phone started ringing at just after 10 p.m.

Charlie.

She swiped to reject the call. He called again straight away and she got an alert to say she had a voicemail. She sighed.

'Someone bothering you?'

'Just Charlie.'

'Again? He's still calling you?'

She sighed. 'He came round to the flat this evening. I said I couldn't talk to him.'

'He sounds like a stalker,' James said, stroking the hair back from her face. 'I have an ex like that. She really doesn't take no for an answer. You have to cut off all contact. Otherwise they keep tracking you down.'

Sophie had a flash of memory. 'Charlie knew where I lived without me ever telling him.'

James frowned. 'Seriously? That's... a little concerning.'

'I know. But while I still owe him money, I can't cut him off.' She looked up at him.

'The advance on your salary hasn't come through yet, then?'

'No, not yet.'

Her phone beeped. A text from Charlie.

Are you OK? You said we could talk. I've finished at the theatre. It wasn't as good as I thought it would be. Maybe because you weren't there. I'm outside your flat, ready to talk.

'Is that from him?' James asked.

'Yep. He wants to talk right now.'

'Tell him no.'

She typed a message back.

Still at the party. Sorry.

The screen was a bit blurry and she couldn't quite make out what she'd written but it looked about right. She pressed send.

'Sorted,' she said.

'You need him out of your life completely.'

'I suppose so.'

'Remind me – how much money do you need to pay him back?'

'He's lent me ten thousand pounds. But he was going to lend me more for my dad's next physio sessions.' She swallowed. Ten thousand pounds. It was more money than she could imagine. But if the physio meant her father could walk more easily it would all be worth it.

'OK,' he said, slowly. 'Well, if it helps I could transfer it now. Do you want me to do that?'

Sophie's eyebrows shot up.

'I have access to the business banking on my phone. I can just make a transfer on the app right now.'

'Right now? For ten thousand?'

'Yep,' he said with a cheeky grin. He opened up his phone and showed her. 'Here we go. Just give me the account details.' She found her bank card and read out the sort code and account number, squinting to make out the small digits.

'I'll just double-check that,' he said, taking the card from her. 'Wouldn't want to get it wrong.' He made the transfer and showed her the receipt.

'All sorted,' he said. 'You can boot Charlie out of your life.'

Sophie smiled, and sank back into the sofa. She felt like a huge weight had been lifted.

Sophie wasn't sure how much time had passed when Max stumbled over to them, his eyes glazed.

'There's someone outside, Sophie. Says he needs to speak to you.'

'What?' she said groggily. She thought she might have been having a small sleep, her eyes had closed by mistake and it had taken an effort to open them. 'Who?'

'I don't know who the hell he is. I didn't let him in. It's my party.'

She went to the door and saw Charlie out there, shivering in the cold.

'What are you doing here?'

'You didn't come home. I was worried.'

'Look, Charlie—'

'You said we could talk.'

'Not now, Charlie. It's not appropriate to come here and look for me.' Her mind was foggy with drink, but she only remembered telling him she was going to a party with people from work. She hadn't said where it was.

She put her hands to her head. 'How did you know where I was?'

Charlie looked sheepish. 'I still have that tracking app on your phone. You know, the one you made me install because you were nervous about being out on your own.'

She remembered. He'd installed it after she'd dropped out of university. She'd been afraid because of what had happened with Will, and had wanted someone to protect her.

'Is that how you knew where I lived, too?' She couldn't believe this. She felt herself reddening with anger. James was right, he was behaving like a stalker.

He looked at his shoes. 'Yeah.'

'You should have deleted the app when we split up!'

'Maybe. But I thought it was best to keep it. That way I could still look out for you.'

'But you don't need to know where I am anymore. I'm not your girlfriend. If you don't know where I am, it's not because something awful's happened.'

'I just care about you.'

'Well, you can see I'm fine, can't you? You can go now.'

'You're drunk, Sophie.'

She shook her head defiantly. 'So what if I am? I can have a good time without you.'

'I can take you back to your flat. Make sure you get home safely.'

'Don't be ridiculous, Charlie, I'm fine.'

TWENTY-TWO

Sophie woke, her eyes opening slowly, her eyelids sticking. The light was too bright, too strong, and she closed them again, circles of colour dancing behind her eyelids, her head pounding. Where was she?

Opening one eye this time, she observed her immediate surroundings. Her bedside table with her hairbrush on it, her perfume. Her jewellery; her earrings laid out neatly next to her necklace. She felt a flicker of relief deep in her chest. As if she had expected to be somewhere else. She took a deep breath. It was all OK. But she had no idea why she needed to tell herself that.

The bedside light was switched on despite the open curtains. Her eyes scrolled the room. She could see her wardrobe on the other side of the room. Her chest of drawers.

Why were her curtains open? She felt sick. So sick. Perhaps she had had too much to drink. She wondered if she should run to the toilet now to throw up, or, if she lay very still, she could hold off the waves of nausea. She wanted to retreat into the cocoon of sleep, where there were no thoughts, no memories.

She closed her eyes, but her thoughts wouldn't shut off.

Why *were* her curtains open? She thought back. She couldn't remember. Perhaps she had got in so late, so drunk, from the party, that she hadn't thought to close them. It was possible. Back when she was at university, there had been occasions when she had lain down on her bed after a night out and fallen straight to sleep in her clothes. Back then she would wake up when the sun started to rise and draw the curtains closed, before returning to bed. But she must have been in such a deep sleep that she hadn't even woken at sunrise. She looked at her watch, still on her wrist. She must have forgotten to take it off. Eleven forty-five a.m. The sun must have been streaming through her window for hours.

She ran her fingers across the skin of her collarbone, something that she did when she was confused or unsure. The touch of her fingers was reassuring. It made her feel real. She looked down and saw that she was wearing an old nightdress. It was one she never wore; she slept in old, comfy pyjamas. This nightdress had been a Christmas present from her aunt, and she'd brought it with her to London because it felt wrong to throw it out. She couldn't recall ever having worn it before.

What had happened last night? Her eyes scanned the room once more. Her clothes from yesterday were folded neatly on the chair; her top sparkling merrily, out of keeping with Sophie's mood. Even if she'd come home sober, it would be unusual for her to have made the effort to fold the clothes. Her chest tightened, but she pushed the feeling down.

She got up slowly, closed the curtains, then lay back down on the bed. Shutting her eyes, she tried to return to the safety of sleep. But there was a faint smell in the room, one she couldn't quite place. She sniffed, trying to put her finger on it. Maybe if she could work out what it was she'd be able to sleep. She could identify stale cigarettes. The other smell was more floral and she realised it was a popular perfume. Not hers. She got up and went over to her coat, hanging neatly on the back of the chair.

She smelled it. The cigarette smell was coming from there. Some of the others must have been smoking last night. That was all. Nothing to worry about.

She felt a cold chill on her legs and reached for her dressing gown, wrapping it round herself as she shivered. She searched around for her phone. Perhaps she should do something. Get in contact with some friends. Get out of the house.

Her phone wasn't on her bedside table as usual, but that was hardly a surprise. She looked around for her handbag. It must be in the living room. She peered round the door into the room and was relieved to see it looked the same as usual.

She spied her handbag sitting beside the sofa. She grabbed it and rooted around for her phone. Out of battery.

She felt grubby and dirty. Her mouth tasted of a sewer and she felt like alcohol was seeping out of her pores. She needed a shower. She went back to her bedroom and put her phone on charge. Once she'd had a shower, hopefully it would be charged enough for her to phone Keely. She missed her, and they hadn't spoken since she'd moved. Then Sophie needed to work out something to do this afternoon in London, so the day wouldn't be completely wasted.

She went to the bathroom and peeled off her nightdress, pulling down her cotton knickers. She felt sore all over: her legs ached, her arms ached, she felt tired to her bones. When she stepped into the shower the warmth of the water started to revive her. She focused on her hair first, scrubbing it with two rounds of shampoo, rubbing and rubbing to get the smell of stale smoke out. She had never minded the smell of cigarettes before, but today it was making her feel nauseous. She wanted it out of her hair. She felt better as the water washed through her hair and cascaded down her body. She felt like it was rinsing off layers of dirt and sweat, carving a path through the grime.

She sighed. Today had to get better. Perhaps once she had

something to eat her headache would fade and she would start to feel a little more human.

She let the hot water run over her face, aware that she hadn't washed away the traces of yesterday's make-up, imagining the black streaks of mascara running down her cheeks. When she'd woken, her eyelids had been glued together as if she'd fallen asleep crying. She felt ready to cry again, lonely, silent tears. But she would not allow herself to. Instead, she let the water cleanse her.

She squirted shower gel into her palm and ran her hands over her breasts, her arms, her legs. Why did everything ache? When she reached between her legs to wash her inner thighs, she flinched. She touched the area again and felt a ball of pain, and her stomach clenched. She looked down, and turned her leg to see. She saw bruises, purple-black marks. So many of them. She counted, because she couldn't think what else to do. Five on her right leg. Four on her left.

Her thoughts raced a hundred miles an hour, trying to find an explanation. She was a clumsy drunk. It wasn't unusual for her to wake up with bruises on her legs, where she had caught herself on a piece of furniture in the night while walking to the toilet. Or bruises on her knees from when she had lost her footing and stumbled over on the street.

But these bruises were on the insides of her thighs. They weren't from losing her footing, or walking into furniture. They were from something much worse.

She sank down in the shower cubicle, under the cascading water, and wept.

TWENTY-THREE

Memories crowded into her mind as she sat under the stream of water. Her breathing quickened and she could hardly catch a breath. She put her head between her knees, feeling faint. It was happening again. Everything was rushing into her mind. Everything that had happened when she'd met Will.

It had started like a perfect day. The sun had been shining, her first-year exams were over and everyone was celebrating. It had felt like their youth would never end.

Sophie and her best friend Nicole had lain out on the riverside, drinking prosecco and eating strawberries, as a boat race took place on the Thames. They'd laughed as they watched the clouds go by above them, tinged sepia by their sunglasses.

Then the day had cooled and they'd gone back to change out of their jeans and into dresses for the celebration party at the boathouse. Legs bare against the chilly evening, shawls wrapped around shoulders. As they neared the boathouse they heard the noise of celebration, cheers and whoops and laughter. Sophie and Nicole had promised each other they'd stick together, and leave the party together. The police still hadn't caught the rapist who had been attacking students over the last few months, dragging girls into back alleys on their way home from nightclubs. The university had told them to watch out for each other, suggesting female students shouldn't walk home alone and that they should keep alert at all times. A local charity had distributed rape alarms.

There was a gaggle of students standing by the water's edge, all men. Laughter filled the air as there was a sudden scuffle and shouting. A splash when one of them landed in the water. Then more laugher, as he stripped down to his underwear and continued his pint.

'He must be cold,' Sophie said, wrapping her arms around herself at the thought. The shawl was not enough; as the sun started to go down it was getting colder.

They climbed up the metal steps outside and made their way into the upstairs of the boathouse. On the floor below, the boats and oars were the only lonely residents, but the upper floor was teeming with people standing and chatting in groups close to the makeshift bar, or lounging on comfy sofas around the edges of the room.

Sophie went to the bar, and as she opened her mouth to order wine, the student next to her spoke at exactly the same time, asking for beers.

'You first,' he said, with a lopsided smile, his vowels a slow drawl. His accent was Home Counties, the accent that seemed to outnumber all others at the university. She met his eyes. He was tall with dark eyes and floppy hair and she felt a flicker of attraction as she looked at his muscled physique.

'Thanks,' she said, then asked the bartender for a bottle of wine and two glasses.

'Are you a rower?' she asked, turning to him.

He laughed. 'Yes, we won the race earlier. That's why everyone's celebrating.'

'Well done.'

'University championships next.'

Three pints of beer were placed in front of him in plastic cups and he took one in each hand, then wedged the third one between the other two to carry them.

'Need some help?' Sophie asked, handing the wine glasses to Nicole so she had a free hand.

'Nope, I've had a lot of practice.' He grinned again and Sophie melted.

'Do you girls want to join us over there?' He pointed to a group of men who'd commandeered one of the sofas next to the terrace.

'Sure,' Nicole said, and Sophie nodded. She felt an alcohol- and sun-induced tiredness, a state of relaxation. This was what university was about, she suddenly realised. Meeting new people, afternoons spent in the sun sharing bottles of cheap supermarket prosecco, evening parties by the river.

They went over to the sofa, and a couple of men got up and moved away, ambling towards the bar. The sofa was surrounded by a sea of plastic empties, but no one seemed to mind or even notice.

The attractive guy from the bar distributed the pints and then held out his hand. 'I'm Will,' he said.

TWENTY-FOUR

It was over an hour before Sophie climbed out of the shower, wrinkled and shivering despite the misty warmth of the bathroom. She had turned the shower up to a searing intensity and scrubbed and scrubbed away at her body, trying to remove all traces of another presence. But no matter how hard she scrubbed, she couldn't get rid of the feeling, the sickness inside.

In the shower she had cried and cried. She told herself she couldn't be sure what had happened, that she'd never really know. Why had she drunk so much that she didn't remember? How had she let herself get out of control? How had she let this happen? She should have learned from the last time, should have known better.

She got out of the shower and knelt naked in front of the toilet. Then she threw up again and again until there was nothing left inside her.

She stood shakily and wrapped her towel around her. Her body felt alien to her, like it was no longer hers. Like it belonged to someone else.

She dressed quickly, grabbed her phone and left the bedroom. She couldn't bear to be in it, couldn't bear to think about what might have happened there. She needed to get away, to escape her thoughts.

She went to the living room and looked at her phone. Just one text. From James.

Just wanted to check you got home safely.

It was from last night. Three a.m. Had she really been out that late? What had she been doing?

She didn't remember leaving the party. She didn't remember getting home. What had happened to her between 10 p.m. when Charlie had turned up, and 3 a.m.? Had they all been to a club? She had vague recollections of a mass of limbs on a dance floor, the feel of the cold glass of a bottle of beer in her hand, the cold air of the smokers' area, a mist of cigarette smoke floating around her. Yes, she thought they had been to a club. The dancing would explain why her calves ached. But beyond the jumbled memories, her mind was blank.

She replied, carefully choosing her words.

Yep. At home safely.

She reread the words. Then she deleted the word 'safely' and hit send. Had she been safe? What the hell had happened?

Her phone beeped. *Glad to hear it! Just got up?!?*

Err. Yep. Think I was a bit drunk last night. She hit send.

Ha. We all were. Fancy a coffee to sober up?

She frowned, thinking back, remembering talking to James about Charlie. What had she said to him last night? She needed to get out of the house, away from her thoughts. Away from her room. She didn't want to think about the bruises and how they had got there.

She would meet up with James. She'd get some information from him about what had actually happened last night, piece it together and work things out. There was probably an explanation. She was just tired and emotional. She didn't want to think about what might have happened to her. *Might* have happened. *Might* was the key word. Perhaps nothing had happened. She wanted desperately to believe that.

Yeah sure, she replied to James. *Coffee sounds great.*

I'll swing by and pick you up.

Sophie went back to the bathroom and stared at herself in the mirror. Her face was lined and taut, the stress from this morning etched there. She removed the remaining traces of last night's mascara and then applied her make-up carefully, trying to cover up how she felt inside.

She went back into her bedroom, threw some clothes in the wash, then turned round and went into the living room and switched on the TV. She tried to focus on the characters arguing in the soap opera, but couldn't.

She kept thinking back to her room. The curtains were open. Her clothes were neatly folded on the chair. She was wearing a nightdress that she never usually wore. Someone had come back with her. They must have done. Whatever had happened between them, it had happened in this flat.

Her mobile rang.

James.

'I'm just outside,' he said.

She grabbed her phone and handbag and hurried down the stairs, and there he was. Five minutes early. Finally, she felt safe. She felt like hugging him and never letting go.

'Let's get out of here,' she said, feeling the tears rising in her throat, threatening to overwhelm her voice. She stepped into the street, relieved to feel the fresh air on her face.

They walked to a coffee shop round the corner. Sophie was shaking; the alcohol must still be coursing round her system. She felt a little nauseous.

'You sit down,' James said. 'You look pale. I'll get the drinks.'

When he brought her a coffee, she sat with her hands around it, letting it warm them.

'So, you look like you're feeling a bit the worse for wear,' he said with a grin. He looked fine, as if he hadn't even been drinking last night. He was probably more used to it than her. She'd rarely drunk after she left university. Until she moved to London.

She sipped her latte, the small amount of liquid swirling uncomfortably round her stomach.

'You had a good time last night?' James asked.

She forced a half-smile. 'I was pretty drunk, the evening's a bit of a blur.' She hoped he'd fill her in.

He grinned, and poked her arm teasingly. 'Gosh, you were bad.'

'I don't have much memory of the night,' she said.

'What point do you remember up to? Or don't you remember anything at all?'

She stared into her coffee. 'I remember the party. Well, most of it, I think. And I remember you transferring money to me, then Charlie turning up. After that, not much at all.' She thought of the bruises on her thighs and felt sick. Who'd done that to her? Had it been someone at the party? It had to be.

'Charlie came in for a little while. He was chatting just to you. I told him to get lost, but he ignored me.'

Sophie nodded. Maybe she'd felt obliged to talk to him.

'You were explaining that you didn't need his money anymore. He didn't take it that well.'

'Oh – and then did he leave?'

'No. I wanted to tell him to, but you didn't want to chuck him out. You seemed to be getting on a bit better then.'

'And then what happened?'

'We all went to a club.'

'Oh,' she said. 'Did I—?' She flushed, but she had to ask, had to find out what happened. 'Did I meet someone there?'

He shook his head, looking confused. 'No, I don't think so. Although I wasn't with you the whole evening. You really don't remember anything?'

She shook her head ruefully. 'No. Did you see me leave? Was I OK?'

'You seemed fine. A little tipsy, but nothing more.'

'Did I leave with anyone?'

'I didn't see you leave specifically. But I did see you speaking to Charlie outside the club, when I was on my way home. I think you were walking back together, but I can't be sure.'

Had she gone home with Charlie? Had he done something to hurt her? To bruise her?

Sophie let her tears roll down her cheeks; she couldn't hold them in anymore.

'Sophie – what's the matter?' James put his arm round her shoulder.

'It's nothing, I'm fine. I just hate not being able to remember last night.'

'Is anything wrong?'

'No, I – I guess I'm just worried that I went home with Charlie last night. It would send the wrong signals, that's all.'

'The wrong signals to who? To him? Or to me?' He stroked her shoulder. 'It wouldn't bother me. You're single at the moment, aren't you? Although maybe not forever.'

She felt confused. It was like he was hinting that in the future they might be in a relationship, telling her he liked her. At one time her heart would have leaped at the thought, but now she just felt sick. What had happened between her and Charlie?

'To him, I suppose,' she said. 'I don't want to be with him.'

'You're allowed to enjoy yourself. Have fun. Even if it's not with someone you want to be with forever. You don't have to beat yourself up over sleeping with him.'

She nodded. He was right. But it wasn't about regretting her actions. It was the bruises. And the fact that as far as she could remember the evening, the last thing she had wanted to do was sleep with him.

'Just put it behind you. You don't need to speak to him again if you don't want to. You can pay him back now and block his number.'

He was right. She just needed to forget it.

He wiped a tear from her cheek. 'It will be all right. We all make mistakes.'

'But...' she said, unable to look at him. 'I have bruising...'

'What do you mean?' He looked concerned. 'Did you bump into something when you were drunk? I've done that before. Bumped into the bed frame when I got up to go to the toilet. Had bruises on my shins.'

'No,' she said. 'Not that kind of bruising.' She couldn't describe it to him, couldn't explain.

'Oh...' he said, slowly, realisation dawning. 'Oh... are you OK?'

'Yeah,' she said. 'It will heal. I'm just not sure... that I wanted it.'

She saw him swallow. 'Do you want to go to the police?' he asked. 'Report Charlie? I'd support you all the way.'

She shook her head. 'I don't think I can.' She thought of all the problems she'd had last time, how it had wrecked her life.

And she thought of how it would look if she came to the police with another complaint of possible sexual assault while they were looking into a completely different sexual offence against her. And she'd been drunk last night. She knew that the odds were stacked against her.

'I don't remember what happened,' she said. 'It could have just been rough, I suppose.'

'Are you sure you even slept with him?'

She shook her head, not knowing what to think. It was still possible the bruises were made by a stranger. But what could she do if she didn't remember? 'I really don't know.'

James touched her arm.

'You'll be all right,' he said. 'You should try to put it out of your mind. It sounds like there's not much you can do.'

'No,' she said.

'And you're sure about not going to the police?' he asked her.

'Yes.'

'Do you want another drink?'

'Yeah, I'll have another latte. Sorry for being so miserable.'

He smiled. 'Don't worry about it. You can talk to me any time. That's what I'm here for.'

Suddenly she felt exhausted, overwhelmed by everything that had happened. She rested her head on his shoulder and closed her eyes, blinking back tears.

TWENTY-FIVE

As Sophie walked back to her flat, she felt exhausted and full of regret. It was taking all her energy just to put one foot in front of the other. How had it happened again? A night she couldn't remember. She reminded herself that she had been with Charlie. And although his behaviour had been odd lately, he always looked out for her. But then she thought of the bruises on her thighs. Perhaps he had hurt her accidentally.

She'd promised herself that she wouldn't ever be in that position again, where she couldn't remember what had happened. But she'd felt safe and relaxed at the party, pleased with herself that she was finally able to let go and enjoy herself. That she had put the past behind her. For so many years she'd been so careful, watching herself, watching her drinking. She hadn't wanted to live like that anymore, running scared.

But she had made a mistake thinking she was safe. Just like before. She thought back to when she'd first met Will at the boathouse. They'd fallen into conversation so easily. It had been like they'd always known each other. Unlike his friends, he hadn't been popping pills; he'd wanted to keep his body in top shape, he was a rower.

When she'd told him she had to go, it was already past midnight. She'd lost sight of her friend Nicole long before. Suddenly she was aware of her leg pressed against his, how their knees were touching. His arm was stretched out on the sofa behind her, and now it moved down, wrapping itself around her shoulder.

'Let's have a photo,' he said, with a surprising energy. 'Before you go.'

Will passed his phone to a friend, and then his arm was back around her and they both raised their drinks, and Sophie grinned at the camera.

Will took his phone back and showed her the picture. They looked like a couple, completely comfortable in each other's company. She thought guiltily of Charlie back home.

'I'll keep this,' he said. 'To remember this evening, the start of things.'

She laughed at his assumption, turning her head towards him.

She opened her mouth to speak, but then he brought his face towards her, coming in for a kiss. It took all her strength to turn away.

'I need to go,' she said. 'Sorry.'

'Another time, then.'

She half smiled. She was starting to feel woozy and she needed to get home to bed. She'd lost track of how much wine she'd drunk. Her glass had been topped up throughout the evening.

She'd looked for Nicole. They'd promised to walk home together, aware of the rapist who they'd been told had been stalking the campus, looking for girls just like them. But Nicole wasn't on the terrace or in the toilets, or on the towpath by the river where other couples were leaning against the bridge and kissing. Sophie tried to ring her, but she didn't answer.

She looked warily towards the river, beyond the kissing

couples, to the path home. The walk that had been so easy and relaxed in the daylight now seemed dark and ominous. There were no lights along the towpath and beyond the boathouse it was pitch-black. The meadows they'd walked through to get here were a sea of nothing. The rapist was always at the back of her mind now, lurking just out of sight of the tree-lined footpaths and in the shadows of every pub, club and alleyway. She couldn't walk home alone. Perhaps she should get a cab.

'Looking for your friend?' Will asked, as she went back to the sofa to see if Nicole had left her bag there. She hadn't.

'Yeah,' she said.

'She's already gone,' Will said. 'Went home with Alex.' He exchanged looks with his friend. 'She won't be back.'

'Oh?' Sophie felt a surge of irritation with Nicole. They'd *promised* they'd go back together.

'Are you all right?' Will asked.

'Yeah, I'm fine. Just thinking of how I'm going to get home.'

'I... I heard about the attacker. I can walk you back if you want?'

Sophie nodded gratefully. 'Yes, please.'

Sophie shook as she remembered her mistake. It had turned out Nicole hadn't left her; she'd been round the back of the boathouse with Alex. But at that moment Sophie thought her only option was Will. She'd trusted him. The next thing she remembered was surfacing from a dream, unable to move, his body on top of her, weighing her down.

Sophie hadn't wanted to go to the police, but the university wouldn't suspend Will unless she did, and she couldn't bear to see him around campus. At first, she'd hardly been able to leave her room from the fear of seeing him again. So she'd gone to the police station and answered question after humiliating question, put herself through the physical examinations. The police thought she'd been drugged, but by the time they carried out the medical tests there was no evidence left in her blood or urine samples.

Will was suspended and he and his friends made her life hell. Although she'd been granted anonymity, rumours about what had happened had spread quickly through the university and everyone had an opinion on whether Sophie was telling the truth. Posters had gone up in the streets around campus with her face on, calling her a liar and a slut.

Sophie had just wanted to disappear, to live a normal life. But the taunting wouldn't stop. People whispered behind her back as she walked to lectures. And then she'd started to get the emails. Saying they had naked photos of her. Saying they'd send them to everyone at the university. Sophie had no idea if they actually had photos. She had no memory of that night. But she couldn't bear the thought of her dad and Charlie seeing her like that. After everything her dad had been through when her mum died, he didn't need this to deal with.

She'd just wanted everything to be over. To stop having to talk to the police, for the taunting to stop. To get back to her normal life. At the same time, the police had told her that it was unlikely there would be enough evidence for a prosecution. So she'd withdrawn her allegations against Will.

She'd thought things would get better, but instead they got even worse. Will had taken out a private prosecution against her, accusing her of lying to the police and perverting the course of justice. She'd had to leave university while they investigated. It had all come to nothing, but the taunts and threats had continued in the meantime, and by the time it was decided that Will's case wouldn't go to court, she couldn't face going back to the university.

And now it was all happening again. The bruises on her thighs. The lack of memories. Had she been assaulted? Or had it just been a drunken, regrettable hook-up with Charlie which had been a bit rough?

Sophie unlocked the bottom door of the flats and made her way up the stairs slowly. The house smelled strongly of air freshener, overpowering any other odours. She unlocked her flat and went into the bedroom, and jumped backwards in shock.

There was someone in her flat. Standing by her bed.

TWENTY-SIX

Sophie screamed, the sound coming from deep inside her taking her by surprise.

The person turned and started screaming too. A woman. She was in her mid-forties and tall, holding a tin of polish in her hand.

'Who are you?' Sophie asked.

She looked confused. 'I'm Jo. I'm the cleaner.'

'I never asked for a cleaner.'

'I come every week. Except when the flat's empty. Cassie pays me.'

'But you haven't been round before.'

'No, I'm sorry. Cassie only just told me the flat was occupied again. I can come round every week from now on.'

'OK,' Sophie said, retreating. It must be another perk that came with the flat. She saw that Jo had stripped the bed and changed the sheets. In the kitchen the floor was still wet from mopping. 'I'll leave you to it.' She smiled at Jo, who frowned back at her. 'Sorry for scaring you.'

'It's no problem.'

. . .

On Monday morning Sophie woke up in her clean sheets with a sense of dread. She hadn't slept properly, trying desperately to remember what had happened, what she'd done with Charlie. There was so much of the evening that didn't make sense; the folded clothes on the chair weren't like him at all. And there'd been no trace of him. She'd been with him long enough to know how he smelled, to know the way he occupied a space, how he left the toilet seat up after using it and abandoned empty cups on the side in the kitchen. But there had been nothing like that. The place had been tidy. And now it had been swept spotlessly clean by Jo.

She had thought about calling Charlie, but she hadn't been sure what to say. If he'd gone back with her, she didn't want to give him the idea she was still interested. He'd left by the morning anyway. Perhaps she had chucked him out of her home, after what he'd done.

As she walked to the office she felt nauseous, working away at the black hole of her memory. But all she could remember was Max's party, the comfortable sofa, the free-flowing alcohol, James. She had the haziest recollections of the club.

It had been going so well with James. But at some point she must have split off from him and spoken to Charlie. The evening must have spiralled out of her control. What must James think of her now? She'd thought he might be interested in her, but she'd messed that up.

And what would the others in the office think? She was the new girl, and yet she was the one who'd been blackout drunk. What if she'd embarrassed herself? She felt a ball of anxiety forming in the pit of her stomach as she thought about going in and facing them. Would they be talking about her? Had they seen her go home with Charlie? She imagined them watching as she stumbled out of the club.

When she got to One Pure Thought, she took a deep breath

and stepped inside, nodding hello to everyone and keeping her head held high as she walked straight to her desk.

'Did you have a good time at Max's party?' Pete asked her, smirking.

'Yeah, I enjoyed it, thanks.'

'You looked like you did.'

Sophie's heart sank. 'What do you mean by that?'

'Ignore him,' Harriet said. 'He's just being an arse.'

'Where's Cassie?' Sophie asked. Maybe she'd be able to reassure Sophie about what she had said and done. Besides James, Cassie was the only person she remembered speaking to.

'She's out with a client today and tomorrow. Back Wednesday,' Harriet said. She turned to Pete. 'Did you see that Lydia turned up?'

Lydia? Sophie's ears pricked up. She hadn't realised Lydia had been at the party.

Pete nodded. 'I heard. Crazy. Looking for Max, I guess. She still hasn't got over him.'

'She was drunk. Could hardly put one foot in front of the other,' Harriet said. Sophie flushed, remembering how drunk she'd been herself.

'That doesn't surprise me,' Pete said knowingly.

Sophie thought of the girl in the taxi who'd spoken to Cassie. That must have been Lydia. She'd been in such a state. How badly had Max treated her?

Sophie buried herself in her work for the rest of the morning, trying to distract herself from what had happened after the party.

'How's it going?' James said, coming over to her desk in the early afternoon.

'Yeah, OK.' She was pleased to have got through the morning without being the centre of the office gossip. Everyone was still talking about Saturday night, but the scraps of conversations she heard were about Max and Lydia, and two of the junior staff who'd gone home together. Nothing about her. No one had even joked about how drunk she'd been. Max stayed locked in his office the whole morning and didn't come out.

'Feeling better after the weekend?'

'I've promised myself I'll never drink again,' Sophie said.

'We all say that.' James laughed. 'Look – I don't have much time, but have you had lunch yet?'

Sophie shook her head. 'Not yet.'

'Do you want to walk down the road to grab a sandwich with me?'

They walked together in the smoggy London air. The sky above them was bright blue and clear, but at street level exhaust fumes belched out from the taxis and cars.

'I just wanted to check you were OK after the weekend,' James said, as they went into a café.

'I'm fine,' Sophie said, although she wasn't quite convinced. She'd made a mistake; she just had to stop dwelling on it. They ordered their food and sat down.

Sophie looked at James. 'You know, a cleaner turned up on Sunday. I hadn't seen her before.'

'Oh – Jo? She always cleans once a week.'

'Yeah. She hadn't been round before, though.'

'That's strange. The flat was empty for a short time. Cassie must have only just remembered to reinstate her. Did you speak to Charlie?'

'No – I – haven't plucked up the courage yet.' Sophie wasn't even sure she wanted to speak to him. It must have been him that hurt her, but she couldn't face a confrontation. She just wanted to forget what had happened.

'Look, it's OK. You don't need to explain. I think you just need him out of your life. Have you paid him back now? Can you cut off contact? He's not worth your headspace.'

'I've paid him,' Sophie said. She'd done it on Sunday, texted Charlie to tell him and then turned off her phone. But when she'd turned it back on, she didn't have any missed calls or texts. He hadn't contacted her at all.

'You should block his number, and block him from all your social media.'

Sophie hesitated for a moment. 'I'm not sure,' she said. Charlie had been part of her life for so long and it felt so final. The waitress put down their paninis in front of them and they thanked her.

Sophie bit into her sandwich. She thought about how she needed to move on. It would feel good to be completely free of Charlie, no longer interrupted by his calls and demands. 'Actually, you're right,' she said. 'I don't want to speak to him again.'

She got out her personal mobile, went into her contacts and blocked Charlie's number. 'There we go,' she said, a wave of relief washing over her. 'Done.'

James grinned. 'That was quick.'

'I only needed to block the phone. I don't have social media.'

James grinned at her and lifted up his water bottle and clinked it with hers across the table. 'Here's to a fresh start,' he said. 'You've done the right thing. Believe me, I know. It's best to do it as soon as you can.'

'What do you mean?'

His face darkened. 'I had an ex-girlfriend who stalked me. I tried to be nice, to give her the benefit of the doubt, keep talking to her, but it all got too much. She called and messaged constantly. I had to block her.'

'I'm sorry,' Sophie said, curious. He'd never mentioned an ex before, but she supposed he must have several.

'Don't worry. It's in the past now. I just had a stressful time of it. She was very jealous, she followed me. But it's been a few months now since I blocked her and I feel freer than I've felt in a long time.'

'Relationships can be hard work,' Sophie said.

'Yeah, you don't know the half of it. But she's out of my life now. And I want to keep it that way.'

Sophie thought of Charlie, how he'd known where she lived without her telling him, how he'd known where to find her at the party. 'I've got an app on my phone that tells Charlie where I am. I'll delete that too. I meant to do it earlier, but forgot. He's supposed to be deleting it on his phone, too, but hopefully if I delete mine it should cut him off anyway.' She went back into her phone and deleted the app.

'Could I have a quick look at your phone?' James asked. 'Check he hasn't put anything else on there. He might still be able to track you.'

Sophie shivered at the thought and handed over her phone.

James pressed several buttons and then frowned. 'Did you know there's spyware on here?'

'Oh. Really?'

'Yeah. You want me to uninstall it?'

'Yes, please.'

'Sure.' James scrolled through the screen on her phone. 'He's been doing more than the basic location tracking. He knows everything you're doing.'

'What do you mean?'

'Internet searches, calls, texts, he's got it all.'

TWENTY-SEVEN

As Sophie pushed open the door to the open-plan office on Wednesday, she felt dozens of pairs of eyes glance up quickly at her, and then down again. Her body tensed and she wondered why they were looking at her. The room was deathly silent and the atmosphere was thick with a sense of foreboding. As she walked to her desk, she could see everyone staring at their computer screens blankly. Several people had headphones in, but they must all be switched off or turned down low, because there wasn't even the slightest sound from them. It was as if everyone was waiting for something, listening out. She felt a ball of dread form in her stomach. Something awful must have happened.

As she put her bag under her desk and sat down between James and Harriet, she heard voices coming from Max's office.

'I can't believe you'd do this. It's so stupid.' It was Cassie: her voice, usually so well controlled, was now a high-pitched shriek. Inside the glass office, Cassie was standing close to Max, her hands held up, palms outwards, showing her frustration.

Max's voice was a low rumble in response, but Sophie didn't

catch what she said. She looked at her colleagues, seated at their desks. Everyone was straining their ears to hear the words.

'They've been arguing for half an hour,' Harriet whispered conspiratorially. 'Max will be in a terrible mood now.'

Cassie's voice rose again. 'You need to leave everything alone. Leave her alone.'

'Why should I?' Max challenged.

'For God's sake, Max. You're playing with fire. What about Mercedes?'

Sophie looked over to where Mercedes was sitting, her face pale. She remembered what James had told her about Mercedes knowing the score when it came to Max and other women. Sophie wondered how much she really did know. She didn't look happy.

She could see Max gesticulating as he paced around in his office. He glanced out of the glass wall, as if suddenly aware he had an audience.

Cassie said something quieter now, that none of them could hear. Then she swung open the door and strode across the open-plan office, letting the door slam behind her. Sophie saw Max sink into his chair, turning back to his computer.

Cassie came over and pulled up a chair beside James.

'You won't believe this,' she said. 'He's seeing Lydia again.'

James raised his eyebrows, then glanced around him. 'Let's talk about this outside,' he said, taking Cassie's hand and leading her towards the door.

Sophie got to work on the campaign ideas for the new gin company, focusing on how they could appeal to a young demographic. She was completely immersed when a hand on her shoulder made her jump. She looked up expecting to see James or Cassie, but it was Max.

'Hi,' she said, hesitantly.

'Are you working on the gin company?' he asked. 'I want to see how it's coming along.'

'Sure,' Sophie said. 'I was just looking at the competitor campaigns. And I have a couple of ideas for different approaches.'

Max sat down in the swivel chair that James had vacated. 'Show me,' he said.

Sophie opened the file where she'd begun to pull together some images and ideas for slogans and started to take Max through the details.

Max was completely silent as she spoke, explaining her thinking.

She turned to look at him when she was finished. He was frowning.

'Is this it?' he asked. 'Is that all you've done?'

Sophie's heart sank. 'Yeah. I've been working on several clients at once. There's also the TV streaming company, the energy drinks campaign and the sustainable energy work James gave me. I can show you that if you like?'

Max sighed. 'I don't care about the sustainable energy branding. If we can just master the gin campaign then it will make a name for us.' He indicated Sophie's computer screen. 'But what you've produced simply isn't good enough.'

Sophie shrank into herself. 'I'm sorry, I can spend more time on it, make it better.' She hated the sound of her own voice, so simpering and desperate. She felt so disappointed that she'd let Max down. After everything that had happened with Charlie, maybe she'd been too distracted to give the campaigns her full attention.

'Can you have another go, focusing more on their core demographic? And then get it back to me tomorrow.'

Sophie frowned. The gin company was Cassie's client. 'Sure,' she said. 'I'll work on it all tonight and send it through to you and Cassie tomorrow.'

'Good,' he said calmly. 'No need to send it through to Cassie, just send it straight to me.'

'Right.' She couldn't do that. Cassie would be furious. She thought of Max and Cassie's argument earlier. 'I'll get on it.'

Max looked at her. 'Sophie, you understand, don't you? This isn't an easy place to work. We expect a lot from you. You need to be able to stick up for yourself and to fight.'

Sophie felt a tight knot forming in her stomach. What did he mean?

'I—'

'Look,' he said. 'A lot of people have been employed here and haven't lasted. It's not right for everyone.'

'It's right for me,' Sophie said softly. She loved working here; the buzz of a new project, the thrill of working late into the night, and then powering through a presentation to a client the next day. She liked juggling several projects at once, her mind always occupied. She felt alive and focused here.

'Well, good,' Max said. Sophie thought of Lydia and Felicity. Felicity hated the company now, wanted to warn others about it. Was this the kind of behaviour she'd meant when she'd said the company was toxic?

'I'm determined to work hard,' Sophie said.

'Great,' Max replied, standing up to leave. 'You've still got a couple of months left of your probation, so plenty of time to prove yourself.'

Sophie swallowed at the mention of the probation period. Cassie had told her it was just a formality, that she'd definitely pass. She needed to stay employed. Especially now she owed the company money. If they fired her, she'd never be able to pay it back. She had to throw herself into her work, prove to Max that she was good enough. She'd do anything to stay at One Pure Thought.

TWENTY-EIGHT

Sophie watched the boats pass by on the river Thames, as she sat with James, picking at her salad. She hadn't seen much of him over the last couple of days, but when Friday lunchtime had come round he'd insisted on taking her out. She had said no at first, but when he'd pointed out that both Max and Cassie were out at a lunch and drinks event all afternoon, at a client's, she'd relented.

'I thought you looked like you needed to get away from the office,' he said.

'I did.' Sophie looked out over the river at the London Eye. It rotated so slowly that she could never see it moving, no matter how long she stared. 'You know, I'm not sure I'm going to last at One Pure Thought. Max really laid into me the other day. He said my work wasn't good enough.'

'Really? I don't know why he'd think that. When was that?'

'Wednesday.'

'Oh, I wouldn't worry about that. He'd just argued with Cassie, hadn't he? He was in a foul mood.'

'Yeah, but people are fired, aren't they? Look at Felicity. And Lydia.'

'Felicity had some serious problems. And Lydia left of her own accord. You're different to both of them. And your work's good.'

'Thanks.' She smiled at James. 'I guess now I owe the company money I can't really leave anyway, not until I've paid it back through my salary.' Since Max had criticised her work on the gin company, her debt to the company felt more of a weight, holding her down. It would be a full year until she'd paid it off.

'You don't want to leave, do you?'

'No, I don't. I love the work. And Cassie's been a brilliant mentor. It's just Max, really. I'm not sure what to make of him.' She'd worked all night to improve the branding for the gin company, and the next day Max had been all smiles and compliments. But she hadn't felt he was sincere, and she didn't know where she stood.

'I wouldn't worry about him. You don't need to have much to do with him. Just stick with me and Cassie.'

Sophie smiled, already feeling better. 'This is an amazing location,' she said, looking out at the river.

'It's lovely, isn't it? And not too busy.'

'I love being close to the water. I grew up by the sea and I miss it. The fresh air, the feel of the sand between my toes, the shock of the cold water when you go for a paddle in spring.' She flushed slightly, thinking of home.

'There are lots of waterways in London. The river, and the canals too.'

'I'll have to explore a bit more.' Her university campus had been near the riverside, so she knew that area of the Thames. But she didn't want to go back there.

James nodded and looked down at his sandwich. 'I wanted to ask you – how are you feeling about what happened at the weekend with Charlie? Sorry if I'm intruding, but I know how upset you were. I just wanted to check you were OK.'

Sophie shivered. 'I don't want to think about it.'

'OK, that's fine. You've done the right thing cutting him off.' He smiled at her and squeezed his hands together as if he was nervous. 'When you first started work, I couldn't figure you out. I wasn't sure if you were single. And when Charlie turned up at the party, I thought that maybe you were still interested in him. I was devastated when I saw you leave the club with him.'

Sophie glanced up in surprise. 'Devastated?'

James blushed. 'OK, maybe that's a bit strong. Disappointed might be a better word. We'd been getting on so well. I'd thought... never mind.'

Sophie remembered how they'd sat close to each other on the sofa at the party, how they'd chatted all evening. She'd thought, hoped, that there might be something between them. But after everything had happened after Max's party, she'd forgotten about it.

Now she thought about how he'd messaged her the next day, checking she got home OK. Had that been because he cared? Because he was interested?

'I thought we were getting on well, too,' she said softly.

'We've been getting on well since the day you joined the business. I love being with you, Sophie. There's no one I'd rather spend time with.'

It was her turn to blush now. He was looking at her so intently. 'I enjoy your company too,' she said. 'And I've really enjoyed this lunch. It's been a good end to a horrible week.'

'I've been plucking up the courage to ask you to lunch all week. Sophie – I wondered if you'd come out with me again at the weekend, for dinner?'

She smiled into her starter, hardly able to believe this was happening. 'I'd love to,' she said.

Sophie lay in on Saturday morning, and woke up around 10 a.m. It was the most rest she'd had since she'd started work.

Now the day stretched out ahead of her, empty. She picked up her phone and saw she had a WhatsApp message from James.

How do you feel about doing something a bit different before our dinner this evening? If you're free this afternoon, that is.

Yeah, why not? But what do you mean by 'different'?

Well, you said you liked paddling in cold water...

?!?

I've booked us into paddleboarding on the Thames. I've done it before. It's fun. What do you think?

Sophie hesitated for a moment, then typed, *Why not?*

That afternoon, they stood by the river in borrowed wetsuits listening to the instructor run through the safety briefing. Everything sounded straightforward, but there were lots of rules, and you couldn't go too far down the river, as there was a current.

'Don't look so worried,' James said teasingly. 'I'll look after you.'

'You'd better,' she said, grinning. She was happy to be out in the fresh air, doing something active for once instead of being hunched over her computer. They weren't far from her old university; the campus was only a few miles away. But she tried not to think about that, tried to repress the memories of the boat race and that fateful evening at the boathouse when she'd met Will. Since she'd reported the website that was taunting her, she hadn't heard anything further from the police. But when she'd tried to find the website again, it had been taken down. Maybe speaking to them had had an impact this time.

'Right, are we ready?' the instructor asked.

'Yes!' the group shouted.

She and James carried their paddleboards to the small wooden platform that was perched at the edge of the water. Sophie watched James get on first and then manoeuvred herself onto her board.

Soon she was wobbling on the river, paddling on her knees, while James stood confidently on his board, paddling it back and forth easily. After a while she found the confidence to stand up and she attempted to drift along beside him. Luckily years of Saturday-morning yoga classes back in Dorset meant she was able to stay standing and they cruised along the river together, James pointing out the landmarks and parks as they drifted by. It was blissful; she felt so far removed from her London life and the stress of the office. The hours seemed to speed by and it felt like no time at all before they were called back to the shore.

After they'd returned the wetsuits and gone home and changed, James took her out for a meal in a Michelin-starred restaurant in Mayfair and they got to know each other better. Sophie felt alive in his company. He listened intently to what she had to say and she felt like she'd known him all her life. It was so different to how it had been with Charlie. Everything felt so natural, as if it had always been meant to be.

He walked her back to her flat, and they stood at the entrance by the top of the steps. He pulled her towards him, their lips meeting as his tongue found hers.

'I've been wanting to do that for so long,' he said, as their lips parted.

'Me too.' She grinned up at him, and they kissed again. She lost herself in the sensation of his mouth on hers, the scent of his aftershave.

Eventually she pulled away. 'I need to get some sleep,' she

said, searching his eyes. She desperately wanted him to come upstairs with her, but she didn't want to rush things.

'On your own?' he asked, raising his eyebrows.

'I think so. At least this time. There'll be a next time, won't there?' she said. 'Another date?'

'Of course.' James grinned. 'How about tomorrow? Sunday lunch?'

TWENTY-NINE

Sophie squeezed James's hand as they walked along the London street towards the office. The weekend had been blissful. On Sunday, they'd had a huge roast and then gone for a walk along the river, then they'd gone back to hers to chat more. He'd asked why the bookcase was in the middle of the living room, and she'd explained how she'd heard noises again last night, the sound of footsteps in the house, on the stairs.

'Probably just Max,' he'd said, but he'd seen she was afraid and he'd offered to stay there on the sofa. She loved how he wasn't pushy with her, was letting her take her time getting to know him, enjoying every second of their new relationship.

With James it was so easy. Her hand naturally slid into his as they walked and she felt his fingers intertwine with hers. She held her head high, felt the glare of the early-morning sun, and absorbed the hustle and bustle of the people around her.

They entered the office together, Sophie's heart thudding with nerves. It felt like they were making a statement, and she wasn't entirely sure she was ready. But James had insisted. He was proud to be with her and he didn't want to keep any secrets.

It felt refreshing to have a man be so open and honest, without playing games.

They heard Cassie before they saw her, chatting loudly about her weekend in the open-plan kitchen. She raised her eyebrows as Sophie and James walked by.

As soon as Sophie had settled at her desk and James was gone, she came over.

'So...' Cassie said, her eyes sparkling. 'You and James? Are you an item?'

Sophie blushed. 'It's early days, but...'

'You walked in together. Oh my God.' Suddenly Cassie's arms were wrapped round Sophie tightly, squeezing the life out of her. 'I'm so happy for you. You guys are perfect together.'

'Thanks,' Sophie said, surprised by Cassie's enthusiasm.

'James has been so unlucky in love lately,' Cassie continued. 'And he really deserves someone like you.'

'Oh?' Sophie thought of the ex James had mentioned. The stalker.

'He had a terrible girlfriend before. No one could get on with her at all. She was quite... well, to be honest, she probably needed psychological help. Maybe she's got it now. I hope so.'

'Right,' Sophie said, not sure how to take this. She almost felt sorry for James's ex if she'd been so disliked by everyone. And it must have been horrible for her if she'd truly had mental health problems.

'She's long gone now,' Cassie said breezily. 'Although I did think my hopes of you and James getting together were going nowhere when you kissed that man at the club last week.'

Sophie turned sharply. 'What? Sorry?'

'The man in the club. Don't you remember?'

'I... I hardly even remember going clubbing,' Sophie confessed. 'I had too much to drink.'

'You went home with him, Sophie! How can you not remember?'

'I went home with him? I thought... James said... I went home with Charlie, my ex.' Sophie felt sick. But then she remembered that Cassie didn't know Charlie. 'Maybe you mean him... he's tall with dark hair.'

'Oh, we met Charlie all right,' Cassie said. 'I think he was around at the end of the evening. He tried to get you into a taxi, to take you home. It was about the time James left. But you didn't want to go. You came back to the club. Then you left with the blond guy.'

A blond guy. Will's image came crashing into her mind. Blond, angular, tall. 'Blond?'

'Don't you remember at all?'

'No, what did he look like?'

'Umm... he had glasses, I think. Average height, I guess.'

Glasses. Will had never worn glasses. Not back then anyway. And he'd been really tall, tall enough that Cassie would have noticed.

Which meant... it hadn't been Will... or Charlie... but a stranger. She felt nauseous as she clutched for memories, but found none. It was a stranger who'd been in her flat, touching her body, folding her clothes, digging around in her drawer for a nightdress. Someone had been through her things, someone knew her possessions, someone knew her body, but she knew nothing of them.

'I need to go to the toilets,' Sophie said. 'I'm not feeling well.'

'Feeling sick?' Cassie said sympathetically.

Sophie nodded and rushed to the toilet. She put the lid down and sat down and wept, then pulled up her skirt and looked at the bruises between her legs, which were fading from an insistent purple to a pale yellow. Someone had done this to her. Someone she didn't know.

'Are you OK?' Cassie asked, when she'd wiped her eyes, blown her nose, braced herself and returned to the office.

'I think I might be getting the flu,' Sophie said. 'I've been shivering a lot, feeling sick, a bit crap really.'

'Not morning sickness?' Cassie said, laughing.

Sophie felt the blood drain from her body. Thank God she'd gone out to get the morning-after pill at the weekend, just in case. 'No,' she said, forcing herself to return Cassie's smile.

Cassie reached out and touched her shoulder. 'Oh, you've gone so pale. I didn't mean to upset you. Perhaps you should go home if you're feeling ill.'

'Actually I...' Sophie was about to say that she wasn't ill, but then she realised she needed to go out. Her mind was spinning. If it was a stranger who'd caused the bruises then she needed to get an STI test.

'I have a medical appointment,' she said quickly. 'I'll be back soon.' When she got down onto the street, she started to panic, and she leaned heavily against the wall in the alleyway, trying to control her breathing. *She had been hurt by a stranger*.

She forced herself out of the alleyway and into the Tube station. In the crowded carriage, she tucked herself in under someone's arm, bending her head as she waited for the doors to shut and then leaning back gratefully into the tiny gap that had been created when they were closed. The man next to her was tall and blond and more than a little too close. Suddenly she felt sick. It could be him, and Sophie would never know. The person she'd gone home with, who'd bruised her, could be anyone. She positioned herself so her back was to the door of the train. So no one could approach her from behind.

She was grateful when she emerged out of the double doors and into the air. She walked straight over to the sexual health clinic and filled in the forms, then took the tests when the nurse called her through. Then she went back to the office.

. . .

'Are you all right?' Cassie asked her, when she saw her return. 'You rushed off earlier.'

Sophie nodded. 'I know. I just...' She didn't know how to explain.

'I'm sorry if I upset you when I talked about Max's party. I didn't mean to.'

Sophie sighed. 'It's OK. I just can't remember what happened that night... and...' She felt tears welling up in her eyes.

'Oh, it's OK,' Cassie said. 'Come with me.' She whisked her into a meeting room.

'You were very drunk that night,' Cassie said softly, once they were inside. 'I wouldn't worry about it. It happens to the best of us.'

'Did I look like I wanted to go home with him? The man from the club, I mean.'

Cassie frowned. 'Umm... I think so. I wasn't really paying attention. Are you saying that you think something happened?'

Sophie put her head in her hands. 'I'm just not sure. Which club did we go to?'

'The one off High Holborn.'

'Do you think they'll have CCTV?' Maybe if she saw the CCTV she'd be able to tell whether she'd wanted to go with him.

'Maybe,' Cassie said. 'We could go over there. Find out.'

'We? You mean, you'd come with me?' Sophie looked up at her gratefully. She could do with a friend.

'Of course I'll come with you.' She squeezed Sophie's arm. 'But I'm sure nothing happened.'

They got a taxi together, then Cassie took her to the club, through an archway to an alleyway to the left of Pizza Hut. She'd been to this street before, but had never noticed the discreet entrance to the club. The chipped blue door was completely unmarked. There was no sign of the rope that would hold back the queues of clubbers in the evenings. There was no sign of any activity at all. It could have been someone's home.

Sophie stood looking at the closed door, trying to conjure up any memories. She would have stood here in the queue, with Cassie, perhaps spoken to the bouncer, paid an entry fee at a little cash desk just inside the door, then followed the pounding music to the dance floor.

She tried to remember the inside, where she had kissed the blond guy. She had no memory of kissing him; the only lips she could conjure up were James's. She could imagine herself on the dance floor, getting closer to James, him holding her tight, no air between them. But she couldn't imagine the stranger. She didn't know whether his lips had been dry or soft, if he had tasted of cigarettes, alcohol, gum or something else entirely. She couldn't picture his eyes, couldn't imagine his blond hair. She had hoped that coming back to the club would jog her memory, but the closed door blocked her off, locking her memories inside.

There was the rumble of voices behind the door, and she wondered if they were getting ready for the night ahead. She could knock, but what would she ask them?

'Do you want to go in?' Cassie asked.

Sophie suddenly felt embarrassed. What reason could she give for wanting to see the CCTV? It was over a week since she'd been in the club. Would they even have it anymore? And even if she saw it, it wouldn't prove anything. Cassie had already told her she'd gone home with him.

'I'm not sure.'

'I'll go in,' Cassie said. She knocked and when the men opened the door she followed them through, leaving Sophie outside.

Sophie stood alone in the cold, wondering if Cassie would

convince them to share any CCTV. And how would she feel if she saw it? She'd see *him*, the person who had caused her bruises. Would the police be interested in the footage? She shook her head, arguing with herself. Of course they wouldn't. The bruises wouldn't mean anything to them. It could still have been consensual. Although she knew in her heart it hadn't been.

After a couple of minutes, Cassie came outside, shaking her head.

'It's no good, I'm afraid. They don't have the footage. It's already been wiped.'

THIRTY

At the end of the week, Sophie and James turned down the invitation to the pub with the others and went straight back to her flat. They'd wanted an evening alone, the chance to get a takeaway and relax in front of the TV.

As they passed through the ground floor of the house they noticed a bitter, rotting smell that the air freshener couldn't disguise. Sophie coughed.

'What's that?' James asked. The smell seemed to be emanating from the lower flat.

'Could it be the rats?' she asked, uncertainly.

James frowned. 'I doubt it. We should look into it later, just to check.'

'Sure,' Sophie said, pulling him towards the stairs. 'Later.'

As soon as they went through the door of Sophie's flat, James started kissing her hungrily and she gave in to him, kissing him back, her back against the hard wall. Sophie ran her fingers through his hair as he reached for the buttons of her shirt. She felt the air touch her skin, and she broke away to pull his T-shirt over his head. As she kissed the dark hair on his chest lightly, out of the corner of her eye she noticed that the door hadn't shut properly behind them.

She pulled away and closed the door, locking it with the key and pulling the bolt across.

'Definitely safe now,' James said with a smile. 'No one can interrupt us.' He took her hand and led her through to the bedroom, sat down on the bed and pulled her towards him.

'Don't you want a drink first?' she asked, going back over to the door. Seeing him sitting on her bed made her stomach twist and turn. It was her room, and being with a man in this room, even James, made her feel nervous. She remembered waking up the morning after the party. In her mind's eye she saw her clothes folded over the chair, the curtains open.

'No, come over here.'

She stood in the bedroom doorway, holding her breath.

'What's wrong?'

She forced a smile. 'Nothing,' she said.

'Sit down.' He patted the bed beside him and she sat down obediently.

He put his arm around her and turned her head towards him to kiss her. Their lips met, but she couldn't concentrate. Her shoulders tensed as his tongue explored her mouth. She couldn't stop thinking of that night. Had she sat on her bed and kissed the blond man from the club too? Before the bruises? She felt tears threatening to fall and she pulled away from him.

The light smell of his sweat made her gag. Flashes of a face above hers, a body bearing down on her. She squeezed her eyes shut and forced the image away. She felt her body tense up.

'Sophie – what's the matter?'

'I— It's complicated. It's just what happened after Max's party... it makes me nervous.'

How could she explain that when he got too close she'd get flashbacks – the pressure of being held down, unable to move, the sense of being frozen in panic? She wanted to scream, to push him away. She thought she was just remembering what had happened with Will, but what if she wasn't? What if some of the memories were from the night of Max's party? Everything was a blur now, the past and present weaving together.

She sighed and met James's eyes, saw his bemused expression. This wasn't going to work.

'I'm sorry, James.'

'Don't be sorry.'

'I can't do this. It reminds me.'

'Reminds you?'

'Yeah, I'm sorry, I'm not ready. It makes me think about it – that night.' She'd told James it wasn't Charlie that she'd been home with, but a stranger. They'd agreed it was best to forget about it, put it behind her. But it wasn't that easy.

'I remind you of him?'

'No, of course not.' She felt the need to make amends. She put her arm around him and gave him a peck on the cheek. 'It's just what we're doing that reminds me. When I kiss you, it makes me wonder... it makes me wonder what he did to me. Here, in this room.' She collapsed into tears.

'You still can't remember?'

'No.'

'Look, you don't really know what happened. You just have to forget about it.'

'I know.'

He put his arm around her. 'I should go. Leave you to your own space.'

She felt desperate. She couldn't let one night affect her whole life.

'Don't go,' she said. 'Stay. Stay for a drink.'

'Why don't we order a takeaway?' he said.

Sophie looked around the flat. She didn't want to be alone, could feel the walls closing in on her.

'Why don't we just go out to dinner?' she said. 'I could do

with a bit of a walk, some fresh air. Then we can find a good restaurant.'

James smiled. 'I know a few places that I think you'll love in Soho,' he said. 'I'll give you a little tour. You can choose.'

She unbolted the door and they left, Sophie double-checking she'd locked the flat three times before she finally went down the stairs.

'You're not quite OK, are you?' James said.

'No,' Sophie admitted.

'It's totally understandable,' he said, reaching over and tucking a stray hair behind her ear. 'You don't know who you were with after Max's party. I can see how that's upsetting.'

'I'm never going to drink like that again.'

'Don't worry,' James said. 'Because I'm never going to let you go off with anyone else ever again.' He gripped her in a tight, jokey hug. 'I'll be your bodyguard. There'll be no getting past me.'

She smiled and they walked down the echoey stairs, Sophie leading the way.

On the first-floor landing, James noticed the light bulb flickering. 'How long has that been like that?' he asked.

Sophie shrugged. She'd stopped noticing.

'I'll change it now. There are some light bulbs in the cupboard.' He went to the cupboard in the corridor where Cassie had found the curtains, and pulled out a selection, checking the wattage. After turning the light off, he went to find something to stand on.

'I'll wait for you outside,' Sophie said.

As she passed the ground-floor flat, she wrinkled her nose. She was going to have to do something about the smell. But for now, she just needed some fresh air. She pushed open the front door and breathed in deeply.

As she did a voice called out to her. 'Sophie!'

The woman remained on the other side of the street, shrouded in a long black coat, her eyes covered by dark glasses.

Sophie walked over.

'You cancelled our meeting,' Felicity said. 'So I've had to come back here.'

'No – James said not to talk to you.'

'You're dating him, are you? You know he's as bad as the rest of them? He'll only hurt you.' Felicity's eyes flashed. 'You need to stay away from him—'

Just then they heard the door to the flats open. Sophie turned to see James staring across at them.

'James?' Felicity said. 'I need to speak to you.'

He shook his head and his voice became hard and cold. 'You need to leave, Felicity. I'm not telling you again.'

Felicity looked from him to Sophie and then back again. Then she turned on her heel and rushed off down the road.

THIRTY-ONE

James came down the steps to Sophie and put an arm around her. 'Was she bothering you?'

'Yeah.' Sophie looked up at James. 'She told me to stay away from you.' She felt uncomfortable. Sophie had always assumed that Felicity had been talking about Max and Philip when she criticised the company, but now her focus was James. Was it possible that her dismissal had had something to do with him?

James gripped her harder. 'Typical Felicity. Always into the dramatics. She'll say anything. She just wants to get you away from us.'

'But why?' Sophie asked.

'I'll explain this evening, I promise.'

Sophie looked at him. She didn't want to be fobbed off. 'What do you need to explain?' she asked. There was obviously something going on, something he'd omitted to tell her about. When she thought about it, she knew so little of his life, his background. She'd got caught up in the whirlwind of the office and then the whirlwind of their attraction.

'I'll explain... But now... I've had an idea. I want to treat you. I just looked online and there's a table for two free at the top of the Shard tonight. I've booked it.'

'Really? Wow,' Sophie said. She'd never been to the Shard, and she'd always wanted to. For a moment she thought of the cost of all the things they were doing together; the Michelin-starred restaurant, the paddleboarding and now the Shard. He'd said he should pay for everything as he was senior to her and she wouldn't be able to afford the activities otherwise, but it made her a bit uncomfortable.

She took his hand as they made their way towards the Underground station. She thought of how she had rejected him earlier, how he hadn't made a big deal of it. She felt grateful he was on her side, looking out for her, and she squeezed his hand tighter, feeling his fingers grip hers in return.

At their table by the floor-to-ceiling window in the Shard they could see the twinkling lights of London spread out before them. Around them the other diners were all looking outwards towards the view. There was a strange silence, not like the usual hustle and bustle of a restaurant. Everyone seemed in awe of their surroundings.

The portion of food in front of her was beautifully laid out. The flavours went perfectly together and she savoured the taste of each tiny morsel.

'I need to talk to you,' James said. Sophie's heart fell through her chest. She knew what was coming. After everything that had happened earlier, he was going to suggest they just be friends. It was the last thing she wanted. She really liked him.

'What about?' she asked, trying to harden her nerve.

'About Felicity. I haven't been completely honest with you.'

'Oh?'

'I haven't lied to you. I've just... omitted to tell you something.' He reached out for her hands, squeezing them across the table.

'What?' Sophie asked, feeling a rising panic.

'Well, Felicity is suing the company for unfair dismissal. But it's a little more complicated than that. She and I, well, we were in a relationship. Only for a short time. It went sour pretty quickly, when I learned what she was really like. She's probably targeting you because she knows you're going out with me. I think even her suing the company is more to do with me splitting up with her than anything else. She's got no chance of winning.'

'Oh,' Sophie said. 'So it's all about revenge?'

'I think so. And she wants to get you away from me. She's jealous. If I hadn't got a restraining order out against her she'd still be following me every day. But as it is, she's not supposed to go anywhere near me.'

'You took out a restraining order?' Sophie raised her eyebrows. It sounded so harsh.

'She left me with no option.' He looked down at his plate for moment, as if trying to find the right words. 'She was so persistent. And her behaviour was getting more and more aggressive. She keyed my car – my Maserati. It caused thousands of pounds of damage. She's crazy. And a liar. She'll say anything to get closer to me.'

Sophie swallowed, shocked. Felicity's behaviour seemed so extreme. 'So she's the difficult ex you were talking about?' Everything had started to click into place in Sophie's mind. Why Felicity had told her to stay away from James; why James never spoke about her. They'd had a bad split. And Felicity was jealous of him moving on.

James nodded sheepishly. 'Yeah, she is. She's caused me all sorts of problems.'

'I understand. Charlie was similarly obsessed.'

James grinned broadly. 'I knew you'd understand. You're

completely different to her.' He took her hand across the table and looked deep into her eyes. 'Thank you.'

After they finished their meal, they went down in the lift, Sophie leaning into James's warm body, appreciating his strong arms around her. The movement of the lift was almost imperceptible as they dropped through the floors and then arrived at the bottom.

They walked back along the river, the lights reflecting on the Thames.

'I'm so glad I met you,' James said, stopping for a moment to turn and kiss her. She savoured the kiss, the moment. She thought of her parents, how happy their marriage had been until her mother died. Nothing lasted forever. She needed to enjoy this moment with James, not think about Felicity, or the police, or the bruises that lined her thighs.

When they got back to Sophie's home, James took her hand and they climbed the steps together. She smiled at him as he unlocked the door. She felt safer when he was staying with her. As the door opened, Sophie gagged. The smell from earlier had intensified and they both recoiled.

'What is that?' James said, his hand over his mouth. It was definitely coming from the ground-floor flat, filtering out around the woodwork of the door.

She shook her head slowly. 'I really don't know.'

'This is the flat that Max uses sometimes.'

'For what?'

James's face gave way to a grimace. 'For his liaisons, I suppose. The ones he doesn't want Mercedes to know about.'

Sophie nodded, thinking of the footsteps she'd been hearing. 'Maybe he left some food out,' she said. 'It could have rotted.'

'Maybe.'

They stared at the door together, their evening at the Shard forgotten.

'I have the master key,' James said. 'For all the flats. We could just have a look. Clear up what's causing this.'

Sophie nodded, but they both hesitated. She imagined a kitchen counter with rotten food, rats crawling all over it.

He smiled at her, a lopsided grin. 'My imagination's going crazy. Shall I just open it?'

'Yeah, it can't be worse than what's in my head. Go on...'

He pulled the key from the bottom of his bag and placed it in the lock.

The door opened slowly, and Sophie coughed uncontrollably, putting her hand over her nose and mouth as the rotten smell invaded the corridor.

They stepped slowly inside. There was a half-full glass of wine on the counter, a black handbag on the floor.

'Whose is that?' Sophie said.

James shook his head, frowning. 'I don't know.'

They followed the smell into the bedroom, Sophie's heart beating wildly in her chest.

On the bed was a girl in a dress, lying down, her blonde hair covering her face, a bottle of vodka knocked over on the floor beside her.

'Oh my God,' Sophie said, putting her hand to her mouth.

James retched, then went over to the body, turning the face towards him.

'Is she dead?' Sophie asked. Although the smell and the flies told her the answer.

James nodded, his face pale. 'She must have been here a while.'

'Do you know who it is?' she asked.

James wrung his hands. 'It's Lydia.'

THIRTY-TWO

'What?' Sophie stared in horror. The woman suddenly changed from just being a body to being a person. A person like her, who'd taken a job at One Pure Thought, who used to live in this house. A woman with her whole future ahead of her.

'I'll call the police,' James said quickly. He pulled Sophie towards the door. 'Let's get out of here. It might be a crime scene.'

They stood by the front door, and Sophie tried to catch her breath. The stench of the body was overpowering. James spoke rapidly into his mobile, explaining to 999 what they had discovered.

'The police will be here soon,' he said when he'd hung up, putting his arms around Sophie. 'There's nothing we can do for Lydia. Let's wait outside.'

They sat together on the steps, waiting for the police. Sophie couldn't get her head round what might have happened. Why had Lydia been in the flat, and how had she died? How long had her body been there, with Sophie walking by several times a day, and then sleeping, oblivious, in her flat in the same building?

. . .

An hour later the police were combing through the ground-floor flat and the whole house had been sealed off with police tape. A policewoman had briefly interviewed James and Sophie about finding the body and their relationship to Lydia.

'You're free to go now,' the policewoman said after she'd taken their details.

'But I live here,' Sophie protested. 'I live in the top flat.'

'Is there anywhere else you can stay?' she asked kindly.

Sophie looked at James. 'Of course you can stay with me,' he said, squeezing her arm. Sophie had never been back to James's place before. Her flat was so near the office that it had always been more convenient to stay there.

They left together, and then got a taxi to the other side of London to James's apartment. James had never said much about where he lived, and when they pulled up in front of a sparkling glass tower block by the river Sophie was surprised. She'd assumed he lived in a small house, or an old building like hers. She'd seen these kinds of flats advertised before and they went for millions of pounds, mainly to foreign investors.

James took her through the building's reception and nodded to the concierge. It was late now, the middle of the night, and as they went up in the lift, Sophie caught sight of her pale face, her red-rimmed eyes. She didn't remember crying, but she must have done. For the first time she was aware of the pressure behind her eyes, the headache starting to form.

In the lift, James swiped his key card into the slot, and they rose quickly. Then the lift stopped and James placed his finger on a sensor and the doors opened, straight into his flat. Sophie stepped out into the apartment. She felt slightly dizzy. The whole apartment had floor-to-ceiling glass windows. As she went over to the window she could see the river far below her.

From the windows on the other side, she could see south London, the railways criss-crossing over it.

'This is amazing,' she said, but her voice was dull, her mind occupied by Lydia.

'I wish we were here in better circumstances. I was really looking forward to showing you the flat.'

Sophie nodded. She felt like she was just going through the motions, making conversation. 'You never said you lived somewhere like this,' she said, trying to distract herself.

'I don't like to tell people straight away. It attracts gold-diggers.'

'I'm not like that.'

He wrapped his arms around her. 'I know. And Felicity didn't like it for a different reason. She seemed jealous, like she thought I'd got above myself.'

'So, how—' Sophie stopped herself before she completed the sentence. She wanted to know how James had ended up living here. He'd said he'd had an ordinary background, like her.

'How did I afford it?' James asked, grinning. 'Well, I'm actually paid quite well by Max and Cassie. The company couldn't run without a Creative Director, so I'm paid accordingly. And of course, I have a huge mortgage.'

'Right,' Sophie said. 'You've done so well for yourself.'

'I've certainly worked for it. I'm not planning to stick around at the company forever, though.'

'Why not?'

'One word: Max.'

Sophie froze, thinking again of Lydia. 'What do you mean?'

'He's incompetent, doesn't know what he's doing. Cassie's the real brains in the family. We're planning to set up our own business together without him, once we can get the finance. I hope you'll come with us. We could use your skills.'

Sophie didn't need to think twice about it. 'I would.'

'Brilliant. Now, would you like some wine? It's been a difficult day.'

Sophie looked at her watch. She felt overwhelmingly tired. 'It's nearly 2 a.m. I think I want to get to bed.'

'Sure,' James said. He took her through the sparsely decorated flat and into the bedroom. Aside from generic prints of famous works of art on the walls, there was hardly anything in it, no clutter on any surfaces, nothing superfluous amid the sleek design.

'This is like a show home,' Sophie said.

James laughed. 'Well, I'm not here much. Always in the office.'

When Sophie lay down in James's vast bed, she couldn't sleep. The image of Lydia's dead body lying on the bed kept flashing into her mind.

She thought about how Lydia had left the company under a cloud. Why would Lydia have been back at the flats? How had she got in? She remembered how Cassie and Max had argued about him seeing Lydia again. James had told her that Max used the ground-floor flat for hook-ups. Had she been there to see Max?

THIRTY-THREE

Sophie was grateful when James's blinds rose at 6 a.m. on Monday morning and the lighting in the room slowly brightened to simulate daylight. She hadn't slept all weekend, and she wanted the day to start to distract her from her swirling thoughts. When James left for the gym, she finally managed to get half an hour's sleep before he was back, shiny and sweaty. They each had quick showers, and Sophie had a slice of toast before they set off for the office together.

'I'll drive today,' James said. 'Can't face the Tube.' They took the lift down to the underground parking and he led her to a polished sports car and opened the door for her.

'There's secure parking down the road from the office. She'll be all right,' James said, wiping a smudge off the dashboard. It took her a moment to realise he was talking about the car.

They pulled out of the car park and the engine roared.

'I've wanted to take you for a spin in my Maserati for a while,' he said, as they turned into a street of stationary traffic. 'It's a shame it has to be like this. I'll take you properly one day. Out to the countryside. We can have the top down.'

'That sounds lovely,' Sophie said, imagining the wind through her hair.

'It was my boyhood fantasy to have a sports car. Max and I met at school, but I was a scholarship boy, so I didn't have anywhere near as much money as the others. We could hardly afford the uniform.'

Sophie nodded, thinking of James's expensive lifestyle. He wanted the best of everything because he felt he'd missed out as a child. It was understandable.

By the time they got to the office it was 8 a.m. and James was stressed because he was at his desk much later than usual. Almost everyone was already in the office, and their whispering stopped as James and Sophie walked in.

'Hi,' Sophie said quietly to Cassie, as she swung her bag onto the desk beside her. She was wearing a new outfit James had bought her at the weekend, as she hadn't been back to her flat yet.

'We heard about Lydia,' Cassie whispered, putting an arm around Sophie. 'It must have been so awful finding her body. Are you OK?'

Sophie sank heavily into her seat. 'I think so. It was just a big shock. Although I didn't know her. So it can't be as bad for me as for others. I keep thinking of her parents, how horrible it must be for them.'

Cassie rubbed her shoulders. 'I'll get you a coffee.'

'Yes, please. That would be great.' Sophie could feel her lack of sleep catching up with her.

When Cassie came over with the steaming mug of coffee, she took it gratefully.

'So what exactly happened? Where did you find her?'

'She was downstairs. On the bed in the ground-floor flat.'

'The one that Max uses?'

'Yes, I think so.'

'Gosh, it must have been so traumatic. How long had she

been there?'

'I don't think anyone knows. It must have been at least a couple of days.'

'And did the police say how she died?'

'We haven't heard anything.'

Cassie gave Sophie a squeeze, her silver necklace swinging into Sophie's top. 'Poor you, Sophie. You know, if you want the day off, you can have it. To process what happened.'

'No, I'd rather be distracted by work. And besides, I don't want to go back to the flat.'

'Of course you don't.' Cassie shivered. 'It must bring back bad memories.'

'I stayed with James last night.'

'Oh, good idea. Things getting serious between you?'

'It's early days,' Sophie said, a smile forming on her lips as she thought of him, in spite of everything. 'But things are going well between us. I really like him.'

The rest of the day passed in a blur. The results of her STI tests came through, which were thankfully negative. Everyone at work was preparing for the big retreat that was coming up: a whole weekend away on a golf course, entertaining clients. It happened every quarter and was one of the top drivers of sales for the company. But Sophie could hardly concentrate on her work, her mind constantly spinning. She wasn't sure if she could face going back to her flat. She didn't feel safe there, especially after what had happened to Lydia. And yet, she didn't want to move in with James by default. They'd only just started seeing each other and even though she loved being around him, she still needed her own space.

Sophie bumped into Cassie in the kitchen in the afternoon. She looked pale and drawn.

'Are you OK?' Sophie asked.

'Yeah, I guess so. I found out that Lydia left a suicide note.'

'Oh,' Sophie said, thinking of the bottle of vodka beside her. Poor Lydia. What had driven her to that? 'Do you know why?' she asked.

'Apparently, she was desperately unhappy. Something to do with Max. The police have already questioned him. They want to speak to my father too, and me, but there's not much I can tell them.' Cassie sighed. 'I really wish Max would be more careful with the way he treats women. I keep wondering... I mean, why was she in the flat? Was she there to see him?' Cassie shook her head. 'I wish he'd be kinder, think about the ways he might hurt people.'

'It must have been awful for her,' Sophie said, wondering if Lydia had come to see Max and he didn't turn up.

'I've been in touch with her parents, expressed my condolences on behalf of the company. I had their number from Lydia's file.'

'They must be going through hell.'

'I know. I really had to brace myself to ring them, I was worried they'd blame Max and they'd take it out on me. But they told me that Lydia had been unhappy for a while. They'd been worried about her, and they were planning to borrow the money to fly over from Australia so they could be with her. She'd been troubled for the last few weeks.'

Sophie rested her hand on Cassie's arm to comfort her. 'I can't imagine how she felt.'

Cassie let out a sigh. 'She was in such a bad way and I never even knew. I feel guilty about how she left the company. Her work wasn't good enough, but maybe we should have been nicer to her.'

'It's not your fault, Cassie. You can't blame yourself.' Sophie squeezed Cassie's arm.

'I just wish I'd reached out to her. Checked she's OK. But now she's gone.'

THIRTY-FOUR

Sophie could feel something digging into her back and she shifted in the bed, wrapping the sheets tighter around her. The footsteps got closer, a shadow above her. She froze in fear, but she couldn't bear to turn her head, couldn't bear to look.

And then she felt the weight on top of her. The crush of his body. Every muscle in her body tensed, every molecule frozen in place. She wanted to scream. She could feel it caught at the back of her throat, feel the pressure of it building, reverberating round her body. But she couldn't release it, couldn't get it out.

She turned her head, and her eyes met the man's, felt the shock of familiarity. *It was him.*

She bolted up in bed, suddenly awake. Her heart pounded as she noticed a looming shadow across the room. But it was just a suit in its dry-cleaning bag, hanging on the front of the cupboard.

She picked up her phone. Looked at the time. Three twenty a.m. She needed to calm down. Get back to sleep.

The dream was already fading from her consciousness as she lay back down. She turned and curled up into the foetal position, freezing for a second when she saw a man in the bed beside her. It was just James. He was breathing deeply, fast asleep.

What had the dream meant? She remembered the shock of the familiarity of the man. But the details were fading. She'd recognised him. But she couldn't remember why. Who was he? The details slipped from her grasp. *It was only a dream*, she told herself.

She reached out to touch James, to feel the comfort of his warm skin. He stirred in his sleep, but didn't wake. Sophie didn't feel any better.

She stared around the room, trying to orientate herself in his home. The penthouse was breathtaking, but it didn't feel like her space. She'd been here a week now. Cassie had collected her toiletries and clothes in a holdall and given them to her at the office so that she could make herself comfortable. But she felt like she'd been here too long; it didn't feel like home. James was neat and tidy compared to her, and every surface was always spotless. When she made a coffee here the mug had to be put straight in the dishwasher. It was his space, not hers.

It was kind of James to let her move in, but they'd ended up living together by necessity, rather than choice. She didn't want to outstay her welcome. She'd thought about looking for another place to rent, but she couldn't really afford to live anywhere else on her own when so much of her monthly salary had to go towards paying back her loan from the company. And she couldn't face living in a house share with strangers, not when she was feeling so anxious. She'd have to go back to her flat, try and forget what had happened to Lydia.

'Good morning,' James said with a smile, once he'd slowly woken up. He rolled over and kissed her and she wrapped her arms around him, kissing him back. She cherished these small moments of intimacy. A few days before they'd slept together for the first time, and he'd been gentle and respectful, letting her take the lead. But since then she'd started to have the nightmares.

'Are you OK?'

She nodded. 'I'm fine, although I didn't sleep well.'

'I'm not surprised,' he said, stroking her hair. 'It's been a stressful week for everyone.'

'I know. The thought of going back to my flat makes me so nervous. I don't feel safe there anymore.'

James turned in the bed and gazed deeply into her eyes. 'You know Lydia did that to herself, don't you? She was... very messed up.'

'I know.' He was right. It wasn't rational to be afraid. There was no one to be afraid of.

'I can't understand why Lydia was even in the flat. I suppose she might still have a set of keys. We took one set from her, but she might have had a spare set cut. Or maybe Max let her in.'

Sophie thought of the noises at night. Could they have been Lydia as well as Max? She thought of Felicity with a jolt. 'What about Felicity? Does she still have a key?'

James shook his head. 'I made sure I took her keys. And besides, I've never seen her go inside.'

'What do you mean?'

'When she was stalking me, Max put up a camera at the entrance. It was to deter her from entering. This was back when she was harassing Lydia. She never tried to get in, at least not through the front.'

So Felicity had been right about a camera.

'I've never noticed any camera,' Sophie said quietly, thinking how it had been there all along, watching her come and go. 'Did the camera catch Lydia going in?' Perhaps if it had they could see if she was with anyone.

James shook his head. 'There's been some kind of problem

with the camera in the last few weeks. I think the battery might have run out, but I haven't looked into it yet. Once the restraining order was deterring Felicity, it didn't seem as important to fix the camera.'

Sophie thought back to Max's party. If the camera had been working then, it would have caught her going into the building with the stranger. 'When exactly did it stop working?' she asked. 'Was it before Max's party?'

'Yeah, a week or so before.'

Sophie nodded. Another dead end. She'd never know what had happened that night. Her thoughts returned to the flat, to moving back in. 'I'm not sure that I'll feel comfortable back in the flat. Not after everything that's happened.'

'You can stay here as long as you like.'

'Thanks, James, but I don't want to intrude.'

'Don't be silly. You're not intruding.' He stroked her matted hair back from her face.

'We haven't been together long. It's too much of a rush for me.'

He nodded. 'I understand. I can help you look for somewhere else to live.' He kissed her cheek. 'Although I'll miss you. I've loved every moment with you.'

They were interrupted by Sophie's mobile ringing. Her father. Sophie had been putting off calling him. After Max's party and Lydia's death, she'd been in too emotional a state to speak to him.

She picked up the phone as James went off to have a shower.

'Hello, Sophie. How are you?'

'I'm OK, Dad. How are you? How's the physio?'

'Oh, I'm fine and the physio's going well. Although I don't think I'll need it for much longer.'

'Why not?'

'I'm getting better, aren't I? Plus Charlie said it cost a lot of money. I thought it was free. I didn't realise you'd paid for it.'

'I paid for it because I wanted to.' Sophie thought uneasily of her debt to Charlie, that had now become her debt to One Pure Thought. She didn't like owing the company money either, it made her feel trapped, like she couldn't leave.

'OK,' her father said. 'But maybe time to stop paying for it now. How's London? I've been worried about you. Charlie said—'

'What did Charlie say?' She wished he wouldn't interfere in her life. It had nothing to do with him.

'Just that you were very busy, working all hours.'

'I love my job, Dad. The people are nice and welcoming. And I'm really enjoying it.' She thought of Lydia and changed the subject. 'Everything's going well. I've met someone. At work. Someone I've started dating.'

Her father was silent. 'You be careful, Sophie. That all seems a bit rushed to me.'

Sophie was taken aback. She'd expected her father to be pleased for her. But maybe he was being overprotective because he hadn't met James.

'I'm sure you'll like him. I'll have to introduce him to you.'

'Is this the man Charlie mentioned you were with? He didn't sound that nice to me.'

'Charlie mentioned someone?'

'Yeah, he did. James, I think he said. He warned Charlie off, threatened to hurt him if he went near you.'

THIRTY-FIVE

Sophie glanced towards the shower room. James had turned the water off and he'd reappear soon in his towel.

'What do you mean, Dad?' she asked. James had never mentioned speaking to Charlie.

'What I just said. James threatened Charlie. Said he would beat him up.' Sophie almost laughed. She couldn't imagine James saying that. Charlie must have made it up. Or at least exaggerated.

Sophie took a deep breath. 'It's Charlie's behaviour that's been threatening, Dad. He's practically been stalking me.'

'I find that hard to believe. He just wants you back, that's all.'

'Well, I'm dating James now. He might have warned Charlie off, I suppose. But only because of Charlie's behaviour.'

It was a moment before her dad spoke again. 'OK, love. Well, I'm sure you know what's for the best. Just make sure you look after yourself.'

'You too, Dad.'

When she hung up the phone, she turned to James, who was now towelling himself off by the bed with an expensive pure white towel. 'Charlie's claiming you threatened to hurt him...'

James pursed his lips. 'I spoke to him at the club. Told him to stay away from you, that you weren't interested.'

Sophie nodded. 'Was that all?'

'I'd had a bit to drink. I probably raised my voice.'

Sophie smiled at him. He'd only been trying to protect her. It was kind of him.

'Charlie's really turned my dad against you,' she said, sadly.

'He's a nasty piece of work, isn't he? But I'm sure I'll change your father's mind once he actually meets me.'

'You're right,' she said, smiling. 'He won't be able to help but like you. I was thinking I might go down and see him next weekend. Do you want to come with me?'

'Not this weekend. It's the company retreat at Philip's golf course. I thought you were coming?'

'Of course,' she said. 'It just slipped my mind.' Cassie had invited her a while ago and she'd been working on the presentations for it, alongside her other projects.

'Great,' James said enthusiastically. It will give you a chance to meet new potential clients. Maybe even get in on the bonus if they sign up with us.'

Sophie felt a shiver of excitement run through her. If she could get a bonus then she could use it to pay back some of the money she owed the company early. 'I'd love to sign a new client.'

James laughed. 'Wouldn't we all? The retreats are pretty regular, so there'll be other chances. Philip loves using the golf course he owns to entertain his mates, and persuade them to buy overpriced branding projects from us. The course is beautiful, surrounded by woodland, and there's a huge lake. And it's one of the top courses in the country. The whole trip's a lot of fun.'

'Who else is going?'

'It is quite exclusive. About ten of us go. Me, Max and Cassie and our best people.'

'Oh,' Sophie said, her enthusiasm fading. She had thought that all the staff went. 'I don't want anyone thinking I got to go on the retreat because... well, because I'm in a relationship with you.'

'No one will think that.' He came closer to her, gave her a light kiss on the lips. 'I promise.' She stepped backwards. 'Besides, it's hard to turn down,' he continued. 'You'll love the opulence. Max and Cassie just think it's normal, but the level of wealth is unbelievable. We stay in these chalets on the edge of the golf course – they're gorgeous. The first time I stayed was when I was just a kid. Max had invited me on his family holiday in the half-term break from school. It was life-changing for me. I finally saw what you could buy if you had that much money. He and Cassie had speedboats that they played with like they were toys, and Max didn't think anything of it.'

'It sounds like fun.' It was so different from anything Sophie had done before.

'It is. And it would be good to get you away, too, have a bit of a break from London. The retreat's exhausting and draining, but it's also the chance to let your hair down and enjoy yourself. Us and the clients. They're mates of Philip's, or Max's old school friends, who've set up their own companies.'

'Where would I be staying?' She didn't want to stay in the same chalet as Max. He made her feel uncomfortable.

'Oh, don't worry. We can sort it out however you want. You can share with Cassie if you like. Or with me?'

She shook her head. 'It doesn't feel appropriate to stay in a chalet with you on a business trip.'

He laughed gently. 'OK, if you insist. The trip's a great opportunity to prove yourself to Max, make yourself indispensable to the company.'

'It sounds great,' Sophie said, feeling a shiver of excitement. 'But I'd like to go back to my flat before then,' she added.

'Oh, are you sure?'

'Yeah. I'll feel a bit odd going back, but I need to, sooner or later, don't I?'

'I suppose so.'

'And you changed the locks, didn't you?'

'Of course.'

'So there's nothing to be scared of.' Sophie could hear the doubt in her own voice.

James put his arms around her and squeezed her tightly. 'There's nothing to be scared of,' he repeated.

An hour later, Sophie walked up the steps to her house with James. There were sticky remnants of police tape on the railings, but all other signs of any disturbance were gone. Cassie had paid a team of cleaners to clear up any mess the police had made. The rotten smell was gone and instead the whole hallway smelled of bleach and air freshener. It was like nothing had ever happened there.

Sophie took a deep breath and carried her case up the stairs towards her flat. As she moved away from the ground floor, she felt safer and more at home.

'Are you OK?' James asked, as she put the key in the lock.

She nodded. 'Yeah.'

Inside the flat, the milk in the fridge was off, but otherwise everything was as she'd left it, a messy pile of shoes by the front door, her work clothes still hanging on the back of her chair in her bedroom. She breathed deeply. She was home.

'I feel better being back,' she said to James.

She wandered out onto the balcony, looked down to the street below. Turning, she noticed that the flowers that had been planted in the window box were all dead. No one had watered them while she'd been away. She felt a tinge of sadness and vowed she would replace them.

'Do you want me to stay tonight?' James asked, appearing behind her.

'Yes, please.' Sophie looked round the flat. It looked the same, but felt alien.

'I can stay as long as you need,' James said, putting his arm around her.

Later, they left the flat and strolled through Covent Garden, browsing the jewellery shops.

'I want to buy you something,' James said. 'To show you how much you mean to me.'

'You really don't have to,' Sophie replied.

'I do,' James said. 'I know we haven't known each other that long... but, well, Lydia's death has made me realise how short life is, how important it is to seize the day. It's...' He looked at her and then down at his feet for a moment, as if he was struggling to find the words. 'It's as if we just fit together. We click. And when I'm with you I feel like I'm the best version of myself. The happiest I've been in a long time.'

'I know what you mean,' Sophie said, thinking of how, despite everything that was going on, she always felt better when she was with James. It felt natural to have him by her side, like he'd always been there.

'I think I'm falling in love with you, Sophie,' James said, placing his arms round her waist and leaning forward to kiss her deeply.

THIRTY-SIX

Max paced back and forth in his office in his suit, clutching a handwritten piece of paper, practising saying the words over and over again. Everyone could see him through the glass panels, and out in the open-plan part of the office, the mood was sombre, a dark cloud over all of them. Max had hardly left his office since Lydia's death, hiding away from everyone. A few days before he'd opened the door and gathered everyone round. He'd told them that Lydia's parents were arriving this week from Australia. As the coroner had finished the post-mortem and the police had concluded the death wasn't suspicious, Lydia's parents were going to take her body back to Australia and bury her there. Before they took her home, Max wanted to hold a memorial, for everyone at the office and any of her UK friends that they could get hold of.

Today was the day, and Max had been nervously practising his speech all morning. Sophie had volunteered to stay in the office and deal with anything urgent while they were out. She was the only one who hadn't known Lydia.

Max looked at his watch and then opened the glass door to the office and cleared his throat. Sophie's colleagues rose from their desks in their dark suits. She watched them file out of the room, talking in whispers, aware of the solemnity of the occasion.

Max was the last to leave. When Sophie looked up at him, she saw the trace of a tear forming in the corner of his eye and wondered if he was feeling guilty. Lydia had named him in her suicide note and the police had spoken to him. He was probably trying to make amends with the memorial, but Sophie wondered how he'd manage seeing her parents, what words he'd find to say to them.

He dabbed his eyes with a hanky from his breast pocket, took a deep breath and left without saying goodbye.

Sophie looked round the empty office. It was always occupied, even early in the morning and late at night. She'd never been there alone. Realising she should use the peace and quiet to power on with her work, she turned back to her preparations for the retreat.

Half an hour later her phone beeped. It was Felicity. Sophie had kept her number just in case there was a kernel of truth in what she said about a toxic culture at One Pure Thought.

I can't believe Lydia's dead. What did that company do to her?

Sophie sighed. She didn't like the way Felicity immediately linked Lydia's death to the company. She was just looking for ways to further her own case. Sophie wasn't going to engage with it. She put her phone back down, ignoring the message, went to the coffee machine and made herself a drink and settled back down to work.

It was deathly silent as she worked, the only noise her fingers clacking on the keyboard and the ticking of the clock. Surrounded by faces smiling from advertising posters, it felt surreal being the only living being in the office. The lights in the other areas had automatically turned off and she was sitting alone in a little pool of light, which she had to keep on by occasionally waving her hands around.

The afternoon passed quickly and she felt more prepared for the retreat at the weekend. She was excited, but nervous. It was her chance to prove herself, and yet she felt uncomfortable around Max, particularly after everything that had happened with Lydia.

She heard footsteps on the stairs, and the sound of chatter and laughter. The memorial must have finished. Then the door flew open and the volume rose, light automatically flooding the room as her co-workers walked across the office.

Sophie checked the time on her phone. It was 6 p.m. already. She saw she had a new email in her freelance account.

The title of the email made her blood run cold.

Pictures of you, it said. It was from an anonymous sender, an email address of random letters and numbers. It was just like before. Just like when Will's friends had taunted her.

She opened the email, her heart thumping.

We have pictures of you that you won't want the world to see. Don't talk to the police again.

They must know that she had referred the latest website about her to the police. They wanted to shut her up.

Sophie calmed her breathing, and tried to think straight. For years she had believed that they had pictures, and she'd been too scared to say anything else about what had happened to her because of their threats. But no pictures had ever appeared. It was all a bluff. She wouldn't be scared by them anymore.

She took a deep breath and replied. *I don't believe you. You don't have any pictures.*

She felt relieved after she'd sent it. Proud of herself. She really had moved on.

She glanced round the office. Her colleagues weren't back at their desks yet; they were standing in small groups chatting.

Sophie's email pinged again almost immediately. *Yes we do.* it said.

She opened the email. There were four attachments.

She couldn't calm her breathing, couldn't focus. They did have photos from back then. They'd had them all along. Will's trophies of a night Sophie couldn't even remember. She gagged, swallowing the bile that rose in her throat.

And then she opened the photos.

The first image was definitely her. Lying naked on a bed.

She didn't remember it being taken.

But the photo wasn't from years ago. She recognised the bedroom, her wardrobe. The wardrobe inside the flat she lived in now.

She looked at the other three photos.

They were all her, in various states of undress. All taken in the same place. In her flat in London. In one she was still wearing her sparkly black top. They'd been taken after Max's party.

THIRTY-SEVEN

A shadow appeared above Sophie and she jumped. It was just James.

'How are you? Coped all right on your own all afternoon?'

'Yeah,' Sophie said distantly. She locked her phone quickly so that he wouldn't see the images, and put it face down on her desk.

'Is everything all right?' he asked, looking at her with concern. 'You've gone really pale.'

'I—' Sophie felt the tears welling up. She was still trying to compute what the pictures meant. The blond guy she'd met at the club after Max's party was somehow connected to Will, to the people who'd been threatening to share photos for years. Now they finally had some. Had he drugged her? Had Will paid him just to get her in this position again? To blackmail her so she wouldn't speak to the police? It seemed too much. But then she thought of his political career, how the police investigation had the power to ruin it. How lots of claims against him in the papers would lead to people thinking 'no smoke without fire'. Of course, they'd be right. Would he really go this far to protect his reputation?

It was like history was repeating itself. Now when she thought back to the night of Max's party, she realised she must have been drugged again. Just like last time. Otherwise, she was sure she would have remembered something.

James's arms were around her, comforting her. 'What is it? Have you been upset by Lydia's memorial? Maybe you should have gone too, rather than staying here to mind the office. It might have helped you.'

'No, it's not that.'

'What is it?' He wiped a tear from her cheek. 'Look, let's go to a meeting room and talk about this.' He took her hand and led her to one of the glass-walled meeting rooms, closing the blinds as soon as they were inside.

He sat her down and handed her a bottle of water from the fridge in the corner. 'What's wrong?'

Sophie swallowed. Should she tell him about the photos? He'd only want to help. And she had nothing to be ashamed of.

Sophie took a deep breath. 'You remember after Max's party, how I thought something had happened to me? I have evidence it did.'

'Really?' His eyes crinkled in concern.

'Yes, someone's sent me photos. Of me. Intimate photos.'

'Oh my God, I'm so sorry.' His face went pale.

'It's worse than that. I think the person who did it might be connected to my past. I was...' She paused, glanced up at him, wondering if she could confide in him. 'I was raped before. At university. And... I don't remember everything that happened, I'd blacked out.'

'I'm so sorry,' James said. 'That's horrible.'

'The police were reinvestigating it. There'd been a fresh complaint. And I started to receive threats, that someone would share naked photos of me. They'd threatened me before – but the photos are from after Max's party. Now I don't know what to think.'

James paced up and down. 'And they emailed them to you?'

'Yeah.'

'Can I see?'

She shook her head, embarrassed. 'I'd prefer it if you didn't.'

He nodded. 'Did you recognise the email address?'

'No.'

'This is awful, Sophie. What are you going to do?'

'I'm not sure.' Should she go to the police again? Maybe she should move out of the flat after all. She didn't feel safe there.

'You can't do anything about it, I don't think. Not if you don't know who it was. The only thing you can do is put it behind you. I can support you.'

Sophie nodded.

James squeezed her hand. 'I came over to tell you that the others are going to go to the pub, to raise a glass to Lydia. But I don't think we should go. Let's do something more relaxing, just the two of us. How about a river cruise? Dinner on a boat?'

Sophie shook her head. She needed some space to think, to work out what to do about the pictures. 'I think I just want to go back and rest,' she said. 'It's been a draining day. And I need to pack for the retreat, too.'

'Whatever you think's best. I'll come with you.'

'Sure,' she said. She didn't want to be completely on her own in the flat.

He leaned over and kissed her gently on the lips. 'You're special, Sophie. Don't get caught up in the past. I really think we have a future together. We should both focus on that.'

THIRTY-EIGHT

Sophie's taxi pulled up on the gravel, in front of the huge country house hotel and golf course that belonged to Philip. The hotel was made of traditional limestone brick and had been the home of an aristocrat before it was bought many years ago and its gardens turned into a golf course. Philip was the latest in a long line of well-off owners. As Sophie stepped out of the taxi, the bitterly cold air hit her. A porter came out and took her case from the boot of the taxi and carried it inside. She rubbed her hands together and quickly followed.

As she went into the reception area, there was a blast of heat from overhead and a strong floral smell, which complimented the huge vase of fake flowers perched on a pedestal in the middle of the room. She paused, unsure what to do. It was 1.45 p.m., fifteen minutes before the time she'd been told to arrive. She'd come up on the train on her own, eating a slightly soggy chicken salad sandwich as she watched the fields roll by outside the window. Cassie and James were coming straight from another meeting, and she didn't know how the others were getting there.

She walked to the other end of the reception area and saw

the entrance to the spa. There was a menu for a range of expensive treatments and she looked at it longingly. Cassie had mentioned that there might be time for some pampering before they met the clients for dinner later. James would be making the most of the golf. He'd told her that he was going to play nine holes with Max, and Cassie's husband, who was coming as a client.

In the corner of the room there was a map of the resort. The country house made up just a tiny part of the estate. The map showed the golf course to the west, and an expanse of blue marked a lake which stretched out beside the golf course and onwards. The chalets were marked in the far corner of the map, in the middle of a wooded area, close to the lake. Sophie hoped that she'd be able to go out and explore the grounds later. It was nice to be away from the smog of the city, in the fresh air.

She wandered back to the main reception area and sat down in one of the stylish armchairs as she waited. Ten minutes later her colleagues appeared, chatting and laughing in a cohesive group. Cassie and James had come straight from their meeting. The others must have met at the station and taken taxis over together. She had probably been on the same train as them, in a different carriage. They probably hadn't even thought to ask her to share a taxi, probably hadn't realised she was on the same train.

She took a deep breath and walked over to the others.

'Hello, Sophie,' James said with a smile. 'Welcome. The porters are going to take our cases to the chalets and we're going to head across in the boats. You'll need your coat.' Sophie shrugged her jacket back onto her shoulders.

'The boats?' she asked, remembering what he'd said about Max and Cassie racing their boats as children.

'Yeah, you'll see in a minute.'

Max led them all out of the back of the hotel and onto a small pier where there were two speedboats. A little sign on the pier said PRIVATE – KEEP OUT but Max pushed it aside. A mist had settled over the lake.

'Who's coming with me?' Max asked, as he climbed into one of the boats and stood at the helm. A few of Sophie's colleagues climbed into the seating at the back.

'These boats are amazing,' James whispered to Sophie. 'They're called cabin cruisers. They even have a kitchen and sleeping area in the hull. When I came on holiday with Max here as a kid, Philip let us have a night out on the lake. Just shows the kind of life you can lead with money.'

'Wow,' Sophie said.

Cassie had hopped onto the other boat and was gesturing for them to get on.

'Dad bought these boats for us when we were teenagers,' she said, with a smile. 'When he and Mum got divorced. A present to keep us on his side. They're designed for bigger waterways really, but Max and I have always raced them here.'

Sophie got onto the boat. It was more spacious than it looked from the outside. She peered down the stairs into the kitchen area. She could just about make out what looked like a wedding photo stuck to the wall, and a door at the end of the work surface which presumably led to a tiny bedroom.

Beside them, Max's boat left the pier and raced ahead. Cassie started her engine and they followed across the lake, the icy wind blowing into their faces.

When they arrived at the other side, they got off the boat onto a rickety pier and walked past a dilapidated wooden hut. Sophie shivered from the cold.

'It's this way,' Cassie said. 'Through the woods. It's not far. Just a ten-minute walk.'

'It's beautiful here,' Sophie said, as she walked through the mist over the hard ground.

'Thank you,' Cassie said. 'My husband and I come here on our own sometimes. When we need a break from the city. It can be good to get away from everyone. That said, the phone reception is terrible. The best place is actually here, in these woods. There's none at all in the chalets.'

Sophie pulled out her phone and saw she had two out of four bars of reception.

The twigs crunched beneath them, and Sophie wrapped her arms around herself. It was colder than she'd thought.

Max appeared beside them. 'Have you seen the latest on Dad?' he asked Cassie quietly. Sophie wondered if she should move away, give them some privacy.

'What now?' Cassie asked, irritated by his question.

'Another scandal. Another girl.'

'Another one?'

Sophie swallowed. She didn't like hearing about Philip's bad behaviour.

Max sighed loudly. 'Yep. I don't know where they all come from...'

Cassie stretched back in her seat. 'Let's not talk about this now. We're here to enjoy ourselves. And sell projects to Dad's friends, of course.'

They walked in silence for a minute or two, and then Max started humming a tune under his breath.

'Was that the school song?' James said, punching him in the arm.

'Yeah,' Max said. 'Getting myself hyped up and in the right mood. Like we did before rugby matches. Doesn't this remind you of school? Tramping through the wood. A bit like the Duke of Edinburgh Award.'

'I miss our Farman's days sometimes,' Cassie said, wistfully. 'Life was fun back then, wasn't it?'

'Farman's?' Sophie said, feeling faint. She must have

misheard. She'd known that Max and James had gone to the same school, but hadn't known the name of it.

'Yep.' Max put his arm round James. 'We're Farman's boys through and through.'

Sophie stared at them, her heart racing. She remembered the article she'd read in the newspaper about Will's political aspirations. It had mentioned the school Will had gone to. One of the top private schools in the country. He'd been to Farman's too. He would have been around the same year as Max. They would have known each other.

THIRTY-NINE

Sophie was quiet the rest of the way to the chalets, trying to convince herself that the Farman's connection between Will and Max meant nothing, telling herself not to worry. Just because they had gone to the same school around the same time didn't mean they were friends. It didn't mean anything. But they'd both treated women badly. And the intimate photos of her had been taken in her flat, which Max's family owned. It seemed like too much of a coincidence.

They emerged from the woods at a row of wooden chalets. As they approached the buildings, two blackbirds swept down from the rooftop and flew into the trees.

'Here's our chalet,' Cassie said excitedly, leading her to the first building.

'It looks so peaceful,' Sophie said, looking up at the three-storey structure.

'I don't know about that,' Cassie said. 'But I'm glad we've got one all to ourselves. It means we can escape when the guys get a bit carried away.'

'What do you mean?' Sophie asked.

'Well, there's going to be a lot of drink. And a lot of drugs.'

Cassie tapped the side of her nose. 'James knows a good dealer round here. A mate of his.'

'James does?'

He'd never mentioned doing any drugs to her; he didn't seem the type. And at Max's party, when everyone was taking them, he'd declined. At least, as far as she could remember.

'Yeah. It should be a lot of fun later. We do the dinner first, with all dad's old golfing buddies. More money than sense, most of them. Old men, too. I can usually charm them into investing in new campaigns.' Cassie winked, and Sophie started to wonder just what was expected of her. James had told her to bring her nicest clothes as the golf club was expensive, and she'd been out to buy a couple more dresses for the occasion.

Cassie saw Sophie's worried expression. 'Honestly – you'll be fine. Don't worry. Just show a bit of cleavage and you'll have them eating out of the palm of your hand.'

Sophie smiled half-heartedly. Was this why she'd been invited to the retreat? As bait for lecherous old men?

'Oh, and don't worry about what Max said in the woods about Dad. Dad's harmless. He just always has money-grabbing girls accusing him of things.'

Sophie frowned. 'Oh – he didn't do anything?' That hadn't been how the papers reported it.

'Falsely accused,' Cassie said casually. She looked at her watch. 'I've booked us both into the spa for a massage and then a manicure in an hour. A car will come and pick us up. I thought we'd have a bit of time in the chalet first to unpack.'

'Oh,' Sophie said quickly, thinking of the money she owed Max and the company. 'I don't think I can afford it.'

Cassie linked her arm with Sophie's. 'Don't be silly. It's on me. I thought we should do something nice while the boys are playing golf.'

. . .

An hour later, they returned to the hotel for their massage and manicure. Sophie was keen to get some time alone so she could search online to see if there was some kind of connection between Max and Will, if they'd been friends at school. But when they arrived at the spa, they had to put their phones in the lockers for the massage, and they weren't returned until the end of the manicure.

'I feel so relaxed,' Cassie said. 'Totally ready to take on the clients this evening.'

'Me too,' Sophie said, wishing she'd had the chance to look at her phone.

Cassie arranged for a porter with a golf buggy to transport them back and they bounced along the single-track road to the chalet. Sophie couldn't google Max while she was sitting right next to Cassie, and when they returned to the chalet she had no phone reception at all.

'So... what are you planning on wearing to the dinner?' Cassie asked, once they were back.

They went to Sophie's room and she showed her what she'd bought and Cassie dismissed each dress in turn. 'I'm not so sure. But don't worry. I thought this might happen. I did a bit of shopping before we came and I have the perfect dress for you.'

The perfect dress that Cassie had selected was a little too short and revealed a bit too much, but Sophie had to admit, it did suit her. Once she'd applied her make-up she felt ready to take on the world.

'You look absolutely gorgeous,' Cassie said, hugging Sophie. 'You know, I think you're really starting to learn my sales techniques.'

Sophie smiled at the compliment. 'That's good.'

'It's so important for women to use their sexuality. It's our advantage. How we can get more business.'

Sophie shifted awkwardly, suddenly embarrassed by the

dress. She wanted to impress with her knowledge. She'd spent so long preparing for the retreat.

'James will be blown away,' Cassie continued. 'And so will the others. You're sitting next to Chris, from the pet food company. Max has high hopes you'll be able to convince him he needs a new brand strategy.'

'I'll do my best,' Sophie said. She'd spent a lot of time researching the pet food company, working out what they might need.

'Great. I'm sure you'll nail it. No pressure, though,' she said, smiling. 'Anyway, the fun will really start later. After the dinner with Dad's buddies, we're hosting drinks in Max's chalet with loads of up-and-coming start-ups. They're young and drowning in venture capital money.'

Sophie felt a shiver of nerves. That would be where the drugs came in. Just like at Max's party.

'Will it be the same people who were at Max's party?'

Cassie raised her eyebrows. 'Not really. But there'll be some crossover. Why? Are you worried that man you went home with after the club will be there? I don't think he was even at Max's party. Just a random in the club.'

Sophie nodded. Cassie could be right. He might not have been at Max's party. But whoever it was had managed to get the photos to Will and his friends. They knew a lot more about her than a random stranger.

Cassie and Sophie were the first to arrive back at the hotel reception. Cassie excused herself to make a business call to follow up the client meeting she'd gone to that morning, and Sophie was finally alone. She went into the hotel ladies' room and checked her phone. She was relieved to find that she had mobile reception.

The ladies' room was huge, with a low sofa on the furthest

side, next to the sinks. There were expensive soaps and moisturisers everywhere, and real towels to dry your hands with.

Sophie sat down on the sofa and googled Max's name and his school. There was an article about a talk he'd given years ago where he'd mentioned the school he'd gone to, but that was it. Then she googled Will and the name of the school. This time something came up. A newspaper article from this morning.

She opened the link.

The headline made Sophie gasp, and she felt as if all the blood had drained from her body.

Lydia's rape ordeal: before her death, tragic Lydia had accused aspiring politician and banker, Will Baron-Taylor, of rape.

FORTY

Sophie's chest tightened, her world contracting around her like a noose. Max had been to the same school as Will. Lydia had worked for Max and wound up dead, after accusing Will of rape. It didn't seem real, or possible. How could the new company she had joined, the perfect job, with the perfect colleagues... how could their lives be so entwined with her past?

How could Lydia have known Will? He'd done the same thing to her as he'd done to Sophie. She had been the second accuser, the reason the police were reinvestigating. And it explained why the investigation had gone quiet after she'd died. She wasn't a witness anymore.

Sophie read the article quickly. It implied that the stress of the accusation had made Lydia, who was already unhappy after a difficult break-up, suicidal. The article couldn't suggest that Will was guilty as he hadn't been tried. Instead, it portrayed Lydia as a mentally unwell woman. It almost implied she'd been lying. Just like Will had accused Sophie of lying to the police.

'Sophie?' Cassie called out as she opened the door of the ladies' room. Sophie stood up so quickly she felt faint. She reached out for the armrest of the sofa to steady herself.

'Are you all right?' Cassie asked. 'We need to get going now.'

Sophie forced herself to smile. 'I'm ready,' she said. She followed Cassie out of the room, her mind still racing, trying to work out what it all meant.

When Sophie entered the dining room at the golf club, she was struck by how plain it was. After the trip across the lake on the boat and luxurious spa, she was almost expecting there to be chandeliers hanging from the ceiling. But the room was old-fashioned and a little tatty, with dark red wallpaper and a 1970s tartan carpet.

There were two long tables in the middle of the room, with name places at each spot. Sophie quickly found hers and slid into her seat, beside Chris, from the pet food company. Philip, who was sitting opposite them, introduced them, before telling them in great detail about the wines he'd chosen to serve with the food. Chris was a grey-haired man in his sixties, who seemed to take an unnatural interest in Sophie's personal life and upbringing. He claimed to be hard of hearing, and used this as an excuse to lean in just a little bit too close and peer down her dress. She gritted her teeth and explained what the company did and how they could help with his brand strategy. It was going to be a long evening.

Chris nodded politely and started talking about the food. It was delicious. Sophie took a gulp of her wine. The waiters were attentive, and seemed to be constantly topping up glasses. Sophie tried to keep an eye on how much she was drinking, but the wine slid down easily and she lost track as the evening wore on.

'You really pick your staff well,' Chris said to Philip, looking approvingly at Sophie. It was possible that he was talking about her qualifications and her skill set, but she knew that wasn't really the case. She swallowed back her annoyance.

Philip laughed drunkenly. 'I've always known how to pick them. But of course, it's Max doing the choosing these days.' He laughed. 'He does have good taste, like his father.'

'Cassie interviewed me,' Sophie said quickly. 'And James. Not Max.'

'Ah,' said Philip jovially. 'A good choice, nonetheless.'

Sophie couldn't wait to get away from them all, and after she'd finished her main course, she made her excuses to go to the toilet. She felt drunk and exhausted and she desperately needed a break from Chris and Philip before she said something she regretted. Their attitudes were stuck in the past. No wonder Max had turned out the way he had if he'd been brought up by Philip. She wondered how Cassie had managed in that kind of a family. She supposed it had made her stronger, more determined to prove herself.

Sophie washed her hands, then dried them with the white towels and spent a few minutes rubbing the expensive moisturiser into them and checking her make-up. She was almost ready to go back.

As she walked out of the ladies', she saw the fire escape door was open. She heard voices coming from outside. She stepped out into the darkness and saw James and Cassie smoking together, whispering. She wondered what they were talking about. Planning some kind of strategy for the clients they were wooing at the other end of the table?

She was tempted to join them, if only to moan about Chris for five minutes. But something about their body language stopped her. They were close, their elbows almost touching, her head bent in towards his.

He said something, his voice low and deep. He was frowning and gesticulating as if he was angry. He stepped closer to her, his voice rising, although Sophie couldn't hear the words over the loud chatter from the meal inside.

Cassie shook her head and then laughed. Then she stroked his arm, leaning in as if to kiss him. She moved her head at the last minute and kissed his cheek, laughing still. He stepped away. Then she dropped her cigarette and stubbed it out with her foot and began walking back towards Sophie.

Sophie ducked away and back into the dining room. What had they been talking about? Securing a new client? Or something else?

At the end of the evening, Sophie felt exhausted and slightly nauseous. She'd had no luck persuading Chris to invest in the brand strategy for his company. He'd only seemed to want to talk to Philip about golf. When he'd spoken to Sophie, he'd steered the conversation back to her personal life quickly, more interested in enquiring about her love life than potential projects.

'So,' she said, standing up and reaching out her hand. 'It was great to meet you.'

'Can I have your number?' he asked.

She frowned. 'Umm... I'm not sure you need it?'

'Of course I do!' He laughed heartily. 'So I know what number to give the CEO if he wants to talk to you about branding strategy.'

She flushed. 'Yes, of course. Sure.'

She took out her business card and handed it to him.

He looked down at it and read the details. 'I'll be in touch, Sophie,' he said. And then he reached over and pecked her on the cheek, the bristles of his beard brushing her face for just a bit too long.

FORTY-ONE

When the dinner concluded at around midnight, the older clients veered off towards the bar with Philip, while the team from One Pure Thought and the younger clients made their way towards the minibus that Max had arranged to take them back to the chalets.

'This is where the evening really gets interesting,' Cassie said with a smile, as bodies piled into the vehicle. Soon the bus was on the move and full of singing and laughter as it bumped over the dirt track. Sophie looked out at the golf course. In the dark, it looked like an expanse of black. There were no lights anywhere, and with the booming voices ringing in her ears, and the wine rolling around in her stomach, the journey seemed to go on forever.

At the dinner she'd been distracted by Chris, but now she couldn't stop thinking about Lydia's rape. By Will. She needed to get away for a moment on her own so she could find out more. And work out if Max and Will had been friends.

When they arrived back at the chalets, the lights were already on in the main building and she could see there was a crowd of people inside.

'The fun starts now,' Cassie whispered to her as she slid out of the minibus. Suddenly, Sophie felt like she was in the middle of a game but she didn't know the rules. Her heart beat faster, afraid of the crowd of strangers.

James appeared beside her. 'Everything OK?' he asked.

'Yeah, fine,' she said, quickly.

'Great. Well, let's get in there. There are lots more clients to network with.'

'Of course,' she said. She wanted to be anywhere but inside the chalet, yet she wasn't sure she'd be safe on her own. She'd be safest if she stuck with James.

James put his hand on her shoulder. 'Don't be nervous,' he said. 'They can't fail to be impressed by you.'

As they walked into the living room, she saw a man leaning over the wooden coffee table, snorting a line of cocaine. A crowd of others were standing up drinking. James went to get them drinks and Sophie took a deep breath and plucked up the courage to introduce herself to the group.

'Hi, I'm Sophie,' she said, offering her hand.

Just then someone put the music on and she wasn't sure if they'd heard, but it didn't matter because she felt a slap on her back and turned round.

Max.

He wrapped her in a drunken hug. She tried to pull away but he hugged harder.

'You did it, Sophie!'

'What?' she asked.

'Our first sale of the evening. Chris has messaged to say he wants us to create a new brand strategy for them.'

'Oh,' she said, relieved, as he let go of her. She grinned, hardly able to believe she'd managed it.

'Time for champagne!' he shouted. 'Congratulations, Sophie!' He kissed her on a spot somewhere between her cheek and her lips and then went to get the champagne.

When he came back, Cassie handed round the glasses as Max gave an impromptu drunken speech.

'Sophie,' he said, 'only started at our company recently. And yet she has excelled, not only producing great work, but also bringing in new business worth tens of thousands of pounds.'

A crowd was gathering around now, warm and jovial. Sophie felt a flush of pride.

Max eased the cork off the champagne and it flew across the room before falling to the floor. The fizz cascaded over the top of the bottle.

'Here's to Sophie!' Max said, holding the bottle high, as the liquid careered over the edge and onto the sleeve of his shirt.

'To Sophie!' the crowd shouted, raucous and drunk and mostly completely unaware of who she was.

Cassie was beside her, handing her a glass. 'Enjoy your moment,' she said. 'You deserve it.'

Sophie scanned the group of men in front of her, trying to take in the cheering, trying to enjoy it. This was her moment. Around her people came forward, holding out their glasses towards Max's overflowing bottle. As they came nearer she spotted the blond hair, the familiar profile. He was slightly behind the others, immersed in conversation.

Her heart stopped. It couldn't be.

Everything seemed to slow down. The room got smaller, crowding in on her. She couldn't hear the music anymore or the voices, just her pulse pounding in her head. She couldn't focus.

She remembered what Cassie had said before the retreat. *We mainly sell to Max's old friends.*

Like Will.

Sophie woke up from her stupor and felt hands patting her on the back, congratulating her. She was still staring at the man. He was facing away from her. Then he turned slightly, laughing at something the person next to him was saying. She could see his face properly now. His face was older, his body broader, but it was him. It was Will.

As if sensing her stare, he turned. For a second their eyes met and Sophie froze. She could almost feel the heaviness of his body on top of her and her breathing stopped.

Slowly, a smirk formed on Will's face. Then he winked at her.

FORTY-TWO

Sophie's legs buckled underneath her, and then she steadied herself. Will had turned away from her now, back to his conversation with his friends. But he had *seen* her. She felt ill with fear. She'd told the police everything he'd done. On the train over she'd sent an email to DCI Jameson to let her know about the intimate photos she'd received over email, the ones from the night of Max's party. Had the police spoken to Will about that? She knew he'd be furious.

Max was pouring the champagne into her glass now. Her hand was shaking and she could hardly hold the glass straight.

'Hey,' he said. 'You should be happy, you've done really well.'

'Thanks,' she said weakly. Her eyes searched the room for James. She needed to tell him Will was here, the man who had raped her. She needed to escape.

But then she remembered. They'd all gone to the same school. Max, Will, James. What if James had been friends with Will too? She thought about how critical James had been of Lydia. What if James hadn't believed Lydia, what if he'd taken Will's side over hers?

'Drink up,' Max said, 'it's time to celebrate.'

'I need to go,' she said.

'Don't go now. We can't celebrate your success without you.'

Sophie thought on her feet. 'I don't like to celebrate until the contract's signed.' Her voice came out quiet, hardly audible over the thumping bass. 'We can't count on the money until the client has signed the contract, can we?' She managed to smile at Max. 'Could I borrow your laptop?'

Max frowned. 'We have other clients to entertain now... honestly, the contract can wait.'

'I know... but I think when Chris sobers up he might change his mind. Best to get the contract signed now.'

Max shrugged. 'Can't stop you working,' he said, a slight frown forming on his face. He put his hand on Sophie's shoulder, guided her away. 'My laptop's in the study. I'll log you on.'

She wanted to get away from them completely. The study seemed too close to the party. Perhaps she could take the laptop to her chalet next door. But as soon as she thought of the idea she dismissed it. She couldn't be on her own, not with Will around. He could easily find her. There was safety in numbers. If she went to the other chalet, no one would hear her call out. She needed to stay here.

'Great,' she said, 'thanks,' letting Max steer her out of the living room and to the back of the house.

The study was a tiny room looking out on to the woods. Sophie sat on the dining chair next to the desk and Max logged her into his laptop and pulled up the contract template.

'Just email it over from my account,' he said casually, leaning right over her. She shivered, wishing he'd hurry up and leave the room. She could smell the alcohol on his breath, mixing with the cloying scent of his overpowering aftershave.

'Sure,' she said.

'You'll be all right in here on your own?'

She nodded, and half smiled. 'Yes, of course.'

'I can stay and help you, if you like?'

'No, thank you.'

He moved towards the door and then stopped.

'It was James who wanted you to come on this trip, wasn't it?'

She frowned. 'Because he thinks I'm a good salesperson. And you can see I am. I persuaded Chris to invest in his brand strategy.'

'Only because Chris's a lecherous old man,' Max said. Sophie felt her stomach tighten.

'No one else has brought in any new business this evening. I'm the only one.'

'You're dating James, aren't you?' he said, and there was something hard in his tone, something she didn't like. Was it jealousy? Or something else?

'I am,' she said. She wanted to say it wasn't anything to do with him, but that wasn't really true. They both worked for him.

'It's going OK, is it? Is he... is he all right with you?'

'What do you mean?'

'Nothing.' He shook his head vigorously. 'Nothing. I shouldn't have said anything. James is a mate. I just... you seem so nice, Sophie. I just want the best for you... maybe... I don't know. Just be careful with James. There are better men than him.' He stepped closer to her, and for a moment she thought he was about to lean down to kiss her. She sank into her seat. She was trapped by the desk, by the window. There was nowhere to go.

She coughed and he backed away a bit.

'Do you feel safe here?' he asked, suddenly.

She nodded, although she didn't. Not now.

'I know there are a lot of men here, and it can get a bit

raucous. Sexist, even. I just... I just wanted to check you were OK.'

'Cassie's here too.' Why was he suddenly treating her as if she was fragile, as if she needed looking after?

'That's different. She's different. She's been around a bit, knows how to handle herself.'

Sophie cringed at the comment, but didn't say anything. All she wanted was Max out of the room, away from her.

'I'm OK,' she said firmly. 'I have my own chalet to escape to.'

'It's very isolated, though. Will you be OK on your own there? At night?' She frowned, trying to make sense of what Max was saying, her head fuzzy from the alcohol. Was that some kind of threat?

She nodded. 'I'm fine.' She smiled weakly. 'You'd better get back to your party.'

When Max left she sat for a moment, her head in her hands, and tried to steady her breathing. She'd work on the contract, then she could try and escape out of the room without anyone noticing. But where to? There was no safety here. Like Max had said, her chalet was isolated.

She needed to work out what was going on, if Max and Will had planned to hurt her together, if somehow they'd coordinated her assault after Max's party. Max had known where she lived; he could have told Will, let him into her flat. They could have taken the photos together. And then emailed the threats. Sophie swallowed. How had she ended up working in Max's company? Perhaps it wasn't a coincidence that she was there, at the company, in the flat Max's father owned.

On Max's computer she googled Max's and Will's names once more. The only new things that came up were multiple articles about Lydia's allegations of rape. They all repeated the same content about her accusations and her suicide. But there was nothing to suggest any of it was connected to Max.

Sophie realised she needed to quickly produce the contract, so she'd have something to show for her time in the study. She put in the name of the client and changed the price, then went to save the contract on Max's computer. The computer suggested it saved it in a 'recent folder' – one named 'Security Photos'. She saved the document on his desktop instead, then went back and found the 'Security Photos' folder and clicked into it curiously. There was a subfolder with her name on. And another with Lydia's. And Felicity's.

She swallowed and clicked on her name. In her folder there were twenty photos. She felt sick as she clicked on the first one. It was of her in bed, asleep, her bare feet sticking out of the side of the bed. The next one was of her getting changed for bed, her naked body in the line of the camera.

Sophie's heart pounded. Max had been spying on them.

She opened the photos in Lydia's and Felicity's folders and found the same. Max had been watching all of them, taking intrusive photos. There must be cameras in the flat, trained on the bed.

There was another subfolder there, titled with just a random string of numbers. Sophie opened it and saw four photos. She could see immediately what they were. The photos that had been taken of her after Max's party.

FORTY-THREE

Sophie needed to get out of the chalet now. Max had been taking photos and videos of her through his security cameras. He had the photos taken of her after his party saved on his computer. She needed to find James, tell him what Max and Will had done. Get him to help her.

She tried to call him, but her phone reception wasn't good enough, and it disconnected before it even started ringing. There was no mobile data reception either. They were in the middle of nowhere.

She saw the Wi-Fi password by the computer and connected her phone to the internet, then tried to call James over WhatsApp. No answer.

She sent him a quick message. *Call me as soon as you can. I need to speak to you.*

A new message appeared on WhatsApp. It was from Felicity. She'd shared the article about Lydia accusing Will of rape.

Did you see this?

Sophie stared at the message for a moment, her mind whirring. She'd been ignoring Felicity because of everything James had said about her. But perhaps Felicity had the answers about Will and Max and what had happened to Lydia. She'd been right about the cameras in the house. Maybe she wasn't as crazy as James said she was.

Yeah I did. Poor Lydia.

Felicity replied immediately.

It was really awful for her. She went to the police, but I don't know if it went any further.

Sophie thought about when the police had turned up on her doorstep. The second allegation against Will. From Lydia. Lydia had lost everything. And then she'd taken her own life. Sophie wished she'd met her, wished she could have talked her out of it, told her that things would get better, that she could rebuild her life. Sophie shivered. She'd thought that was what she had done herself. But had she really? The life she had at One Pure Thought now seemed like a trap, a way of getting her back into Will's orbit, a way of punishing her.

Will must have been afraid of Sophie coming forward again. With Lydia's evidence, would the police have brought Will to justice?

I think the police were pursuing it, Sophie typed. *Before she died.*

I can't believe she's gone.

Sophie felt tears welling up in her eyes, thinking of Lydia's final weeks, how she was dealing with what had happened between her and Will, how she'd sought comfort in Max, but he'd just hurt her again. Max, who'd been filming them all.

You were right about the cameras. Max had set up cameras inside the flat. I've found the photos on his computer.

I knew it. James always tried to tell me that it was impossible, but I was sure of it. James was completely tied up in that company. He'd do anything for Max and Cassie. They worked him to the bone.

Felicity really hated the company. Sophie wondered if there was more to her unfair dismissal claim than James had told her.

She thought of Will in the other room. Had he hurt Felicity too?

Will has turned up here, Sophie typed. *I don't know what to do.*

Will? At the office?

No, we're at a retreat. On a golf course.

There was a pause and Sophie saw the three dots that showed Felicity was typing appear then disappear, then appear again.

At Max's father's golf course?

Yes...

With Will?

Yes

It happened there. Will raped Lydia on a company retreat at the golf course.

FORTY-FOUR

Sophie squeezed her eyes shut, trying to block out what was happening. Lydia was raped at the retreat. And now Sophie had been brought here too. To Will.

The job, the flat, the lifestyle. She'd embraced all of it. But had it always been a trap?

She needed to find James, tell him Will was here, that he was the man who had raped her at university. James would know what to do. She hesitated for a moment. What if she couldn't trust him either?

But there was no one else she could turn to. James had always treated her well, and just going to the same school didn't mean anything. James had a totally different personality to Max and Will. He'd always been kind to her.

Tentatively, she opened the door of the study, her heart racing. She didn't want to run into Will, or Max. The music was still thumping and she could see a crush of bodies in the living room. She went round the edge of the room, keeping close to the wall, trying to be smaller, to be inconspicuous. She scanned the groups of men standing chatting and lounging on the sofas, but couldn't see James. Quickly, she left and headed to the kitchen, but he wasn't there either. She glanced at the back door, leading out into a dark garden. Perhaps she should just leave now. She could hear boisterous laughter from the living room. She was aware of her vulnerability; she was the only woman there apart from Cassie, with a load of drunken men. She pushed open the back door and stepped into the cold night air, quietly shutting the door behind her. She stood leaning against the wall for a minute, taking deep breaths, wrapping her arms around herself to warm up. Beyond the sheltered veranda she could see snowflakes starting to fall, drifting back and forth in the breeze. The ground below was already coated in a thin layer of white.

She saw the spark of a lighter further along the back wall and looked towards it. The figures were shrouded in darkness. As the man brought the lighter and cigarette up to his face, she felt a flash of recognition. James.

He started coming over to her before she could say anything. Cassie was beside him, but she went through the double patio doors into the living room before she got to Sophie.

'What are you doing out here?' James asked kindly. 'It's freezing.' He put a guiding hand on her back. 'Let's get you back inside.'

'James – I've been trying to get hold of you. I need to talk to you.'

'Oh?'

Suddenly, Sophie felt exhausted. She didn't know where to start. Cassie had already slid away, but there might be others around. She didn't want them to overhear. She had no idea whose loyalty she would be testing if she said anything critical about Max.

'Maybe we should talk about this elsewhere. I...' But she was forced into silence as a crowd of men came out of the back door, laughing.

James led her through the door. 'Did you manage to sort out the contract?' he asked.

'Yeah, I did. But James—'

'Hi, buddy,' James said, patting someone on the back as they went by. He couldn't hear Sophie over the noise. 'Let me introduce you to our major clients,' he said, grabbing a bottle of red wine off the mantelpiece and pouring himself a glass. 'Have you got a drink?' he asked Sophie.

'No, I'm OK.' He didn't hear her, but he saw her shake her head.

'Look,' he said, 'these guys have a lot of money, and I want you to meet them, because I really think you might be able to work your magic on them, persuade them to use us as their ad agency. They work in banking, and they want a new campaign to target students. It could be the biggest project the company's ever seen, if we play our cards right.'

Sophie grabbed his arm, drew him back. Will worked in banking. She couldn't be in this room, risk seeing him again. Her heart was pounding fast, her palms sweating.

'James, I need to get out of here.'

His eyes crinkled in a mix of concern and irritation. 'Now? Really? Do you want me to come with you?'

'Yes, please.'

They walked over to the other chalet, Sophie's teeth chattering in the cold, as snow fell softly around them. James ushered her quickly into the house.

'Are you all right?' he asked.

'Yeah, I feel a bit better being away from the party.'

'OK.' He stroked her arm. 'But you're so cold. I can light the fire, warm us up.'

'That would be good.'

'So what's happened?' James asked, as he put firelighters in among the logs in the hearth and lit them with a cigarette lighter.

'Will's here.'

'Will? From Farman's?' James turned away from the fireplace towards Sophie. 'Yes, I've seen him. Have you been introduced?'

Sophie shook her head, swallowing her panic. James did know Will from school. She had to tell him what had happened. 'James, he's the man who raped me, back at university.'

'What?' James's eyes widened. 'Really? Are you sure it was him?'

'I'll always remember his face,' she said softly. She wished she could forget it. Sophie thought of Will's wink. She knew she hadn't got mixed up.

James reached out and squeezed her arm, hesitating for a moment. 'Will and I go back a long way. I just can't believe... he'd do something like that.'

'What about Lydia?'

James's eyes narrowed. 'She made all sorts of stuff up.' Behind him one of the logs caught light and the fire sprang into life. Sophie rubbed her hands together.

'She said she was raped by Will, didn't she?'

'Yeah, she did. But—'

Sophie felt anger rising inside her. She had just expected him to believe her. She hadn't been expecting him to question what she was saying. She was his girlfriend. He needed to trust her.

'James, she was telling the truth. He raped me too.'

James put his hands to his temples, his face creased in a frown. 'I'm just trying to get my head round all of this. We go back a long way. Me, Will and Max.'

Sophie sighed. 'Max is the same. He's had cameras up in my flat. He spied on me, Felicity and Lydia. He filmed us in the bedroom. Recording everything we did. I found the pictures on his computer when I was preparing the contract.'

'What?' James said, shocked. 'I've had my doubts about

Max recently, but I never thought he'd do anything like this.' He put his arms around Sophie. 'It makes me feel sick, thinking about him watching you, watching us.'

'Me too.'

'You poor thing. But don't worry,' he said. 'You're safe now. I'll be staying with you this evening. Sit down on the sofa, I'll make you a hot chocolate.'

James disappeared into the kitchen. When he came back, he brought her a jumper and a blanket along with the hot drink.

He sat down beside her. 'Here you go,' he said gently, as he stroked her hair.

'Thank you.'

James put his head in his hands. His eyes were bloodshot from tiredness and drink. 'I can't do business with Max anymore. I can't work with someone like that.'

Sophie almost cried with relief. He was on her side.

'You know Cassie and I are planning to set up our own company,' James said. 'We should do that as soon as we can, break away from Max. You can join us. If we can't get funding from Philip we can try and get it elsewhere.'

'That sounds like a good idea,' Sophie said. She felt a glimmer of hope that everything would be all right.

'Look,' James said. 'There's no point in staying at the retreat now. Not if we're both planning to leave the company. I'll call a taxi. Get us out of here.'

FORTY-FIVE

James pulled out his mobile phone and frowned at it. 'No reception. I'll go outside.'

Sophie watched him leave and shut the door behind him, wondering whether to lock it. She didn't feel safe with it unlocked, but surely James would be back soon. Outside the snow was getting heavier.

She stood by the door waiting for him to come back. He was right. They should leave tonight. She needed to get away from Max and Will.

The clock ticked on the wall. Five minutes passed. Then ten. Then twenty. Where was James? He was only supposed to be looking for phone reception. But then Sophie remembered her own difficulties. The only places with reception were the woods or all the way back at the main hotel building, which was several miles away.

Too much time had passed. Her breathing got faster as she took short, shallow gulps of air. She could still hear the echoes of the party next door. She looked at her phone, but it was useless without reception. There was no way of calling for help if she needed it.

Outside, the music was booming but inside her chalet was silent, except for the crackling of the fire. She wondered if anyone had noticed she'd gone, if anyone would come to look for her. As soon as they saw the lights in the chalet, they'd know where she was. What if Will or Max saw them? She quickly went round and turned the lights off and then sat down on the sofa. The only light came from the fire and the glow from her phone. She wished James would come back, that the taxi would arrive and they could get out of here.

Half an hour had passed now. It was too long. Maybe something had happened to James. Maybe she needed to find a taxi herself. If she walked out and tried to find a main road, maybe there'd be reception there.

She was just getting ready to leave when she heard a loud knock on the door. She stood frozen to the spot as the wooden door shook. Whoever was on the other side of the door wouldn't be able to see her. Surely they would go away.

The knocking got more insistent. What if it was Max? Or Will? Why hadn't she locked the door? Sophie's heart pounded.

'Sophie? Sophie? I know you're in there.' A woman. Not Cassie. Felicity.

Sophie stared at the door, unsure whether to let her in. She hadn't said she was coming. Why was she here?

Before Sophie could make up her mind, the door handle turned and Felicity was in front of her, one foot already through the door.

'Hi, I'm so glad I found you,' Felicity said. 'Can I come in?'

Sophie hesitated, looking at the snow falling behind her, whirling around in the wind and landing on Felicity's thick black coat. 'Sure,' she said.

Felicity came in, and Sophie felt a rush of relief that someone else was in the chalet with her. If Will or Max came now, she wasn't alone.

'Where's James?' Felicity asked.

'He's just gone to call a taxi. After I messaged you, I found him. He thinks we should get out of here.'

Felicity nodded. 'That's a good idea. But I need to talk to him. I've come all this way.'

'What do you want to talk to him about?'

Felicity narrowed her eyes. 'I'm not sure that's any of your business.' She was back to being the jealous girlfriend again, someone who didn't like the fact that Sophie was dating James. Sophie wished he'd come back.

'This is where they stayed last time, you know? These two chalets.' Felicity sat down on the sofa. It was warm indoors, but she kept her coat on, holding it tight around her.

'When Will attacked Lydia?'

Felicity nodded. 'Yeah.'

'What happened?'

'I wasn't here, Max and James had fired me by then. I'd tried to warn Lydia about the company but she hadn't listened. I only know what she told me about what happened. She got drunk when she was with the clients, she was having a good time and Will was flirting with her. He offered to take her out for a ride on the lake in Max's boat, and she went off with him through the woods. And then after that she couldn't really remember what happened, she'd blacked out. She thought she'd been drugged. When she came to, she was in a hut in the middle of nowhere, and it was obvious he'd had sex with her.'

'Oh,' Sophie said, struck by the similarities with what had happened to her. Will had a practised way of operating. How many other girls had he hurt? She wondered whether to confide in Felicity that he'd attacked her too. But she didn't know Felicity, didn't know if she could trust her. 'Poor Lydia,' she said softly.

'Yeah. She was so shaken up by it, she couldn't concentrate at all at work. She left in the end. The others were so nasty to her she could hardly stay. I'd persuaded her to join me in suing the company.'

Sophie nodded. 'It must have been awful for her. No wonder she was unhappy.'

'Yeah. None of them took her side, none of them believed her.'

Sophie thought about what James had said about Lydia. He hadn't believed her either. 'She must have felt so let down.'

'It was awful for her. She was seeing Max at the time, and they split up. He thought she was lying about what happened. He and Will had been friends for years. He chose Will over her.'

Sophie thought how convenient it was for Will that Lydia had gone. Her case against him surely wouldn't be going ahead now. Her stomach clenched in anger. She thought about how Max had spent time with her just before she died.

'She still had a thing for Max, didn't she? Cassie said he was mentioned in her suicide note.'

Felicity sighed. 'Yeah, she couldn't let him go. I think they'd started seeing each other again. That must have been why she was in the flat, I suppose, to meet him. I know she'd met up with Cassie too. They'd been friends before she left the agency.'

Sophie sighed. 'Cassie wished she could have done more.'

'Lydia was really the centre of things at the company for a short while,' Felicity said. 'Before she left, she was very highly regarded. It was just at the end they decided her work wasn't up to much. Before then everyone loved her. Even James.'

'Really?'

'He had a thing with her, too, you know.'

'What?' Sophie's eyes widened in surprise. James had never said anything complimentary about Lydia.

'Oh yes,' Felicity said. 'James is quite the ladies' man. He always tries to play the good guy to Max's rogue but in fact he's just as bad as Max. He just does it a bit more subtly. James slept with me when I was in that flat, then after the company fired me and Lydia moved in, he started sleeping with her. That was before she got together with Max. I think he was always pissed off about that, how Max got the girl.'

'I didn't know,' Sophie said, surprised by James's behaviour. She hadn't known he was friends with Will either. Maybe she didn't know him at all.

But she didn't know Felicity either. She thought of all the things James had said about her. That she was a jealous ex-girlfriend, that she'd stalked him. Had James really slept with Lydia, or was Felicity just jealous of any girl she saw him with? After all, James always welcomed new employees to the flats. He would have welcomed Lydia too.

'I bet there's a lot of things he hasn't mentioned to you,' Felicity said smugly.

'He's told me a lot about you.'

'Has he now?'

'He told me you were a stalker. That you were suing the company for revenge.'

'Well, that's not true.'

'So why did you decide to sue the company?'

'I was unfairly dismissed,' Felicity said. 'Pregnancy discrimination.'

'What?' Sophie said, completely taken by surprise. She stared at Felicity. She could see no discernible bump through her baggy black coat.

'Yes,' Felicity said. She parted her coat and it was there. A small, neat bump. Unmistakably a baby bump.

'I'm having James's baby,' she said.

Just then, the door swung open.

James had returned.

FORTY-SIX

'Sophie?' James walked into the living room and surveyed the scene before him, his face darkening when he saw Felicity. 'What are you doing here?' he said to her, his voice hard. 'You're not supposed to come anywhere near me.'

'I was just about to tell your girlfriend a few home truths. About who you really are. What you're really like.'

'Don't be ridiculous, Felicity.' He put a protective arm around Sophie. 'She's never going to believe your lies.'

'Well, I wasn't wrong about the fact the company's toxic. Or the cameras in the flat. And she can see I'm pregnant.' Felicity smiled smugly at Sophie. 'He didn't tell you that, did he?'

Sophie turned to James. 'Why didn't you mention it?'

'It's not my baby,' he said firmly.

'It *is* your baby,' Felicity said, her voice racked with emotion. 'I've told you it can't be anyone else's.'

Sophie's mind spun. Why would James deny the baby? Unless it wasn't his and Felicity had made the whole thing up. He had said that she had a vendetta against him, that ever since they'd split up, she'd tried to punish him.

Felicity turned to Sophie. 'You need to know what he's

really like. When he found out I was pregnant, he gave me money towards an abortion, offered to pay for counselling if I needed it. He wouldn't even admit it was his, but he was willing to pay me off.' Felicity's eyes flashed. 'That seems odd, doesn't it?'

'It wasn't like that!' James protested. 'I was just trying to help. I saw you'd got into trouble, I don't know who with. And I wanted to help. That's all.'

'How helpful did you think firing me would be?'

'That was Max's decision. You weren't doing any work.'

'I was ill with morning sickness. Carrying *your* baby.'

'You fired her because she was pregnant?' Sophie asked. It seemed unnecessarily cruel, not to mention illegal.

'It had to be done,' James said.

'You got rid of me to keep me quiet,' Felicity said. 'You didn't want anything to do with me and the baby.'

James shook his head. 'It wasn't like that.'

'It sounds like that,' Sophie said. 'Because if you hadn't wanted her to leave you could have supported her, insisted that she wasn't fired, helped her out.'

'I need you to acknowledge your baby,' Felicity said desperately. 'Don't deny him. He's your flesh and blood.'

'I'll think about it,' James said. 'If you can prove he's mine.'

'We'll do a paternity test.'

James shrugged. 'OK, then. If you insist. He turned to Sophie. 'Sophie, I've told you she's trouble. She's making things up, stirring things to disrupt our relationship. She's jealous.'

Sophie wasn't sure she believed either of them. Even if the baby wasn't his, James's callousness towards Felicity was hard to witness. But for now, Sophie just wanted to focus on getting out of here, before the snow got heavier.

'Did you sort out the taxi?' she asked James. 'You were gone ages.'

'No, I'm sorry. And I didn't mean to leave you so long. It

took me a long time to get reception. And there are no taxi firms willing to come out in this weather. They don't want to get stuck out here.'

'So we can't get out tonight? What about the minibus?'

James shook his head. 'The minibus went back to the clubhouse. I called them but there isn't a driver available until the morning.' Sophie's heart sank.

Just then, laughter rose in the air from the other chalet, and Sophie thought of Will and Max next door. 'I'm not safe here,' she said. She thought of Will's smirk, his wink. 'Max and Will have brought me here. I don't know why. But I think they want to punish me. I need to leave.'

Felicity looked up. 'I'd better go too,' she said. She looked at James. 'I don't know why I ever thought you cared about me,' she said. 'I really thought that if I came here today, and asked you to support your child, there was a chance that you would. I thought you might turn back into the James I loved. But that was never the real you, was it? It was all an act.'

James shook his head. 'Just leave, Felicity. Get out of my life.'

Sophie winced at his harsh tone.

'Can I come with you?' she asked Felicity.

Felicity looked from her to James and back again. 'Sure,' she said. 'It's not you I have a problem with. My car's in the car park. Follow me.'

FORTY-SEVEN

'Are you sure you'll be OK?' James asked, as Sophie grabbed a moth-eaten coat from the understairs cupboard in the chalet. She'd left hers at the party.

'Of course she'll be fine,' Felicity snarled.

Sophie nodded.

'I'm going to go back to the other chalet,' he said. 'I need to speak to Cassie about everything you've told me. Work out what to do about Max.'

He came over and kissed Sophie lightly on the cheek. She realised in that moment that their relationship was well and truly over. She couldn't trust him anymore. Not after the way he'd behaved towards Felicity. 'See you later, James,' she said.

He shrugged on his coat and went out the door.

'Let's go,' Sophie said, turning to Felicity.

'I wanted to show you something quickly first,' Felicity said, as they stood by the door. 'Look at this.' She took out her phone and unlocked the screen.

It was the end of the newspaper article she'd seen earlier, the one about Lydia accusing Will of rape. 'Look at the comments,' Felicity said. 'I screenshotted them so we can see them offline. I've sent you the pictures.'

Sophie took the phone and read the comments.

I've heard of this guy. He had a reputation for being handsy.

I went to school with him. Everyone knew what he was like even back then.

He assaulted me too, when I was working for him.

There were more comments, people who'd heard rumours, people whose friends had confided in them, people who knew not to be alone with him. And people like Sophie and Lydia, who'd been raped by him.

'Oh my God,' Sophie said, thinking back to university when she'd gone to the police. She hadn't known there'd been so many others.

Felicity smiled. 'I think he'll finally get what's coming to him. Surely they can't ignore all this?'

Sophie nodded, thinking of Lydia. Any justice would be too late for her.

And Will was still here, in the other chalet.

'Let's get going,' she said.

They stepped out into the freezing night air, a sea of white around them. Sophie didn't have the right shoes for the snow, and the moisture quickly soaked through.

'How far is it to the car?' she asked Felicity.

'About ten minutes.' She indicated the dark woods in front of them. 'The path's through here.' Felicity switched on her phone's torch and held it up, revealing a wooden sign to the car park.

They crunched through the snow-dusted twigs in the woodland, overshadowed by the looming trees, the light of her phone guiding the way. Sophie could still hear the noise from the party, the laughter, but as she got further into the woods, less of the light from the chalet cut through the trees and she felt more and more isolated. In front of her, Felicity led the way without speaking. Sophie wished she wasn't wearing a dress. The heavy coat only covered her thighs and her knees were bare. When she reached down to touch them, they were icy.

'Is it much further?'

'Not too far.'

Felicity walked on ahead, checking her phone.

There was a rustling sound behind Sophie and she jumped. Her breathing quickened as she looked behind her and then all around her. Away from Felicity's torchlight, the wood was pitch-black. She sensed movement, perhaps an animal making its way through the undergrowth, looking for shelter.

'Sophie?' She froze as a man stepped out of the shadows.

Max. She shrank away from him, but he took a step closer.

'Are you OK?' he asked.

She couldn't answer, her voice trapped inside her, her heart pounding.

Up ahead she saw Felicity turn around and start to walk back towards them. Max hadn't seen her.

Max reached out and touched Sophie's arm. She withdrew, rapidly stepping backwards. As she did, she found her voice, letting out a piercing scream.

'What's wrong?' he asked. 'You ran away. You seem upset. Not yourself.'

'I'm fine,' she said, her eyes darting round the wood, looking for a way to escape.

'Really? I've been concerned about you. You seemed... well, I thought there might be something wrong.'

'Get away from me,' she said, her voice a whimper.

But he was stepping closer.

Then she saw a flash of light from Felicity's phone behind him. Felicity was running towards him. As he turned in surprise, she shoulder-barged him, the unexpected force of it knocking him down into the snow.

'Felicity?' he said from the ground.

'You were watching us,' Felicity said, spitting out the words at him as he tried to get up. 'Filming us. How could you?'

He was starting to stand now, and Sophie didn't want to stick around. She grabbed Felicity's arm and pulled her away. They started to run.

Behind them, Max called after them. 'It wasn't me,' he shouted. 'I didn't film anyone.'

FORTY-EIGHT

Sophie ran over the uneven ground, Felicity beside her. She slipped for a moment on an icy log, but then recovered. After a few minutes they stopped, breathless and panting.

'We're away from him now,' Sophie said. 'I can't believe you knocked Max down. Thank you.' She'd been terrified of what he might do to her.

Felicity grinned. 'I used to play rugby when I was at school. It felt good. Punishing him for all the things he's done.' Her tone sharpened. 'I wish I'd hit him harder. Really hurt him.'

Sophie frowned, a shiver of doubt running through her, wondering what Felicity was capable of. But at least she was on Sophie's side now. They just needed to get to the car.

'Let's keep going,' she said. She pointed ahead of her. 'Is it this way?'

Felicity frowned, looking around her. 'I'm not sure. We're not on the path anymore.' She pulled out her phone from her pocket and looked at the map.

Sophie peered over her shoulder. The blue dot that showed their location was in a white expanse of emptiness.

'I don't think our location's updated,' Felicity said. 'It's not very accurate out here.'

Sophie swallowed and looked around them. Light snow had started to fall again. She hoped they weren't lost.

'Which way did we come from?' she asked, already unsure. In every direction there was the same view. Endless snow-coated trees.

'That way, I think,' Felicity said, pointing. 'But we don't want to run into Max again.'

'No.' They stood for a moment, unsure what to do. Sophie checked her phone for reception, but there still wasn't any.

'Let's go this way,' Felicity said decisively, pointing down a slight slope. 'I'm sure it's the right direction. I remember walking uphill from the car park.'

Sophie nodded, feeling a growing sense of unease as they set off again. She thought of the stories she'd sometimes read in the papers. Underdressed girls found dead from hypothermia. Boys, too, lost on their way home, falling over drunkenly and resting in the snow. Dead in the morning.

'Hello?' a voice called out. A woman's voice. Cassie. Relief surged through Sophie as Cassie appeared in front of them.

'James said you were out here. He was worried you might get lost.'

'We're fine,' Felicity said quickly.

'Where are you going?' Cassie asked, frowning at Felicity.

'We're—' Sophie paused, not sure if James would have had time to tell Cassie what her brother had done. 'I'm not feeling well,' she said. 'So I'm going home.'

Cassie sighed. 'Is that the real reason? James mentioned something about Max.'

'Felicity was right about the cameras,' Sophie said. 'I found the images on Max's computer. He put cameras in that flat, even in the bedroom. He's been watching us.'

'The bastard,' Cassie said, shaking her head, as she looked

from Felicity to Sophie. 'I mean, I knew he was an idiot, but this... this is just beyond belief.'

'I can't stay here,' Sophie said. 'Not with him.' She didn't mention Will. It was too difficult to explain.

'Oh, I see. Of course.'

'Which way's the car park?'

'The car park?'

'Yes, Felicity's got her car here. She's going to give me a lift back to London.'

Cassie frowned. 'Oh, it's that way,' she said, pointing down the slope. 'It's in a little dip at the bottom of the wood. But you can't go there. You won't be able to get out. The cars there are completely snowed in.'

Sophie's stomach turned.

'Why don't you come back with me?' Cassie said. 'To our chalet.'

Sophie looked back towards the direction Cassie had come from. She couldn't go back to the chalets, not after all this. Not now. She shook her head. 'I really... just want to get home.'

Cassie suddenly smiled. 'Oh,' she said, 'I've just realised. We can go by boat. I can whizz you across the lake to the clubhouse in no time. You can call a taxi from there. It's all main roads round there, and they've been gritted. You should be able to get out tonight.'

FORTY-NINE

Sophie was flooded with relief. She wanted to hug Cassie, but she resisted the urge. 'Thank you so much,' she said, unable to find the words to convey her gratitude. She was getting out of here, escaping.

'It's nothing,' Cassie said. 'It's easy to give you both a ride over on the boat. And besides, it's Max's fault you feel like this. Let's get going. The pier's this way.'

Cassie led them to the little wooden hut at the foot of the pier. It seemed like a lifetime ago when Sophie had first seen the pier and the hut when she'd arrived on Cassie's boat earlier in the day.

Felicity stopped in her tracks and pulled Sophie towards her by the arm, pointing at the hut. 'I think this is where it happened,' she said. 'Where Will brought Lydia...'

'Oh,' Sophie said, her stomach tightening with anxiety.

As they looked towards it, the door of the hut swung open suddenly and Sophie and Felicity both jumped.

James. Sophie stared at him in shock. Why was he here?

'I'm coming too,' he said to Cassie. 'I changed my mind.'

Sophie stared at him. Changed his mind? How did he know

they'd leave on the boat? Cassie must have spoken to him. Her hands started to sweat despite the cold. Something wasn't right. But she just needed to get away. It wasn't far to the other side of the lake. Soon she'd be there, at the clubhouse. Away from Max and Will and close to civilisation.

Cassie glared at James, and Sophie wondered if they'd argued. 'You always want to be the saviour, don't you, James?' she said, standing in his way, blocking him from coming onto the pier.

He stepped towards her. 'Cassie, let me on.'

'You wouldn't hurt me, would you?' she said threateningly. Sophie saw the glint of a knife in her hand.

'I carry it for self-protection,' Cassie said quickly, when she saw Sophie looking at it. 'You need it with the men around here.' Sophie thought of Will, all the comments on the article, the multiple accusations of rape. Had Cassie been assaulted by him too?

'I just want to come on the boat,' James said to Cassie. 'Make sure Sophie gets to the other side safely. You've been drinking.'

Sophie glanced at Cassie. She seemed so calm and collected. Not drunk at all.

'Don't be silly. I could steer the boat with my eyes closed. I think you'll find I'm not quite as accident-prone as you.'

It sounded like a threat. And then suddenly Cassie pushed James into the little hut. He stumbled drunkenly backwards, through the door. 'You're not coming with us,' she said. She glanced at Sophie. 'I know what you did now, James. I know everything.'

'What are you talking about?' James slurred his words. Sophie wanted an answer too. James had been hiding so much from her. He wasn't the man she'd thought he was.

'You know what I'm talking about.'

'Sophie, I—' James looked at her pleadingly. But Cassie was pushing him hard into the room, holding the knife towards him.

'Help me move him,' she called out to Felicity. Felicity rushed over and together they manhandled him into a chair. James slumped into it. He seemed much drunker than when Sophie had seen him in the chalet.

Sophie shivered as she thought of Lydia in this hut with Will, surrounded by boating paraphernalia. Old life vests, rowing oars and a long-forgotten kayak. A shoe rack full of flip-flops and deck shoes. She noticed the shelf to her left. The tools that lined it: hammers, nails, duct tape.

Cassie grabbed the duct tape and chucked it to Felicity.

'There – tie him up.'

'What?' Sophie said. 'No!' Whatever Cassie was angry about, this seemed too much. Unless James had something to do with everything that had happened. Unless he was in on it with Will and Max.

Cassie turned to her calmly. 'I think you'll change your mind when you hear what he did.'

'Don't listen to her, Sophie!' James shouted desperately.

Felicity was busy gleefully putting the duct tape round his waist, securing him to the chair, while Cassie held him in place. Sophie remembered all the times James had said Felicity was crazy, how she'd keyed his precious car. She thought of how she'd barrelled into Max, knocking him over. She was fearless.

Cassie went over to James and placed a final strip of tape over his mouth. 'There you go,' she said, smiling. 'How do you like that, James?'

He shook his head violently, his shouts smothered by the tape.

Sophie's face tightened. A part of her felt sorry for him. 'What's he done?' she said softly. She needed to know. Things were getting out of control.

Outside the window, the snow had stopped. She lifted up

her phone. Still no reception. No data either, although at some time she must have briefly connected, because a WhatsApp message had come through. It was just from Felicity, with the screenshots of the newspaper article.

James was screaming through the duct tape, wriggling in his chair, banging the legs into the floor.

'What did he do?' Sophie asked again. She thought about Felicity, how he'd got her pregnant and then abandoned her, letting her get fired from her job.

Cassie sighed. 'I'm so sorry, Sophie, but James never cared about you. He just went out with you because Max paid him to.'

'What?' Sophie's heart plummeted in her chest. Had their whole relationship been a lie? And why would Max pay him to date her?

'Max wanted to keep an eye on you. He knew you'd accused his friend of assault, and he wanted to protect him. And when he saw you were looking for a job, he knew it was a way to get closer to you. You know what they say. Keep your friends close and your enemies closer. So he insisted we employ you.'

Sophie thought of Philip. She'd been right. Max was exactly like his father.

'Max was watching what I was doing? He knew I was applying for jobs?' He must have been the one protecting Will all along, sending the threatening emails.

'Yeah,' Cassie said. 'He started watching you again when Lydia accused Will of rape. He was worried about what you might do to his friend. He knew you wouldn't keep quiet if you found out, that you'd talk to the police again. Once he had you working at his company, Max made sure he was tracking you on your work computer and your phone. James put spyware on your personal phone, too.'

Sophie turned to James, but he wouldn't look at her. She remembered him telling her he was deleting the spyware that

Charlie had put on her phone. That must have been a lie. He'd been installing his own. Was it true that James had only dated her for money? When she thought about it, it made sense. He'd flirted with her from the first day, always been kind to her, never put a foot wrong. She could tell from the way he was staring at the floor that Cassie wasn't making it up. He'd completely betrayed her, never loved her. He'd only ever wanted money. Her heart felt like it had been torn in two. How could he do that to her? All the time he had been listening to her, sympathising with her, it had all been an act. He had let her cry on his shoulder about Will, when he'd known exactly who Will was. Will was his friend. He'd been helping Will all along.

FIFTY

'I'm so sorry, Sophie,' Cassie said, 'but we'd better get on the boat.' She glanced out the window. 'The snow's stopped for now, but the weather's due to get worse.'

Felicity stood up to leave too. 'No,' Cassie said. 'You sit down. I'll come back for you. We need someone to stay with James.'

Felicity smiled down at James in the chair. 'Maybe I'll enjoy that,' she said, as he squirmed.

Cassie climbed onto the motorboat and switched on its lights. Sophie shielded her eyes from the sudden brightness and saw Cassie standing on the deck, the skirt of her blue dress billowing around her, under her dark coat. She held out her hand and Sophie climbed up beside her. She felt sick with relief. She was finally going to get away from the golf retreat, and everyone in it.

She could hardly believe that Max and James had been helping Will all this time, trying to undermine her, trying to stop her talking to the police. She'd always suspected that there was something off about Max, but James... she had thought she was falling in love with him. And now this.

Cassie wrapped Sophie in a hug. 'I'm so sorry about what my brother and James did,' she said, putting her cold hands on Sophie's shoulders. 'But don't worry. I'll get you to the clubhouse in no time.'

Sophie nodded and sat on the deck, looking over the vast expanse of the lake. She could just make out the lights of the clubhouse on the other side. She couldn't wait to get there, call a taxi and get out of here. She thought of James, how she had always turned to him for protection, had thought she could trust him. He'd never wanted to protect her. In the end it had been Cassie and Felicity who had helped her. Without them, she'd have been trapped at the chalets.

'I'll get you a drink,' Cassie said. 'Hot chocolate – it will warm you up.'

Cassie went down into the tiny kitchen area in the hull and made the drink, placing it in a takeaway cup with a lid. Sophie took it from her gratefully.

She took a sip and was surprised by the sharp taste.

'I added a shot of whisky,' Cassie said with a smile. 'Shall we get going?'

Sophie nodded, desperate to be on her way.

Cassie went to the helm of the boat and turned on the motor.

They set off, cutting through the lake's icy waters. Sophie tilted her head back and felt the freedom of the cold night air on her face. The hum of the engine drowned out any distant sounds of the party, and for a moment she imagined she was completely alone, completely free. The hot chocolate was warming her up now, but she longed to go inside in the clubhouse and feel the blast of the heater.

Suddenly, the engine faltered and then cut out. Sophie jolted forward.

'Is something wrong?' Sophie asked Cassie, in alarm. They were in the middle of the lake.

Cassie smiled at her. 'Don't worry, Sophie,' she said. 'Nothing's wrong. I always wanted to stop here.'

'But we need to get back to the clubhouse,' Sophie said, overcome by confusion.

Cassie smirked, her pretty face contorting. 'No, we don't. We need to talk. I've brought you here to introduce you to someone.'

And then Sophie saw him, the broad shape coming up the stairs from below deck. She recognised him immediately and shrank away from him. But there was nowhere she could escape to in the boat.

'This is my husband,' Cassie said. 'Will.'

FIFTY-ONE

'What?' Sophie said, staring at Will as he reached the top of the stairs. Fear rose in her and threatened to choke her. She took a step back, away from them both, bumping into the edge of the boat. There was nowhere to run.

'I said, Will's my husband.' Cassie reached for his hand, then kissed him gently on the lips, before turning to Sophie. She shook her long, wavy hair behind her head, casually. 'We've been a couple for ten years. Since school. We're strong together. We've supported each other through thick and thin.'

'Sorry?' Sophie said, her head spinning as she tried to comprehend what was happening. 'You're married to him? But you know what he did?'

Will smirked, draping his arm round Cassie. 'Cassie's always stood by me. I don't know what I'd have done without her.' Sophie's body tensed at the sound of his voice as she looked from him to Cassie. In the distance, she could hear the faint sounds of the party continuing in the chalet.

'Especially when you made those malicious allegations against him,' Cassie said. 'He was in quite a state then. I really had to look out for him.'

Sophie's heart rate quickened, as her hands clenched into fists by her sides. 'You mean you supported him when I accused him of rape?' Sophie thought of everything Cassie had told her about James and Max back in the hut. Had she been in on everything too? Had she helped them to target her? Beneath them, the icy water lapped at the sides of the boat.

'You were lying, Sophie. You withdrew the case, remember?'

Was that how she had seen it? That withdrawing the case meant she'd been lying?

'Of course I remember. But I wasn't lying. There wasn't enough evidence to proceed.'

'Oh, grow up, Sophie. There wasn't enough evidence because you made it up. That's why he brought a private prosecution against you. To stop your vicious lies ruining his career.'

Sophie felt the tears welling in her eyes. They hadn't ruined his career. The only person's career that had been affected was hers. When she'd been forced to drop out of university.

'I wasn't lying,' she repeated. The fog was clearing in Sophie's brain, things were becoming clearer. 'It wasn't Max who sent me those threatening messages, was it? It was you,' she said. 'You sent me those messages saying I was a liar, you set up websites about me, you threatened to share photos.'

Cassie nodded, smiling. 'It was the only way to make you stop targeting him.'

Sophie struggled to absorb what she was saying. It was Cassie who'd been tormenting her all these years.

'Max didn't insist on me being employed at One Pure Thought, did he? That was you, too. You're the one who wants to protect Will.'

She nodded. 'When Lydia accused Will of assault, I knew the police would want to contact you. I tried to track you down, scare you off again. But I could only find an email address. And then your friend posted that LinkedIn post saying you were looking for a job. With your name in the post! That was stupid, wasn't it? When you'd been religiously avoiding social media for so many years to get away from me. But it seemed like fate. The perfect chance to get you here, right in front of me where I could see you. To manipulate you. To make sure you couldn't do anything to hurt Will. To make you pay for what you did.'

Sophie remembered Cassie at her interview, how friendly she'd been. How welcoming she and James had seemed. 'And James? Was he really in on all this? Or was it just you all along?' Sophie thought of Cassie tying James up in the hut, and felt filled with remorse that she hadn't done anything to help him. Had he been innocent? He hadn't wanted her to get on the boat with Cassie alone. This was why. He knew who she was, who she was married to.

'I paid him to date you,' Cassie said, shattering Sophie's illusions about James. 'Not Max. And he knew it was about Will. He was just happy to take the money. Will has known James since school. They were friends, although not close. James was always a social climber and Will wasn't interested. James was just a scholarship boy, always lusting after the other boys' wealth, totally uncouth. But he was good at one thing: spying on women. It's what he always did. We found out he set security cameras up at the flat when Felicity put in a formal complaint. Of course, we let her believe that Max set up the cameras. In fact, we wanted everyone to believe he had set them up. We thought we might be able to oust Max from the company if people thought it was him. My father hates a scandal.' She laughed. 'Although he does attract them himself.'

Sophie felt sick. James had set up the cameras. Not Max. James was the one who'd spied on her. James had dated her for money. She'd thought Cassie and James were her friends. She'd trusted the wrong people. The whole new life that she thought she'd found had been a mirage. She hadn't escaped her past; it had been there all along, waiting in the shadows to catch up with her.

'James didn't need much persuading to date you,' Cassie continued. 'He was never picky. I think he might have done it without us paying him. After all, he was quite attached to that flat. He'd dated the two employees who'd lived there before you. When he dated you, we asked him to find out everything about what you were thinking, doing, feeling. And stop you going to the police. Maybe undo you a bit, too, your mental health. We wanted to make you suffer.'

FIFTY-TWO

Sophie stared at Cassie, shocked by her cruelty. Around them the lake was still, barely a ripple on the water. Sophie could see the lights of the hotel ahead and when she looked the other way she could just make out the little hut. No one except Felicity and James knew they were here. They might as well be hundreds of miles away. No one would come to look for them.

'Why don't you just withdraw your lies, Sophie?' Cassie asked, angrily.

'Because they aren't lies. I can understand you believing him over me. But Lydia too? Isn't that too much of a coincidence?'

'Not when someone's got money. It's no coincidence at all. Lots of girls like you come out of the woodwork. They just want paying off. The same thing happened to my father. Will explained to me how you'd been coming on to him that night. I know he slept with you. It was a huge mistake for him. But you threw yourself at him.'

Sophie stared at Cassie defiantly as the water lapped below them. 'I didn't. I didn't want to sleep with him. He drugged me.' She glared at Will, who was watching them in silence.

'You disgust me,' Cassie said, stepping towards Sophie, so close they were almost touching. 'You were jealous of our relationship. You only accused him because he didn't want to date you, because he went back to me. You wanted to punish him for being with me.'

So that's what Will had told Cassie. That Sophie was a jealous ex-lover. Not his victim. 'That's not true. I didn't even know he had a girlfriend.'

'No one believes you, Sophie. And look what happened to the last money-grabbing girl. Lydia's gone now,' Cassie sneered. 'I saw her just before she died. Gave her a few home truths.'

Sophie's heart raced. Did Cassie have something to do with Lydia's death? Sophie looked down at the cold water, then glanced towards the shore. She'd swum in the cold sea in Dorset, but this was something else. The temperature was below freezing and the shore was over a mile away. She wouldn't make it.

'What do you mean about Lydia?' Sophie asked, although she wasn't sure she wanted to know. She thought about how Cassie had tied James up. She was capable of violence.

'Oh, nothing. I just met her before she died. In the flat. She thought she was meeting Max. I emailed her pretending to be him, said his phone was broken. But then I turned up and surprised her. Reminded her that no one was on her side, that we had photos of her.'

'And that was the night she died?'

Cassie nodded smugly. 'Yeah. But I can't be blamed for that. That was her own doing.'

'I don't know how you could do that,' Sophie said incredulously, thinking about how Cassie had threatened Lydia with photos too. They must have been the ones from the cameras in the flat.

'You've seen the photos we have of you,' Cassie said. 'We

can send them to everyone you know. Your father, your friends, everyone at the office.'

The photos from Max's party. Cassie must have been there at her flat, after the party. But Sophie had already told the police about the photos. She refused to be scared anymore, refused to be ashamed.

'Were you with me in the flat that night? When the blond guy was there? Did you know who he was?' Cassie had told her he was a stranger, but now Sophie wasn't so sure. She looked at Will, desperately praying it hadn't been him.

Cassie smiled. 'There was no blond guy. I made him up. It was me and James there that night. He's quite the photographer. I wanted to make you feel like anything could have happened to you. To know how it really feels to be hurt.'

Sophie took a sharp intake of breath. James had been there that night. James, who'd messaged her the next day and sat and listened as she poured her heart out in the coffee shop, admitting she didn't know what had happened the night before and that she had bruises. James, who got her out of the house, so Cassie could get the cleaner round just to be sure there was no sign of him or Cassie from the night before. 'Did James give me the bruises?' she asked, her voice breaking.

Cassie looked pleased with herself. 'You think that badly of him now, do you? No, he didn't do that to you. He was there in the room, though, with you passed out on the bed. I asked him to hurt you, but he wouldn't. He's not that kind of guy. Doesn't get the same thrill out of hurting people as he gets out of spying on women and chasing after money. That's why he didn't want you to come on the boat. He thought I might hurt you. He had some crazy instinct to protect you. I had to give you the bruises myself. And I must say, I enjoyed it.' Cassie spoke with relish.

'You're sick,' Sophie said. But a part of her was relieved that the bruises had only been Cassie, that nothing worse had happened.

'Maybe. But you're the one with photos of you out there. Ones that could easily be sent on.'

'Do what you like,' Sophie said calmly. 'You've already committed a crime, taking the photos and sending them to me. I've told the police about it.'

Cassie laughed. 'Are you saying you really don't care? Don't care that everyone will see your ugly body?' Sophie thought of the time she and Cassie had tried on dresses together, how Cassie had swiped away her concerns about her back fat and told her she was beautiful. Their friendship had all been an act.

Sophie shrugged. 'I said, I don't care. I'm going to keep telling the truth.' Sophie looked at Will, her palms sweating. He hadn't said a word.

'You need to stop talking to the police,' Cassie said firmly. 'Otherwise Will's career will be damaged forever. He's on the cusp of becoming someone. He should be elected as an MP. We've been working on this for years. You can't ruin it for him.'

Will ran his hand through his floppy hair, still styled the same way as it was at university. 'Come on, Sophie,' he said gently, as if talking to a flighty child. 'It was all so long ago, wasn't it? A he said/she said scenario. You can't remember anything, and the police put the idea in your head that I'd assaulted you. I don't blame you. If I blame anyone I blame the police.'

Sophie stared at him, struck by how calm he was. As if he fully expected to be able to talk himself out of it. 'There were others too,' Sophie said, looking at Cassie. 'Not just me and Lydia.'

Sophie reached for her phone in her pocket. Felicity had sent her the screenshots of the comments on the newspaper article. She went into her WhatsApp messages and found them.

'Look,' she said to Cassie. 'Look here. All these other people say Will did the same to them.'

Cassie glanced at the phone, then took it from her hand, began to scroll through.

Will suddenly loomed over them and snatched the phone from her and threw it overboard, into the water. The proof was gone.

'You bitch,' Will said, his voice low and aggressive. He was right beside Sophie now, leaning towards her, his spittle landing on her face. 'What gives you the right to show her that?'

Cassie's face was reddening. 'She just wants to hurt us. We can't let her do this to us, Will. You realise everything we have to lose? Our whole future. If the police believe her, you could go to prison. And then how would we start a family? How would we continue our lives together? You'd lose your job, we'd lose our home. Everything. She can't do that.'

Will shook his head. 'She needs to learn a lesson.'

Cassie turned to Sophie. 'I was starting to like you,' she said, 'when we were working together. But I was completely wrong about you. You haven't changed. And I won't let you destroy my life.'

Sophie needed to get away from them. She looked out at the vast expanse of freezing water. She wouldn't survive long in that. There was nowhere she could go.

Suddenly, Will stepped forward and pushed her right up against the edge of the boat. She struggled away from him, bending over and slipping out of his grip and running to the other side. Cassie grabbed her arm and tried to pull her towards Will. She was stronger than she looked and Sophie couldn't quite escape her grip. Then Will caught her other arm and they were dragging her to the edge of the boat. Sophie fought as hard as she could, thinking of the ice-cold water. She kicked out at them and tried to scratch them with her nails, but they had a firm grip. She was at the edge of the boat now and they were lifting her up. She pulled at Will's polo shirt as she dangled over the edge, and managed to get a grip on the material. She clung on, but it wasn't enough; she was no match for both of them. Cassie gave her one final push and she tumbled over the edge.

FIFTY-THREE

Sophie free-fell through the air, her coat flailing around her like wings. She hit her head on the sparkling-white side of the boat as she went down and landed awkwardly on the water, its surface slapping her legs and arms. The ice-cold water shocked her system and she felt herself sinking, her coat weighing her down and pulling her under. She focused on trying to peel it off. The waterlogged material clung to her arms, and it took every ounce of energy she possessed to remove it. She could feel her body tiring as she struggled to tread water, each movement laboured in the freezing cold. Terror gripped her chest as she tried to focus on breathing. She wriggled out of her clinging dress, tied a knot in the middle and blew it up before tying the other end, so she could use it as a float. It was something she'd learned years ago in her school's water survival class, but she'd never expected it to come in useful. The makeshift float was helpful, but it wasn't enough. The water was too cold to survive for long.

She needed to swim to shore. It was a shorter distance to the hut than the clubhouse, so she turned that way and forced herself to start moving. She managed a hundred metres or so using the makeshift float to support her, focusing hard on every stroke, keeping her eyes trained on the hut. The freezing water restricted her throat, and she felt like her body was shutting down. But then she heard a noise behind her. Cassie had turned on the engine of the boat.

The boat started to come towards her and for a second her jumbled mind let in a glimmer of hope that Cassie might regret her actions, realising how it would look if Sophie died in the water. But she knew in her heart there was no chance of Cassie showing any mercy. As the boat got closer, it gained speed. It wasn't coming to pick her up. Whoever was driving wanted to hit her.

Sophie ducked under the water, trying to hide. She kept her eyes open, turning to look at where the boat was, and then swimming as fast as she could out of its path. They must have lost sight of her because suddenly the boat started turning to the left, and slowing down. She had to come up for air. Her lungs were burning. She forced her way up to the surface, taking in huge gulps of the cold night air.

The dark was on her side now, and if she just stayed still, perhaps they wouldn't spot her. But she wouldn't survive if she stayed in the water much longer.

There was a shout from the boat. 'There she is,' Will shouted.

She saw Cassie turn her face towards her and start to steer the boat her way.

But then there was another sound on the lake. A second boat. She saw it bouncing over the water towards her. She recognised it. Max's boat. Was he coming to help his sister?

Sophie cowered. She thought about hiding, but if she hid now, she would surely die of hypothermia.

Then she noticed Cassie had turned off her engine.

Max pulled up beside Cassie. 'What's going on?' he shouted.

Sophie didn't hear the reply. Her body shivered violently, as she trod water. Soon torchlight was on her, temporarily blinding her. Max's speedboat was coming towards her. She didn't know what to do. If she ducked under the water he could hit her by mistake, but if she stayed above the surface... he might hit her on purpose. But she couldn't stay in the cold water either.

She was still trapped in her indecision when he pulled up beside her... and outstretched his arms to pull her on board.

FIFTY-FOUR

Sophie looked at Max in terror as she pulled herself into the boat, her body shaking with cold. She was dressed in only her underwear, the rest of her clothes abandoned to the lake.

'What do you want from me?' she asked him.

'You're freezing,' he said. 'We need to get you warmed up and then to shore. I've got some spare clothes in the cabin.' She stared after him as he disappeared down the stairs and returned with a pair of joggers and a hoodie.

'Go downstairs, change into these quickly. You can have my coat too.'

She hurried downstairs into the cabin, then took off her sodden underwear and slipped the joggers and hoodie on, struggling to use her numb fingers, which had turned blue. Her hair clung to her face in freezing clumps and she wrapped it in a towel. When she went back on deck, Max handed her his coat and she put it on.

'Why are you here? Why did you come for me?' Sophie's heart was thudding. Max had rescued her; he was treating her kindly. But he was friends with Will. He was Cassie's sister. He couldn't be on her side.

'What do you mean? I came out to check you were OK. You and Felicity ran away from me earlier. You seemed distressed. And then I saw Cassie's boat was missing... and I was worried about you.'

'Why?' she asked, perplexed. She rubbed her hands together, trying to warm herself up.

'I've been worried about you for a long time. I saw what James was doing to you. The same thing he'd done to Felicity, reeling you in, ready to spit you out later when he was bored. And I didn't know what to do. I tried to hint to you that he was bad news, that you should stay away from him, but I didn't know how to get the message through.'

'Oh,' Sophie said. She thought of how he'd said he didn't understand what she saw in James, how he'd pulled her away from him in the pub. He hadn't been trying to invade her space; he'd been trying to keep James away from her. 'I thought you and James were friends,' she said.

He laughed. 'We were. Not anymore. You know he'd put cameras in the flat. He'd been taking secret photos of the girls who lived there.'

'How did you find out?'

'Well, Felicity reported it when she left, but I didn't believe her. I just thought she was angry with James. And I understood why. He'd abandoned her, insisted she was fired. But later, I found the files in the company shared folders. At first I didn't understand why he'd left them there, why he hadn't password-protected them, but now I think he was trying to set me up. He hoped my father would have to take the company away from me, give it to him and Cassie.'

'I think you're right,' Sophie said, thinking of what Cassie had said to her earlier.

'We need to get you back to the shore,' he said. 'But not yet. I'm worried about my sister. Did she seem all right?'

'Cassie pushed me over,' Sophie said.

'Oh, God. I'm so sorry.' Max's face went pale. 'She's been so angry lately. She was furious with Lydia, before Lydia died. It's all to do with Will. I realised who you were this evening. Everything clicked into place. Why Cassie was so obsessed with you. You're the girl who accused him of rape at university.'

'He raped me, Max. I was telling the truth.'

Max nodded. 'I was always on his side before, believed that he'd never do it. But lately, after Lydia accused him too – well, I've started to revisit the past, remembered the rumours that always circulated at school about him taking advantage of girls at parties, how he boasted about it. Before Lydia died, I'd got back in touch with her. I felt guilty about how I treated her. She went into her shell after what happened with Will. And the fact that I didn't believe her tore her apart. It was inevitable we'd split up. Cassie wanted her to leave the company and she did, without too much fuss. I guess she wanted to get away from us all. I let her go... When we started speaking again, she told me more about what had happened with Will, and I realised that it was probably true. Lydia was a good person. I think there might have been something still there between us... but then...'

'...she died.'

'Yeah,' Max's eyes filled with tears. 'I'm sorry, Sophie. For what you've been through. For what Lydia went through.'

Sophie swallowed. Somehow she had got Max completely wrong. He wasn't the one to be afraid of. 'It wasn't your fault. Cassie was with her before she died. She'd emailed her pretending to be you, asking to meet Lydia at the flat. And then she... well, she must have been horrible to her. I know she threatened to share naked photos of her. She did the same to me.'

Max looked distraught. 'I can't believe she'd do that to her. To treat someone like that...'

They were interrupted by the sound of voices arguing.

Sophie looked back at Cassie's boat as the shouts got louder.

She could see the shadows of Will and Cassie talking, gesticulating wildly.

Max stared up at them. 'Do you think she's all right?' he asked again.

'I don't know,' Sophie said. She didn't care.

Will and Cassie's voices rose, carrying on the breeze.

'You've taken me for a fool,' Cassie was screaming.

Will's voice was quieter and Sophie couldn't make out the words.

On the deck of the boat, Will swayed drunkenly.

'There were lots of them, weren't there?' Cassie shouted. 'Even at school. When you were with me. There were always rumours. I never believed them. But they were true, Will.'

Their shadows got closer to the edge of the boat. Sophie knew what was going to happen before it did. She watched Cassie push Will and saw his body bend over the railing and tumble down over the other side, landing with a splash.

'We need to get over there,' Max shouted, switching on the engine. But Cassie's boat was already moving, going full throttle towards the body in the water. There was a gentle thud, and then Will disappeared underneath it.

EPILOGUE

SIX MONTHS LATER

Sophie stepped off the stage, smiling as she listened to the applause. A few weeks before she'd been named one of the 'Thirty Under-Thirties to Watch Out For' in the same newspaper that Max had been named in the previous year. It had been great publicity for her new advertising company, and since then she'd had multiple invitations to speak at conferences. Today over two hundred people had come to hear her speak about founding her own agency. Her business partner, Felicity, wasn't there as she was still on maternity leave. The payout from her unfair dismissal claim had provided the investment to set up their agency.

As Sophie came off the stage, she made a beeline for her father, Charlie and Charlie's new girlfriend, Amy. They'd all come to London to support her, and Charlie and her father had sat awkwardly in the audience in ill-fitting suits. After the retreat, Sophie had had a big heart-to-heart with Charlie, and they'd agreed to be friends again.

Now her father came over to her, hobbling on his bad leg, and gave her a hug. 'Well done, love,' he said, as he wrapped his arms around her. There were spending more time together again these days. She'd founded her agency in Dorset so she could be close to him, and she'd moved back in with him while she looked for a place of her own.

In the corner of the room, Sophie spotted James and Cassie, representing One Pure Thought. Max had left the company, but before he'd left, he'd made sure he'd written off Sophie's debt. It was the only way he could think of to make up for the way Cassie and James had treated her.

Will had died instantly when he'd been hit by Cassie's boat. She'd claimed it was an accident, but Sophie knew better. At first there'd been enormous sympathy for Cassie from the public, but as more details emerged and the police arrested her, the media turned against her, raking over every detail of her life. Eventually, she was released without charge for Will's murder and it was recorded as an accidental death.

But she'd had to face the courts when she and James were tried for taking photos of Sophie without her consent and setting up the spy cameras. They were given community orders, and had to undertake unpaid work cleaning up a local park. Sophie was glad that the cases had gone to court, and glad that they were over. Though Will's death meant he would never be held to account for what he did to her and so many others.

'We'd better be off,' Sophie's dad said, bringing her thoughts back to the present. They were planning to spend the rest of the day exploring London, while Sophie stayed on at the conference.

As soon as James saw that her family had left, he came over. She hadn't seen him since the retreat, and he looked thinner, but he still had the same ready smile, the same piercing blue eyes.

'Sophie,' he said. 'How are you?' He moved forward as if to hug her, but she stepped back.

'I'm well,' she said. 'As you can probably tell. Did you hear my talk?'

'Yeah, I thought it was brilliant. I always knew you were an excellent brand strategist.' He seemed to have no intention of acknowledging what had happened between them, or apologising. The only things Sophie knew about his life now were from Felicity. He was reluctantly paying his child support, but had only met his son twice.

'Thank you,' she said, ready to step away from him. If he wasn't going to apologise then they had nothing to say to each other anymore.

'I wanted to talk to you,' he said. He glanced over at Cassie, who was still standing in the corner, and Sophie saw the look the two of them exchanged. It reminded her of One Pure Thought, where they'd so often been plotting together.

'What is it, James?'

'Well, you may have heard that we've had a few problems. At One Pure Thought. Max has left, and some of the clients have left with him. And we were also hit by a huge financial problem, that has left our finances in tatters.'

Sophie nodded. 'The unfair dismissal case, you mean?'

'Yeah, that. The thing is, it's left us in a rather difficult position. If I can be straight with you, Sophie, the company's likely to go under. Philip will lose all his money. So Cassie and I thought, well, you said in your talk that you were growing so fast you were struggling to recruit...'

'You want to work for me?' Sophie asked, with a wry smile.

'No, no,' James said quickly. 'We thought more of a partnership. And you wouldn't need to tell Felicity, of course. I know she's still on maternity leave. You could pass work over to us, the work you don't have the time to do yourselves. You know we're the best in the business. We'd do a great job.'

Sophie looked at him, trying to work out if he was serious. Then she glanced over at Cassie, not brave enough to come over but clearly pulling the strings from the sidelines. 'You'd both need to ask,' she said. 'You and Cassie.'

James nodded, and beckoned Cassie over. She came reluctantly and then held out her hand to Sophie, forcing a smile. Sophie didn't smile back.

'There's a lot of water under the bridge between us,' Cassie said, 'but I hope you can consider our proposal. One Pure Thought has a great reputation.'

Sophie nodded. This was clearly as much of an apology as she was going to get. 'It did have a great reputation,' she said. 'But it doesn't anymore. I'd never work with either of you. And I wouldn't employ you either. Just so we're clear: I don't want to see or hear from you again.'

And with that she turned her back on them, and went over to the bar area. In five minutes she was due to meet a journalist there to give a media interview on women in business.

A LETTER FROM RUTH

Dear Reader,

I want to say a huge thank you for choosing to read *The New Girl*. If you enjoyed it, and want to keep up to date with all my latest releases, just sign up at the following link. Your email address will never be shared and you can unsubscribe at any time.

www.bookouture.com/ruth-heald

My books often explore the vulnerability of women in everyday situations. *The Mother's Mistake* and *The Woman Upstairs* explored the vulnerability of new mothers. *The New Girl* takes this theme into the office. People can become trapped in a job as easily as they become trapped in a marriage. With bills to pay (and in Sophie's case, debts) most workers are dependent on their employment. And if there is a predator among their colleagues, there is no escape. Sophie is damaged by her past, but appears to have overcome it, when Cassie's desire to protect her husband from fresh allegations leads Sophie into harm's way.

Sophie's assault represents the experience of too many women, and behind the drama of the book, there are some sobering statistics. In the UK twenty per cent of women and four per cent of men have experienced sexual violence since the age of sixteen. The vast majority don't report it to the police, and for those crimes that are reported, the conviction rate is just six per cent.*

Despite the difficult themes, I hope you have enjoyed this book. If you have, then I would love to see your review on Amazon. Reviews really help authors to sell books, and help readers discover new authors. And it's brilliant to hear what you think, too.

If you want to follow me on social media, you can use the links below.

Thanks so much for reading!

Ruth

*Source: *An Overview of Sexual Offending in England and Wales,* 2013 (jointly commissioned by the Ministry of Justice, Office for National Statistics and the Home Office)

www.ruthheald.com

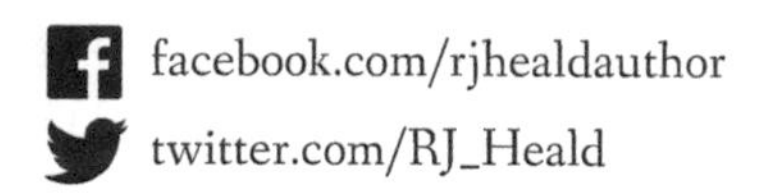

ACKNOWLEDGEMENTS

Thanks firstly to my husband, who is endlessly patient and supportive, and to my children, who bring so much joy and fun to my life. Without them I'd be a different person and most certainly a different writer.

Many people work to make my books the best they can be, and I'm grateful to all of them. Thanks to my wonderful editor Laura Deacon, for her insightful feedback and for recognising the central themes of the book and helping me to stay true to these. As I've come to expect, my beta readers, Charity Davies and Ruth Jones, provided excellent feedback and suggestions which have really improved the book. Thanks to my copyeditor, Jon Appleton, and proofreader, Jenny Page, who have helped further refine my work. I'm also grateful to friends in the police who helped me with details on how the police would handle both historic and current crimes.

It's a real privilege to be published by the exceptional team at Bookouture. There are so many people who work tirelessly behind the scenes. Thanks to the publicity team of Sarah, Kim, Noelle and Jess, Alex Holmes and the production team, the audio team, the insights team, the finance team and the rights team and, of course, the leadership team.

I'm grateful to my cover designer, Aaron Munday, and my audio narrator, Tamsin Kennard, who always does a superb job of bringing my books to life.

Finally, but most importantly, thank you to my readers. It's wonderful to know you're out there, reading and enjoying my books.

CPSIA information can be obtained
at www.ICGtesting.com
Printed in the USA
LVHW031045260122
709219LV00001B/53